HIS DARK E
BURNED INTO HER

"I'll court you, Cleo, but there's going to come a time when courting won't be enough."

Wild spurts of excitement and dread warmed Cleo's flesh. She stood up. "I have to get home now. I'm starved."

His hand shot out, grabbing her ankle. "I'm starved, too."

She moistened her lips. "I'm talking about chicken salad."

"As long as you know I'm not." There it was, said. His hand moved up the smoothness of her calf, then dropped. "I'll see you tomorrow. I'll pick up some steaks and we'll throw them on your grill. How does that sound?"

As if you're giving me time to ponder all you've said, as if you've handed me an ultimatum. "Like a pleasant way to pass the evening," she said, turning and walking rapidly back to her camper.

ABOUT THE AUTHOR

Superromance readers will be delighted with this first Superromance by popular Temptation and American Romance author Jackie Weger. Once again, Jackie has created a unique story written in her very own touching and down-to-earth way. She has a special talent for transforming ordinary characters into real people who live on long after the book is finished. Cleo, Fletcher and Katie are no exceptions.

Home for Jackie is a trailer in Texas with her childhood sweetheart-husband, a large family and a few friendly geese and chickens.

Books by Jackie Weger

HARLEQUIN AMERICAN ROMANCE

5–A STRONG AND TENDER THREAD
48–COUNT THE ROSES

HARLEQUIN TEMPTATION

7–CAST A GOLDEN SHADOW
29–WINTER SONG
53–BENEATH A SAFFRON SKY
89–THE WINGS OF MORNING

These books may be available at your local bookseller.

Don't miss any of our special offers. Write to us at the following address for information on our newest releases.

Harlequin Reader Service
901 Fuhrmann Blvd., P.O. Box 1397, Buffalo, NY 14240
Canadian address: P.O. Box 603,
Fort Erie, Ont. L2A 9Z9

Jackie Weger

BEYOND FATE

Harlequin Books

TORONTO • NEW YORK • LONDON
AMSTERDAM • PARIS • SYDNEY • HAMBURG
STOCKHOLM • ATHENS • TOKYO • MILAN

Published September 1986

First printing July 1986

ISBN 0-373-70227-2

In memory of Misty Heather

CHAPTER ONE

JUST AS CLEO STEPPED FORWARD to tighten the bracing strut that clamped the awning to her Play-Mor camper, a man broke through the overgrowth that surrounded her campsite. He was striding fast and looking everywhere but where he was headed.

Before she could call a warning or dodge from his path he caromed into her. The strut flew out of her hands. The canvas collapsed, enveloping them both. In the space of a heartbeat the sun was shut out. Cleo found herself being dragged to the sandy earth, her arms and legs entangled with those of the man.

"Sorry," he moaned.

"Don't mention it," she said, trying to make sense of what had happened and get her bearings. She tried lifting the canvas away from her face and couldn't. "I think you broke my arm."

The limb felt numb and leaden. She wiggled her fingers and bent her elbow as much as space permitted. Feeling came flooding back, a prickly sensation, so that she knew no great injury was done. But damn! It hurt.

"Okay?" he asked.

"Just terrific," she said uncharitably, annoyed now. It was hot and dark beneath the awning. She could hear herself breathing . . . hear him, too.

The sailcloth, stiff and unmalleable from its winter packing, defied her attempts to throw it off. She sucked in

a lungful of musty air, a prelude to panic. "Are we going
to sit here and suffocate or are you going to get us out of
here?" she asked.

He began scrambling over her legs and burrowing toward fresh air. Cleo crawled behind him.

But he didn't crawl out into the sunlight; he slipped instead into her small camper. Cleo heard the door snap
shut, the lock click.

"What the heck—" She yanked on the knob. "Hey,
you! Come out of there!"

"Lady, please," came his pleading reply, "tell them I
kept going...please?"

A moment later the canvas was lifted by unseen hands.
Cleo homed in on the light and scooted into sunshine and
two pairs of well-tanned legs. One pair was fat and solid,
the other, stick thin.

"Thanks," she breathed as she got to her feet. A rivulet of sweat was running down the back of her neck. She
took a swipe at it.

"Is Fletcher under there, too?" asked the chubby
blonde. She stomped about the canvas until it was flattened, then gave Cleo a sidelong look of reproach—a look
designed to make its recipient feel mildly guilty.

At the moment it would take far more than a look to
make her feel guilty about anything, thought Cleo. After
all, she was the victim here.

"Who?" she asked offhandedly, and got busy inspecting her arm, then she dusted twigs and sand from her
shorts.

"The tall good-looking guy. He ran into you, didn't
he?"

"Something ambushed me. I didn't notice what it
looked like." She took in the women. Two against one.
Since she felt she was somewhat in control now, charity

reared its head. Cleo avoided glancing at the camper. "This guy you're chasing, what's he done?"

"Did you see which way he went?" asked Thin.

Cleo shook her head. Well, she hadn't, had she? Now, if the woman had asked, Do you know where he is? Cleo would have been obliged to tell. She had been raised to tell the truth, but sometimes it clotted in her throat and she could swallow it before it got out and did damage.

Ah, Cleo, you're fudging, said a small inner voice.

I can't talk to you now, I'm in a situation.

Sure you are, and the situation is that there's a strange man in your Play-Mor along with your traveler's checks, cameras and typewriter, not to mention Gram's last four pieces of Limoges.

I'm just doing him a favor.

A man you don't even know?

Why not?

He might be a rapist, a thief or worse—married.

Cleo flushed and forced a smile. "Look, I don't want to get involved in a marital spat."

Blondie laughed. "This is no marital spat. Fletcher's the perennial bachelor. I just want his autograph. He promised and now he's trying to renege."

Thin didn't look happy. "C'mon Clara, if you pursue this, Fletcher'll get mad and refuse to make a fourth at bridge next time we're here." Thin looked at Cleo, explaining, "Women have been hassling Fletcher ever since his book came out. Some want to convert him and some want to kill him. Besides that, it's gotten terrible reviews."

"Book?" Cleo was trying to change the direction of her mind in mid-thought.

The man was a writer. An unmarried writer. His book had gotten rotten reviews. The poor guy. A writer herself, Cleo felt an instant affinity for him.

The woman called Clara was thrusting a thin volume in Cleo's direction. She glanced at the title. *For Men Only. 101 Ways to Stay Married.* In very small print was, *and Still Do What You Want* by Fletcher Fremont Maitland.

Cleo blinked and read the title again. What gall! Her ire rose. Empathy for a fellow writer evaporated. No wonder he was the perennial bachelor. No woman in her right mind would tolerate him.

"You're looking for the guy who wrote this?" She was ready to tell them.

Clara scanned the clearing. "I guess we'll catch up to him next time we're here." She turned to go, stopping in mid-stride. "Say, you're new here, aren't you? I mean this is your first time camping at Big Momma's."

"Yes." Cleo wanted to be rid of the women now. She also wanted to be rid of the clod hiding in her camper.

Clara thrust out her hand. "Well, I'm Clara, and this is Beverly. We're a couple of the regulars. We've been coming here—" she looked to her companion "—six years, now?"

"About," said Beverly. "And if we don't round up the kids before they cause any more mayhem, Big Momma won't let us back." She smiled at Cleo. "We'll see you in a couple of weeks if you're still here. Say, do you play bridge? We usually get up a table or two...."

"Sorry, no," replied Cleo, and watched until the women disappeared around a bend in the footpath, then she faced the camper and sang out, "You can come out now, Fletcher Fremont Maitland."

With her first good look at Fletcher Maitland, Cleo's stomach tightened.

His teeth were of a peculiar whiteness and symmetry. The slight smile he gave her was irresistible. His face was formed of converging planes—wide brow, straight nose, square jaw and deeply set brown eyes. Clad in a black polo shirt, white walking shorts and leather espadrilles, he exuded a buccaneerlike magnetism, as if he was ready to take a swat at the world just to see where it'd land. It wasn't lost on Cleo that he'd taken an inadvertent swat at her.

She wanted more than anything to look away, to be able to ignore Fletcher Fremont Maitland, perennial bachelor, to wave him casually on his way.

She couldn't. She was struck almost with a physical force by his smile. Her insides seemed to go haywire—expanding, shrinking, filling with a gathering commotion impossible to ignore. Her brain darted here and there, landing on random thoughts, flitting away to monitor the spiking waves racing down her spine.

"I owe you one," he said in an easygoing way. "Did I hurt you badly, slamming into you like that?"

"There must be a Neanderthal somewhere in your ancestry," she said, a little testily, almost before he finished asking the question, the tartness evidence of her rallying defenses. "But, don't give it a thought, I'll survive."

"I should hope so. It'd be a shame if you didn't." His voice was vibrant, accented heavily on interior syllables, Southern fashion. He could make it do anything, she noticed. He was making it sweep and enfold her like a caress. At the same time he was studying her with a faint tightening of the muscles of his face, which meant that she had his entire attention.

Floundering beneath his gaze, Cleo noted something more. He was classifying her . . . with some curiosity, but more of habit.

She saw his eyes flicker, inspection over. He thrust out his hand; she hesitated. "Shake?" he asked, taking a step into her space so that all her senses were engaged at once.

He looked good, sounded good, smelled good and her mouth went dry. When Cleo put her hand in his, the clasp was warm and firm, sending a quick rush of pleasure through her. Right then and there she determined never to bite her nails again.

Hold on, Cleo, said her interior voice sharply. *Don't get your hopes up. You've only just met the man.*

I am wholly without hope, she told it.

Cleo, you're such a liar. You forget that I'm right here, that I know everything.

"Since I knocked it down," said Fletcher, "let me help you get this awning back up."

"No thanks, there's nothing to it," she said, extricating her hand from his and anchoring it on her rounded hip to disguise its sudden trembling.

"I insist."

One could only allow a situation to go so far, thought Cleo, making an attempt to dilute the feckless reaction of her body to his touch. "I insist not."

"Okay," he said.

Flabbergasted, she formed a captivating moue with her lips, softening her strong jaw. Why, she'd had every intention of letting him put the awning in place. He was supposed to act on his words despite her protests. It was the least he could do, sort of a friendly atonement for invading her life.

"A chauvinist would help you against your wishes," he said, his eyes so dark as to be almost black. Only in the sunlight did they turn deep umber. "Now me, I believe in equality of the sexes."

"Oh, you do?" she said, utterly vexed now that all her options were closed. "Where do you come by that attitude? Researching *101 Ways to Stay Married and Still Do What You Want*?"

His features hardened. "It was a privately published book and not meant for public consumption."

"Maybe that's why it got panned by the critics." Almost in spite of herself, Cleo was fascinated by him, repelled yet attracted. So attracted she was shifting from one sandaled foot to another in a useless attempt to dislodge an airy, floating sensation making its way toward her stomach.

His dark eyes were briefly penetrating, then amiable again. "I think I'll fade into the woodwork now. I'm detecting a slight trace of sarcasm."

One up for him, thought Cleo. "If you don't mind my saying so, you don't look the type to fade into anything."

"I'm not. Well, if you're sure I didn't hurt you and that I can't help you with the awning..."

"I'm tip top and the awning is a piece of cake."

"There you are, Uncle Fletch," piped a sprite of child as she appeared from behind Cleo's camper. "Dad sent me to see if you were still in one piece."

"Just barely," said Fletcher dryly, leaving it up in the air for Cleo to decide whether he meant that she had discommoded him or if it had been his autograph seekers. He clasped the child's frail hand in his own. "See you later, Miss...?"

"Anderson."

"First name?"

"Cleo," she said with reluctance.

"Cleo. That's nice, and it fits you. I like it. You're not likely to forget my name?"

"No."

The child tugged at Fletcher. "Hurry. Dad's got the boat in the river. We're waiting on you."

"Don't let me keep you," said Cleo, lifting her hand in an abbreviated gesture of dismissal.

She turned her back and began to wrestle with the awning. She felt Fletcher's eyes on her for a lingering moment. Instinct told her when he turned away. She chanced a look over her shoulder and caught the youngster doing the same, staring at her with . . . not curiosity, but something else, something more elemental, Cleo thought, struck by the whimsy of the face and the large gray eyes.

She shrugged, giving the child a half smile. She meant to return to the task at hand, but she noticed that Fletcher Fremont Maitland looked as good from the back as he did from the front. No, she wasn't likely to forget his name. Or anything else about him. But there was no need, really, to remember him, since she had no intention of ever expecting anything from a man again. A little flirting when she could get the nerve up once in a while was fun, but that was about as far as her expectations went.

AT LAST the camp was quiet.

Quiet enough for sleep, Cleo thought as she stepped outside the Play-Mor and sat on its tiny step. The only sounds were her own breathing and the sluggish swishing of the Suwannee River as it brushed the sandy bank and swept around boat keels.

Dusk filtered into the clearing and blurred the outlines of the low matted growth of swamp oak, palmetto shrub and old pine that hemmed her in, separating her from the rest of the world.

It was all so peaceful. Chicago seemed far away, separated by more than miles. She found it good to sit there in silence, letting the dusk thicken about her and draw her into it.

She had read much romantic literature of the south and she began to wonder if there might not be something for her in this way of life. The friendliness of the natives, their generosity, their casual manner of revealing their lives, seemed to keep the wolf pack of loneliness at bay.

She was aware of her inability to sustain communication with another human being. Most people, given the chance for personal speech, loved hearing themselves talk, so they didn't seem to notice her silence.

Then, in Georgia it had begun to happen, as though it had been arranged long before, as though a pre-knowledge that something of importance awaited within her in the South. She had begun to respond to people, revealing tidbits about herself...to gas station attendants who noticed her license plates and struck up conversations. To waitresses in off-road diners, curious that she traveled alone. And to the woman who insisted Cleo join her for lunch while the woman's husband changed the flat on the camper.

She had picked a good place, thought Cleo, observing the landscape. She felt it in her bones.

A faint light still shone dimly above the copper-colored Suwannee to the west of an ancient cypress. The tree cast an unnatural shadow. Her gaze strayed to the source of the aberration. Boards had been nailed up the narrow trunk above its squat base, rundles that climbed fifteen feet to a limb where a thick rope dangled above a deep hole in the river. She imagined the fun youngsters must have swinging from that rope to drop with a great splash into the cool coppery water. She could also imagine their laughter, their thudding hearts, the act of bravery or bravado it took to be first.

She swallowed a whimsical sigh. She had never been first at anything. It wasn't that she was a follower, but that she felt driven to do her own thing, and that put her out of step with the rest of the world.

It kept her alone. Although the isolation had nothing to do with any attempt on her part to be different. She had been different from the very first.

Leaning her head back against the metal door, her eyes half-closed, she let the dream come, the recurring daydream that took different shapes.

In this dream she was not alone. She never saw his face, only arms, legs, a muscled torso. Sometimes her fantasy man would hold out his arms and she could see herself rushing into them, anticipating a warm, loving, safe embrace. Before she got there, before he could speak, before she could see his expression, he would melt back into her subconscious.

The meaning of the dream plagued her. She had even gone so far as to make an appointment with a psychiatrist famed for interpreting dreams. Then she had learned he treated his patients with hypnosis, regressing them back to childhood. Cleo could not see the use of reliving a childhood fraught with unhappiness.

She had gone instead to Madam Zutu who read tarot cards and kept rooms in the corner building of the street on which she lived.

"I don't understand why I can't see myself in a loving situation, why love escapes me," she had said to Madam Zutu. "Do you think that it means I'm frigid? Paul said—"

"It means you're scared of commitment."

"That's not true. I give my all to my job. I do volunteer work at the charity hospital on Sundays. That's commitment."

"Busy work," countered Madam Zutu. "The cards don't lie." She had shuffled the deck, turned the cards up, spreading them out upon the baize-covered table. "This Paul used you and he wasn't very good at what men do."

"I wasn't very good at what women—"

"Ah, you used him, too, in the name of love."

"No! Not in the name of love . . ." but something more desperate. If Madam Zutu had sensed this inner turmoil in Cleo, she never let on as she shook her head and tapped another card.

"When you rid yourself of her, the old woman, your dream will change." She read on. "Ah, the old woman is dead. It is her words that live on and torment you. Troubled, insecure words from a troubled, insecure old woman."

Cleo had never mentioned her grandmother to Madam Zutu. Gram? Insecure? Madam Zutu might as well have asked her to believe the earth was flat. That day she had left Madam Zutu's, pale and trembling. She never went back. It had been a stupid idea. Tarot cards were a farce anyway. Everyone said so.

So Cleo had arrived at the conclusion that her dream was wishful thinking, nothing more.

But now, because he had been on her mind all day, she tried to fit Fletcher Maitland's face to the dream. It wouldn't go. Nice try! she thought, letting her mind wander back to Madam Zutu.

The fortune teller had been so right about Paul. He had used her.

She had married him while still in college and discovered too late that what Paul had wanted was someone to do his laundry, keep house and to help pay his way through law school. He had no intention of continuing their marriage once he passed his bar exams.

There had been bitter scenes, but in the end he had packed his bag and left her, with two months back rent due and unpaid utility bills. Left her with an aching unfulfilled need that lay buried inside. His very first legal procedure had been to file for his own divorce. Nothing in her whole life had been as bad as that.

The finality of it made Cleo feel empty and afraid. She still felt afraid sometimes. The feeling was too strong to deny.

Marrying Paul had meant escape from Gram. Divorce had forced her to return to the small dark rooms with their shabby furnishings where she'd spent her childhood. And to Gram, who had never been a great respecter of tender feelings.

"If you had listened to me, Cleo," Gram had railed. "If you had! But no! You told him, didn't you? Of course you did, I can see it in your face. For shame! That's why he didn't want you for the mother of his children. He thought you were a trollop. I warned you! I told you—no man of good family is going to take you to wife and keep you."

"Paul wasn't... That's not the reason—" She stopped, for she knew she could never tell Gram the ugly truth. Or anyone else. Just thinking about it made her feel shame so deep and thick it seemed to clot her blood.

"No? He's gone, isn't he? He took his name back, too, didn't he, when you tried to keep on using it? You're part and parcel of your own mother's sin. Tainted. You have bad blood, just like your mother."

Sick at heart, weary of spirit, Cleo had crawled into the plain iron bed that had been her mother's, lying there, staring into her past.

On good nights she fell asleep. On bad nights she remembered Paul—her awkward approaches, his refusals.

The image was still so clear and strong it made her throat ache.

Then, one morning Gram hitched herself over the threshold. "I said you'd end up like Ellie and you will. Just look at you. Day in, day out, shriveling, shriveling. Lust! For a man. That's all you know. Cast it out! Cast out the sin." Cleo wanted to deny it, but she felt all her devils gathering and closing in, and she had to stave them off.

End up like Ellie? A small, desolate thing? Sickly? Dead at twenty-nine? The next day she got out of bed and began to put her life back together. She went back to work; she looked fine on the outside. Yet, no one part of her seemed to fit as it had, for the essential element that would give her life meaning was gone forever. She was not loved. In loving others, she had been rebuffed.

However, Gram's prophecy lingered and fed her superstitious nature.

She didn't walk under ladders. She was careful with salt. It was partly because of her superstitious nature that she worked Sundays at the charity hospital. Patients were sick. She was well. The line was easily definable.

Because her mother had died at twenty-nine, Cleo had been chary her entire twenty-ninth year. Reaching thirty had been a milestone. Cleo had come to regard this, her thirtieth summer, as the watershed year in which all that she had been would be separated from what she would become. She had a wonderful sense of buoyancy, as if anything were suddenly possible—even love.

She only had to figure out what she needed, wanted, could get. She didn't expect to live happily ever after. That wasn't the way life went, but somehow—by instinct perhaps—she knew she had a force inside her and that it was just waiting to burst forth.

Yet the force could hardly burst forth while Gram's voice lingered like an old ghost whose honor had been slighted. Cleo could still hear Gram speak, could still see Gram's face looking like an argument you couldn't win.

"You get settled a'right?"

The voice, coming out of the night to mingle with the voice in her mind, startled Cleo. It took her a moment to adjust, to separate the two.

The spare, angular body of the park owner appeared as a bent shadow at the edge of the campsite. A young moon, hot and burnished, hung over the camp. The old woman stepped into its sliver of light.

Mrs. Freeman was holding a silver-gray tabby, and Cleo could see one of the veined old hands slide gently down the velvety fur. Before she spoke, Cleo rose to her feet, a gesture of deference to an elder. It was an old habit, one ingrained into her during childhood.

"Yes, I did, thank you." She tried not to let pride creep into her voice. There had been times when she'd had to ask help, but now she was adept at parking the camper, unhitching it from her car, leveling it with wooden blocks, and plugging it into whatever hookups were provided.

"You be a writer you said," observed Mrs. Freeman. She had not moved from the sliver of moonlight, nor adjusted her stance. Her hand still stroked the cat. "Another writer come here oncet, long about the time I was on my second mister. She lived in the swamp and writ about the people. You aim to write about me, mayhap?"

"I write about animals mostly, and plants sometimes, for children."

"Oh. I be mistaken then. It don't matter none. I got no call for reading and writing nohow."

"I might need your help though, to tell me places to go and how to get there," Cleo said, discerning a hint of disappointment in the old voice. "This is my first trip to Georgia." There it was again, Cleo noted. Volunteering information. Whatever it was, she was in its grip.

The old woman nodded. For several long seconds her dark eyes tracked the tall pine and low scrub. "The first thing I be telling you, be to take a flashlight when you go along the path to the toilet. It be snake weather certain t'night." The cat wriggled, then leapt from her arms into shadows, becoming a part of the grayness. "Waal, I be going. You let me know something you need."

"I will," said Cleo. "Good night." She watched Mrs. Freeman stop on the moonlit path and look back over her shoulder.

"Don't forget now, you keep a mind out fer snakes."

"Yes. Yes, I will. Thanks for the warning." Cleo shivered. She hated snakes. Even in zoos. In her articles she stuck to birds, frogs, lizards and from a distance, alligators, bears and other predators.

"Fowkses who stay in my camp be reg'lars and call me Big Momma. If you reckon on it, you can, too."

Cleo didn't know what to say. Big was a misnomer for the reed-thin old lady. "Big Momma," she repeated. "You can call me Cleo."

"Twas planning on it," said Big Momma. "I don't hold with uppity fowkses." She took another step into the moss-draped shadows and the low matted growth swallowed her up as it had the cat.

Solitude once again overtook Cleo. She was more watchful, sensitive to the slightest noise or to a change in the nightly hum of insects. She began to feel apprehensive. She had the eerie sense that she was being watched. The cat, hoping for a scrap of food? she wondered.

Her gaze swept the clearing, the tangled growth at each side. It was just the talk about snakes and seeing the cat disappear as if it had been tapped by a magic baton. It made her jumpy. No need to tempt fate her first night in camp, she thought. She gave a last look and went inside.

The camper was tiny; there was space to stand, a bed beneath which she stored her things, a stove top beneath which was a refrigerator, and a table for two. The camper was her pride and she liked the cocoon effect of having the walls so near. It made her feel safe.

Above the table was a narrow shelf that supported a cracked mirror with an air of shame. Cleo didn't dare throw the mirror away. She didn't know how long it had been broken. She was counting seven years from the day she'd bought the camper secondhand. Five years to go before she replaced it, she mused, glancing at her reflection.

On the other hand, perhaps she would never discard the mirror. It knew her old image and now, her new.

Since her teens she had worn her red hair long and pulled back in a ponytail, but this, her milestone year, she had felt ready for a change. Now her hair was short and...curly. She hadn't expected the curls that coiled up tight at the first touch of sun or salt or wind. She wasn't sure she liked them. However, the new style did show off her eyes and her eyes were her best feature. They were oval, tilted at the corners and colored amber, a golden brown rarely found in redheads.

Her lashes and brows were so fair as to be almost invisible unless she dabbed them with mascara. She supposed she could make a virtue out of having a straight nose if her mouth wasn't so ordinary or the chin below it, too sharp. Even more humiliating were the freckles. She shouldn't complain about her chin. She'd won a scrap or two by leading with it. Never with Gram, though those chilly battles had taught Cleo to guard well her secrets and vulnerabilities.

When Cleo walked, she knew she looked as if nothing could stand in her way, not other people, not a barricade, not even a brick wall. That look was a facade, she decided, for she had crashed into a lot of life's brick walls.

She strode from place to place with a purposeful, no-nonsense manner. In this she had no choice. She was too tall to take short, wiggly feminine steps. Better to get where she was going, she always thought, face whomever she had to and find out if they liked the way she was up close.

Since both her mother and Gram had been small boned and dainty, Cleo surmised she took after her father. Not that she knew who he was or what he looked like.

She hadn't realized that she was supposed to have a father until she started school, and the other kids had them—like possessions.

She had asked about her own father on one of the rare occasions Gram had allowed her mother to table. Ellie had responded to her query with a painful wince. But Gram had yanked Cleo from her chair, switched her legs with a flyswatter, then stood her in a corner for hours. Later that week Gram had marched her down to the minister's house to have the devil cast out.

The preacher had put his hands upon her head, praying in a language which she did not understand. After the devil was cast out, she asked where he went. "Behind you, in front of you—everywhere," said Gram.

After that she had played elaborate games with herself to keep the devil at bay, but she knew he followed her to school. It worried her sick that the devil might sneak up and get back inside her without her knowing. He was under her bed at night, or in the tiny closet where her clothes were hung. She woke sometimes with her whole body pulsing and fear thundering in her head.

Once the devil began to stalk her it had made her sad to look at her mother, sad and guilty and angry. Why couldn't her mother have a husband and so provide her with a father like other children? Fathers were big and strong and could keep the devil at a distance. Maybe even make the devil move into somebody else's house. It wasn't fair.

At six, Cleo did not understand any of it. At thirty, she understood too much.

She looked in the mirror again. Who am I, really? she asked. The twin selves that she had been plagued with for a long time stared back at her.

Why, plain old Cleo Anderson, came the reply. *Won't that do?*

Not so old, retorted Cleo, and I'll make it do.

As she climbed into her bunk she wondered if Fletcher Maitland had liked the way she looked up close. But then she veered away from the answer, as if it wasn't her business to know.

You can't get him out of your head, can you, Cleo? You were something else today. You almost melted at the center when you saw that man. Ripe, that's what you are—for the first man who says a kind word to you. For shame.

Looking at him made me feel good.

You certainly felt something. What do you think Gram would have thought if she'd seen how you behaved today?

Cleo recoiled from the question. Gram thought all passion was sin.

Really? How did she come by having your mother, then?

I don't know. I've often wondered. Osmosis? Sympathetic alchemy?

Cleo folded her hands behind her head and sighed, wishing she could've known her mother as a child. Wondering if Ellie had ever been carefree, or if she played hide and seek, or if...

Know your own mother as a child? Cleo! What a silly idea. How like you to wish for the impossible.

I know, but together—maybe we could have outwitted Gram.

Dreams and tarot cards and silly wishes. What will you come up with next?

Cleo reached up and switched off the bedlamp. Sleep, I hope.

WHEN THE LIGHTS WENT OUT in Cleo Anderson's camper, eleven-year-old Katie Miller let loose a disappointed sigh. She allowed the sharp palmetto frond behind which she was hiding to snap back into place. Muscles aching from lying so still, she longed to stretch, but Big Momma's warning to the newcomer still rang in her ears.

Snake weather! Goose bumps erupted on the nape of her neck as her eyes swiveled, investigating the shadows and black gloom of the underbrush. She knew about venomous snakes, the shoe-button black eyes with no perceptible iris, the elliptical pupil like a thin vertical line of cold jade green that gave the eyes a brilliance during nocturnal hunting. She didn't sense any danger, couldn't see any unblinking eyes or angry fangs.

Maybe, Katie worried, Big Momma had spied out her hiding place. It could be true, what people said about Big Momma—that she had cat eyes, that she could see in the dark, that she could see through things like a "hant" did. Katie didn't believe in hants which were said to be swamp ghosts that took the shape of any dead thing. So it was hard for her to believe that Big Momma could see through things.

Katie had been trying to interest Big Momma in taking a scientific test—to no avail. Big Momma just accused Katie of trying to court glory for her own self. But Katie suspected Big Momma's refusal was to keep her see-all reputation intact among the children. Some of the littler kids did believe in hants and Big Momma kept them in line by threatening to call one up.

A small slithering sound intruded at the edge of Katie's thoughts, then melted away into nothing. She was back to the crucial immediate worry of whether or not she was sharing her nest of moss and pine straw with a snake.

She let awareness wash over her as they had taught her at the hospital. She could feel her heart pumping, her pulse throbbing. Through her thin shirt and shorts she could feel pine needles and twigs pressing into her flesh. The twigs didn't hurt because the ground was spongy. She couldn't feel any bugs or creepy crawlies scooting over her body anywhere. But she'd just lie here another minute, she thought, just to be on the safe side. She rested her chin on her hands and watched the camper for signs of life.

You could tell a lot about people when they thought no one was looking. Like Uncle Fletcher. Twice today he'd gone looking off into space with a silly grin on his face. Katie had put two and two together and came up with the new camper in number eleven. After supper Uncle Fletcher had walked down to the boat ramp. Katie had been positive he was aiming to visit number eleven and raced ahead to get into place, but he hadn't come.

Now there was nothing going on in the clearing. Katie yawned. She might as well go back to the cabin. She'd have to sneak in the side door and pretend she was just getting up from a nap, though, or Daddy'd start yelling at Roger for letting her out of his sight.

She hated having Roger tag behind her everywhere. At ten, he was old enough to be a real pest. If there really were hants, she wished Big Momma would call one up to tote Roger off. If there was anybody she knew of who was out for glory, it was Roger. He courted it by tattling. So far as Katie was concerned Roger could have all the glory he wanted, as long as he didn't get it from traipsing along behind her.

Katie squinted at the clearing once more. Nothing moved. She didn't think there were any snakes in her vicinity, but all the same she was cautious as she began wriggling backward. She could hear the buzzing of insects, nothing else. That's when she felt the sudden harsh sting on her ear and knew the snake had got her. She opened her mouth to scream. And couldn't, for the snake had slammed across her lips. Lights going out! thought Katie.

"Don't you dast give a holler and get ever'body riled," hissed Big Momma.

Katie came back from a dark place where her mind had gone fuzzy. She felt herself being hauled to her feet. "Ooooo, turn loose my ear, Big Momma. That hurts."

"It orta. What d'you call y'self doing? Spying on my new fowkses?"

"I was just looking." She wouldn't be made to feel guilty about spying. She wouldn't! "How else am I going to find out about life? Nobody tells me anything!"

"What you're hoping to find out ain't fitten for a child to know. Now get on back to your place afore your pa turns ever'body out a-looking for you. And no more sneaking, you hear me?"

"You scared a year off my life, Big Momma," Katie said in parting.

"Well, you come up to the house tomorry. I'll bake you some cookies and put it back on. That is, if you can stand to relive it again."

"I won't pass up cookies, but it wasn't a year I've already lived that you scared out of me. It was a year I got coming."

"The only years a body can count on is the ones they had a'ready. Now scoot afore a hant comes outen the swamp and carries you off."

"Big Momma, wait! Did you see me, or did you just guess I was there?"

"I smelled you. You been eating peanut butter. Now, get."

It wasn't until Katie was well along the path that it occurred to her that all the kids ate peanut butter and that Big Momma had reached out and yanked her ear in the dark. She wished now she hadn't asked.

She still didn't believe in hants though.

CHAPTER TWO

THE AIR CONDITIONER HUMMED, shutting out night sounds of buzzing insects, hooting owls and the lazy swish of the Suwannee as it flowed out of Georgia on its journey into Florida and the Gulf of Mexico.

Lying in bed, propped up against the headboard, Fletcher was as taut as an overwound spring, a condition that was directly related to his mind being full of Cleo Anderson. She had pushed all other thoughts aside, even thoughts of his work, and no woman had ever done that. Women were an after-hours extravagance he allowed himself when he had the time. He didn't have time to squander; nonetheless, he found himself doing just that.

Earlier, when he had been reading through the transcript of his most recent trial and taking notes for an appeal, Cleo's face kept appearing before him. Mildly chagrined that she was disturbing his work, he had closed his eyes for a moment, and then the whole of her materialized. He hadn't even noticed himself putting his work away.

He was not a man to daydream, but then it wasn't really daydreaming that he was doing now. It was thinking, an act of conscious whimsy. Looking at it in that light, Fletcher guessed he could do it once more.

He let the entire scene float into his mind's eye again—from the moment he emerged from Cleo's small camper to the instant when he was walking away, knowing she was staring after him. It had made him feel...well, *good*, to know her glance lingered upon him. He had savored the sensation all day, likening it to the excited feeling he had in court when he knew he was closing in on a trail of evidence.

In shirt and shorts of no particular distinction, no single part of her was designed to draw undue attention. Then, he had taken in the whole of her. Now, he separated the parts.

He didn't think she had worn makeup, but the color in her face, its liveliness, was pleasant to look upon. Her thick glossy red curls emphasized a smooth brow, high cheekbones and the unblemished perfection of her skin. Her nose was narrow, the splash of freckles charmed him; her jawline was strong, but the lips were full and curved and pink—the kind of mouth that made a man have thoughts of sexual excesses.

Such bothersome thoughts had plagued him at the oddest moments all afternoon. On one occasion he'd been sitting on the sofa trying to read while Katie and Roger were engaged in an argument not two feet from him. Cleo had somehow appeared on the page of text and he discovered himself growing hard. Stunned, he'd had to whip a newspaper over his lap until he got himself under control.

Confusing as these feelings were, they were made worse by the realization that it hadn't been the first time. When he had noticed the lace on Cleo's panties peeking out below the cuff of her shorts his gaze just naturally went to her thighs. Then suddenly he was seeing her without shirt and shorts, seeing her naked so that he could trace his fingers up and down those perfect thighs. The vision had been so arousing he'd had to check it before he made himself out a fool right in front of her.

Refusing to help her install the awning had been a protective gesture. Next he would have offered to help her make the bed.

He recalled the surprise in her face, the shape her lips had formed. It was sweetness itself, that sudden air of vulnerability that clung to her. It hinted at a soft core, a fragility requiring a tough exterior. It was apparent that Cleo thought she had that tough exterior. Yet it was so blatantly *transparent* a nitwit could see through it.

He wondered what secrets were behind her facade, what caused her to need that tough exterior. He had a knack for seeing beneath subtleties and had no doubt of his ability to find out what made Cleo tick.

It came as a shock to him that he wasn't considering Cleo Anderson as just another interlude. His thoughts were leapfrogging into the future, his brain offering solutions to every obstacle he might encounter in his pursuit. His muscles contracted, sending a tension throughout his body, a fright into his heart.

Marriage was a road not to be taken. Women never seemed to grasp that. It was amazing how deaf they got when he told them in plain English that he wasn't about to enter into any permanent liaisons. He'd been in a ticklish spot once or twice, too. It was something, how mad a woman could get when she found out a man wasn't leading up to matrimony.

He knew how marriage could drag a man down. Keep a man from being the person he wanted to be. His own father had aimed himself down a dozen different paths trying to be his own man, but his mother had yanked him back every time. Willis had tried for a while to work himself up to a fight, but he was no match for Mattie, and he knew it.

Thus, Fletcher lost his first hero by seeing his father sink into apathy. Being a fun-loving man, Willis had put on a good face, but as he grew older, Fletcher realized the frivolity was only for his sake.

He lost his second hero, a football coach in high school when the coach was discovered flagrante delicto on a bench with a male student. After that, Fletcher did not model himself on anyone and he trusted few. The center of his life became work.

Taking any job available, he worked his way through college and law school, graduating fourth in his class. Upon passing the bar he accepted a position as an assistant district attorney with Fulton County in Atlanta. If he had any lingering heroes it was the law and the peace officers who protected society. He soon lost his innocence. He learned the halls of justice closed in on the poor and swelled to purge the wealthy.

Late one afternoon a young pregnant and poor woman was brought to jail. She was bruised, bleeding from a knife wound inflicted by her husband whom she had killed in self-defense. She had hit him with a hot, grease-filled frying pan.

The district attorney insisted upon presenting prejudiced evidence to the grand jury. The woman was indicted for murder. Appalled, Fletcher resigned from the district attorney's office to take the young woman's case. It was a lurid trial that caught the public's attention. He won an acquittal. That had been ten years earlier.

The young woman had since remarried, had two children and sent him Christmas cards each year.

So now he had no heroes, only the Law, and even then the American criminal justice system tested his faith.

His clients were never innocent until proven guilty. Prosecutors thought them guilty from the moment of arrest. Fletcher saw his advocacy in life to make the prosecution *prove* that guilt.

As legal counsel, even if his client was guilty, he must do, and always did, the best job possible to guard against a false conviction. His dedication and fierceness in the courtroom had made him one of the more controversial personalities of the city.

During his rise to prominence as a criminal lawyer some had called him an opportunist, immoral and ruthless. The name-calling and gossip only added a piquant touch of mystery to his reputation. Oddly, it got him entry into some of the best homes in Atlanta. His mystique was augmented by his recently published book.

The book, *101 Ways*, had been a tongue-in-cheek catharsis, a protest to his married friends to stop using him as a dumping ground. After all, the very reason he remained a bachelor was so he wouldn't *have* to listen. However, what he had told Cleo was the truth; he had never meant it for public consumption.

It had begun as a joke. But who believed him? Certainly none of his colleagues. The book made him come off sounding as if he didn't like women. Now he had to suffer their challenges.

Women wanted to change him. They wrote him letters proposing marriage so that they could convince him of the error of his ways. They came into the courtroom wanting his autograph, wanting him to dine, or…just wanting him. It was crazy! The last thing in the world he wanted to be was changed. Or married.

He wondered if Cleo would believe him about how the book came into being. By the time he had mulled the prospect for ten minutes, the idea that she might not had swelled beyond reason. Yet the fact that she had provoked him to thinking back on it all annoyed him, too. He didn't want to start working over his memories, like an old man. It was a dangerous pastime, taking the measure of what you've done and been and holding it up to the future. It made the forward road look too short.

Fletcher had a reputation for having the coolest head in a courtroom, but he couldn't stop himself from feeling anxious about Cleo, what she might be thinking of him. *If* she was thinking about him at all.

He had another anxiety, too, of a different nature than appearances. It was between his thighs and affecting him more than he had supposed anything could.

He moved off the bed and began dressing in the dark. So what if she was asleep? Sleep was something you did when there was nothing better. He was taking a risk and he knew it. He could feel his heart pumping faster.

With one leg inside his slacks, the other out, he stopped. He was behaving like a teenager. Behaving as if he'd never known a woman. The thought aroused amused irritation. It was only that she pricked his curiosity. And once pricked...

He finished pulling on his pants.

Moving silently through the cabin, he was careful not to awaken those with whom he shared it; Ward Miller, Ward's wife, Marilyn, and their two children.

Fletcher had known Ward for thirty-one of his thirty-eight years. They had undertaken their adolescent rites of passage together—Ward usually playing a straight sort of man, solid, stoic and methodical to his own flamboyance and articulateness, skills that now served him well in drawing rooms and the halls of justice.

Marilyn had entered both their lives in college. She was small, petite and in those days, had been just zany enough to tolerate both himself and Ward as emerging adults. Ward had been almost apologetic when he informed Fletcher he was marrying Marilyn. "Look at it this way, Fletch, she can cook...well, not yet, but she's willing to learn, and she does laundry. You can appreciate that since you're always borrowing my socks.''

''She must do something else, too... almost,'' Fletcher recalled saying. ''She's got you following her around like a puppy looking for scraps.''

''Yeah,'' said Ward dreamily, and Fletcher had decided not to tease him further. Marilyn wisely did not intrude on their long-standing friendship. Instead she just accepted it and the three-way relationship had proved durable.

Fletcher himself took a dim view of the utility of wives, particularly ambitious wives. Marilyn had learned to cook and she did do laundry—until Ward started earning enough that she could hire help. As for himself, he ate out and took his clothes to the cleaners. As far as he was concerned, people's moral turpitude rendered marriage obsolete. The fact that he spent most of his own evenings working or alone was a minor irritant—female companionship, when required, was only a telephone call away.

However, all in all and despite a slight nervousness about Marilyn being on the bossy side, he did like her. He was godfather to both of her children. He liked that, too. It salved some atavistic quality in him.

Katie and Roger slept on the sofa bed in the big room that served as kitchen, dining and family area. He glanced their way as he slipped through the room. In the dim glow of the night light, Roger was sprawled atop the coverlets. Katie was curled into a ball on her side.

The cabin creaked and shifted in the dark. The hinges on the screened door squeaked as Fletcher emerged into the starlit night.

The throaty cry of a great horned owl greeted him as he walked briskly along the path. He watched a dark shape plane swiftly, soundlessly down upon unsuspecting prey. There was a squeal, a flutter of broad wings, and then, as

silently as it had come, the big owl floated upward, a limp
form dangling in its claws.

The old owl worked his territory the same way Fletcher
worked the courtroom. The analogy made him smile.

CLEO WAS JUST REACHING that first stage of good slum-
ber—body relaxed, thoughts pleasant but with no discernible direction, when there came several quick raps on
the door. Drowsily, she sat up, listening, thinking perhaps
she had dreamed the sound. The raps came again. Soft, yet
insistent.

A quiver of fear streaked down her spine. Nothing good
happens in the middle of the night, she thought. And how
was she to protect herself if it was some kook, some
blackguard bent on evil?

"Who's out there?" she called warily.

"Me, Fletcher Maitland. We met earlier today. I
couldn't sleep wondering..."

The quiver changed, no less a fear, but one that was far
more titillating. Cleo swung her legs off the bed, sitting
there for a few hesitant moments to track what she knew
of Fletcher Maitland, deciding whether or not to open her
door to him. He was a writer, single, attractive...
harmless? No, a man such as he was never harmless. But
he was somebody's uncle; she'd heard the child call him
that, so probably his intentions were good and honest.

Her logic was hackneyed and she knew it, but she moved
off the bed anyway, took the one step that put her at the
door, unlatched it, opened it only a crack to preserve her
pajama'd modesty and peered through the crack with one
amber eye. "I remember that we met, Mr. Maitland. I've
hardly had time to forget."

"I thought we agreed. I'm Fletcher, you're Cleo."

"We didn't agree on anything."

"I guess you think I'm crazy, knocking on your door in the middle of the night like this . . ."

"The thought is crossing my mind this very minute."

"I couldn't sleep. I wanted to explain about the book. I'm not a writer, I'm . . . you see I have all these married friends—"

"Mr. Maitland—"

"Fletcher."

"All right . . . Fletcher . . . I really don't want to know anything about your book. I don't think I'd like your book. The title puts me off. I can just imagine what pearls of wisdom you've got between the covers."

"If you'd just let me explain—"

"Listen, up until two minutes ago, I was thinking some very nice things about you. It meant overlooking the book, but nobody's perfect."

He drew in his breath sharply. That she had been thinking about him delighted him. That she would admit it left him bereft of his usual verbal eloquence. "What things?" he asked baldly.

His face was touched with shadows, his expression indiscernible to Cleo. "Now I'm thinking you're an eccentric egomaniacal insomniac," she said. "Good night."

She closed the door, set the latch and crawled back into bed.

The rapping began again.

"Go away."

"What nice things?" he persisted.

"I can't think of any now. I'm too sleepy."

"What about tomorrow?"

"I won't be able to think of any tomorrow, either."

"I've been thinking nice things about you, too," he said. Turn and turnabout was only fair, thought Fletcher, bringing in his courtroom skills.

Cleo sat up. "You have? What?"

"I like your hair."

Cleo fluffed up her curls.

"And, you have spectacular legs."

Cleo wrapped her arms around her knees.

"Are you listening to me, Cleo?"

"I can hardly keep from it. You have your mouth right up to the door."

"I feel pretty stupid standing out here on your step talking to a door."

"Ever think about quitting while you're ahead?"

"Am I? Ahead, I mean."

Cleo smiled into the dark. "Maybe."

"Are you smiling?"

"No."

"You sounded like you were smiling."

"That sound you hear is me putting a pillow over my head. Good night!"

"I'll be here in the morning, for coffee," he said. "Decaf. Folger's, if you have it. I always did like Mrs. Olsen."

"Would you...would you just please go away," begged Cleo.

"Have we got a coffee date?"

"If I say yes, are you going to leave and let me get some sleep?"

"Sure am."

"It just so happens I have some Folger's decaf."

"I know," he said. "I saw it on your table this morning. Sweet dreams."

Sweet dreams? mused Cleo with no small derision. Sweet dreams came behind sweeter sleep. Fletcher's appearance put her in such perplexity of spirit that sleep was going to be impossible.

RETRACING HIS STEPS along the path, Fletcher, hearing a leaf crackle now and then, wondered in an aside if squirrels were still about so late. But mostly his thoughts were focused on Cleo.

Looking back on it now, it was an insane thing for him to do—traipsing over to her camper like that. Still, he was trying to assess how he had made out, and he took infinite pleasure from the contemplation.

Maybe it wasn't so insane after all, though. If Ward or Marilyn got wind that he was interested in a woman, a terrible amount of ribbing would ensue. He was already getting ribbed terribly about *101 Ways*. Enough was enough.

On the cabin steps he stumbled, then felt soft flesh against his legs. A tight little squawk shut itself off in mid-squeal.

Fletcher caught himself on the screened door before he fell, though his flattened palm tore the screen from its lath.

"Crimey! Uncle Fletch," whispered Katie. "You tryin' out for the Jolly Green Giant, or what? Parts of me are mashed flat."

Fletcher gained his balance and reached down to help Katie to her feet. "What're you doing hiding out in the dark?"

"I wasn't hiding. I couldn't sleep, so I came to look at the moon. Sometimes deer come right up to the steps in moonlight."

"You were sound asleep twenty minutes ago."

"I was not!" she said adamantly to thwart his suspicions. "I was trying to will away a stomach ache. Then I heard you sneak out."

There were rocking chairs on the porch. Fletcher felt around in the shadows until he located one and sat down, stretching out his long length. "Grownups don't have to sneak, unlike some eleven-year-olds I know. Now come over here and let me make sure you're okay."

"I'm fine."

"You're being coy. Come over here anyway, and sit in my lap." Her very youngness moved Fletcher to a charity unusual for him. He thought the tender feelings he harbored for Katie might be the sweetest he would ever have. Though the older she got the more persnickety she was, watching her grow up was giving him insight into the female psyche. Katie had begun to get possessive about him around the age of four, and she collected and stored up little happenings between them to flaunt it. At the moment she was torn between acting adult and the lure of his arms.

The breeze off the river was cool, cutting through her thin pajamas. Katie shivered, then opted for Fletcher's lap. When she was comfortable, her back braced against his chest and her legs hanging over the chair arm, he put his arm around her and squeezed.

"You followed me, didn't you?"

Katie burrowed into his shoulder. "I went for a walk," she said, avoiding outright denial and so a lie. She was trying to watch her p's and q's. No telling what was going to be held against her in heaven.

"I suppose you overheard everything."

"No." A truth easily told. She had been too far away and had not dared to creep closer. She lifted her head and glared at Fletcher. "You like her?"

"I just met the woman," he answered. "How's the tummy now?"

"Okay. You're changing the subject, Uncle Fletch."

"That subject is changed," he said in his most authoritative courtroom tone.

Katie emitted a lugubrious sigh, and the exaggeration of it was not lost on Fletcher. "You want something, Katie. What is it?"

"I just want to talk. Nobody talks with me. Everybody just talks through me or around me."

"What do you want to talk about?"

"Me. Do you remember when I was little?"

"I remember you before you were born."

"Huh? That's impossible."

"It was right here in this cabin, matter of fact. It was Christmas and money was tight, so your mom and dad and I and Horace—"

"Horace? The big detective you fight with all the time?"

"We don't fight. We have differences of opinion. He wasn't a detective then, he—"

"It sounds like fighting."

"You want to hear this or not?"

"You're talking about everybody else, not me."

"I'm just setting the scene."

"Don't make it boring. Children don't have long attention spans, y'know."

"As I was saying," Fletcher muttered, sorely tempted to dump Katie off his lap, "we pooled our money for the Christmas tree and dinner and came down to the cabin."

"Why?"

"We were romantics then. We didn't have money for presents. We thought we ought to have Christmas before a roaring fire, and this was the only place we knew that had a fireplace."

"You have a fireplace at your house."

"I didn't have the house then. I was poor."

"Were Mom and Dad poor?"

"All of us were."

"Boy, I'll bet Mom didn't like that. So, go on. How did you see me before I was born?"

"We were playing pinochle, your mother had her hands resting on her stomach. All of a sudden her cards flew every which way. She said you kicked her. Then we all put our hands on her stomach, and sure enough, there you were, racing around like you were playing a game of tennis or something. Of course, none of us met you face to face until Valentine's day...."

"You're not makin' all this up?"

"Nope."

"Was Big Momma here, too? I could check it out...." Katie operated on the childish logic that if any two adults told the same story, it was true, if three adults told the same story, it was a conspiracy and not to be believed.

"She came by later with a pumpkin pie, which was a good thing. Marilyn didn't know the first thing about how to cook a turkey. Big Momma had dinner with us."

"Did she meet me?"

"We told her about you."

"What'd she say?"

"She told us how her own daughter, Francine, before she was born, had kicked her third husband out of bed and that he kept on going. She predicted you'd be a girl. Before that, Marilyn was certain you'd be a boy."

"I'm glad I wasn't a boy. I'd be Roger and the worst pest in the world."

Fletcher let that float on by. He wasn't about to discuss genetics. So they sat in semisilence for a few minutes. He, waiting to see where the conversation would go, hoping he could cope, while Katie gave another of her giant sighs.

"I can't imagine being in Mom's stomach. Musta been dark in there."

"I imagine so."

"I guess Mom and Dad had to do it to get me there, right?"

Fletcher choked. "You want to know about sex, talk to Marilyn."

"Don't get uptight, Uncle Fletch. I already know everything about sex. I know how sperm swim like fish and find the egg to make a baby. I just can't imagine it, is all." What she couldn't imagine was exactly how. She knew about anatomy, the difference between a man and a woman. She'd seen Roger naked often enough. The mystery of it all was which body part went where? The impression she got was that sex had to do with what was between a man's legs. But after she'd observed Roger's limp little worm, she'd dismissed that out of hand.

Fletcher settled back. "The creation of life is an awesome thing." Truth to tell, it scared the hell out of him. He'd never understood how Ward and Marilyn just seemed to take it in stride.

"I think having a baby is a brave thing," Katie mused. "I'd be scared to do it myself."

"Me, too."

Katie scoffed. "You're not afraid of anything."

"Yes, I am. I'm afraid if I don't get my beauty sleep I'll look like made-over sin in the morning."

Katie refused to take the hint. "Do you remember the first time you took me to the zoo?"

"Not that story, not tonight."

"Please...?"

Fletcher made a soft pinched noise in his throat. "Yes, I remember the first time I took you to the zoo...."

"It was July Fourth and Mama was in the hospital having Roger and Daddy couldn't find Grandma to watch me, right?"

"You're leading the witness," he told her, "and telling the story."

"I was just setting the scene," she said sweetly. "Did I have a good time?"

"You know you did."

"No, I don't. I was only one and a half. I can't remember that far back. Did I laugh at the monkeys?"

"Yes."

"What else?"

"You said 'bird' for the first time."

"I was a smart little thing, and so cute, too. What else?"

"You petted the lambs."

"What else?"

"I can't remember anything else."

Katie lifted her head away from his chest. "You can too! I want to hear the best part."

Fletcher expelled a groan laced with asperity. "You made a bigger blob in your diaper than an elephant."

"Did you change me?"

"I tried."

"Then what?"

"Then I went home and drank a bottle of Scotch. Now hop down, no more stories."

"Only one more? About—"

"No, the jury's in. I have an early date."

"Rock me to sleep, then." She waited, giving him a chance to respond. She hoped he didn't think she was a baby. But she felt as if no bad things could happen to her while she was in his arms. Sleep was scary now. Suzie

Stahl, with whom she'd roomed on a recent overnight stay in the hospital, had gone to sleep and never woke up.

Fletcher kicked the rocker into motion with his foot. "All right, for ten minutes. After that, asleep or not, off to bed you go."

"Deal," she said, and snuggled deeper into his chest.

When Fletcher finally tucked Katie in beside Roger, she was smiling.

Compared to his goddaughter, he thought, he was emotionally poor. A sad plight for a thirty-eight-year-old man who considered himself a success. It was only with Katie that he lamented what he might have had, the ordinary things that most people held dear, that could have been his, if he'd chosen marriage instead of bachelorhood.

But domesticity was not for him. That kind of destiny could wait in the wings forever as far as he was concerned. He undressed and pulled on pajama bottoms, which he was forced to wear since privacy in the cabin was nonexistent, even behind a closed door.

Then, fluffing his pillows, he spent a drowsy minute probing Cleo's self-protective facade, another few minutes in the wonderment of anticipation of their coffee date and a good portion of the remainder of the night trying to ignore the adamant sexual signals his body was sending.

CHAPTER THREE

THE NOTE WAS ATTACHED to the camper door with a Band-Aid. It said:

In the words of Ann Landers— Wake up and smell the coffee. That means there's a pot of Folger's decaf on the stove—help yourself. Friends?

Cleo.

P.S. Don't forget to unplug the pot.

Fletcher reread the note, smiling to himself. Cleo was having a joke at his expense. He liked a woman with a sense of humor. If he had to rate sex and humor, humor would be number one.

He rapped once on the door, then yanked it open. Cleo wasn't there and she wasn't hiding. Coffee service for one was set out on a small counter next to the stove top. Another note, another Band-Aid: Remember! Unplug the pot. No signature this time.

It dawned on him with stupefying swiftness. Cleo Anderson had stood him up! Women just didn't do that—not to Fletcher Fremont Maitland.

He had a certain elegance, didn't he? One that women adored? He knew how to behave with instinctive gallantry. He was adept at small talk; he knew well how to dance the social minuet. Plus, he was well respected inside the courtroom and out.

Fletcher puffed up with indignation, stiff pride and a stab of disappointment. He had regarded the coffee date and all that he planned to come after it as a fait accompli. He felt dazed, numb, astonished, outraged, above all—cheated.

He unplugged the coffeepot and stepped outside. The camp was beginning to stir. Voices drifted to him on the breeze. The sun crept up the sky, leaving the backdrop of the swamp the color of wild orchids that in spring laid a shell-pink coverlet over the Suwannee.

Cleo Anderson was out there somewhere laughing her head off. It wasn't funny. It wasn't funny at all! He hated women with a sense of humor. They never took anything seriously. With long strides and a growing sense of injustice—done to himself—he walked back to the cabin he shared with his long-time friends.

Ward Miller was sitting on the front porch, still in pajamas and robe, having his coffee. He had a receding hairline, which embarrassed him, an overhanging belly, which he blamed on Marilyn's cooking, and the kind of sweet smile that women of all ages envied. Behind the pleasant facade was a good, if methodical, mind. "Coffee's made," he said as Fletcher approached.

"I'm not in the mood for coffee."

"Did the kids roust you out of bed this morning? Marilyn told them—"

"Nope."

"You don't look happy. A case worrying you?"

"Do I have to look happy twenty-four hours a day? Is that some sort of prerequisite for camping? A man can have a bad day without the whole world coming down on him, can't he?"

Ward gave him a cherubic smile. "You can have all the bites out of my hide you want. I can spare it."

Marilyn came out of the cabin bearing a tray with coffee and doughnuts. She pulled up a chair, poured herself and Fletcher a cup. "You two fighting already this morning? You're worse than Katie and Roger. Speaking of which, did they go off with you, Fletcher?"

"They were still in bed when I left."

Marilyn frowned. "Maybe they're at Big Momma's."

"They can't be far. Leave them alone," suggested Ward.

"That's easy for you to say," Marilyn shot back. "You always think things will be fine. But they aren't. Suppose something happens to Katie while she's with Roger. He'd be traumatized for years."

Ward squirmed. "Doctors don't know everything."

"They know about Katie. Why can't you accept that?" She turned a pleading face to Fletcher. "Tell him. Explain to him. Make him— Oh, I give up!" She jerked to her feet.

The men watched her retreat into the cabin, flinching when the door slammed. Ward slumped in his chair. "I don't know why I thought it, but I did, that spending some time here this summer, where we've had such good times . . . well, I thought that good memories would prevail."

The thick cabin door swung open again. Marilyn pointed to the porch door. "And, one of you bums had better fix that screen before Big Momma sees it."

Fletcher decided he needed coffee after all and took a sip. A moment later they could hear Marilyn rattling pots and pans in the kitchenette. Ward sighed. "Do you think she's in a bad mood?"

In spite of his own bad feelings, Fletcher laughed. Ward's simple, direct optimism was always disarming. "I'd say she's leaning that way."

Ward shook his head, contemplating his lot. "Why don't you suggest to Marilyn we drive over to Jacksonville for dinner one night. Get Big Momma to watch the kids?''

"If charisma worked on Marilyn, she'd have married me instead of you."

"You're right," said Ward with friendly vindictiveness. "Give her an hour to cool down and ask anyway. She's not always immune to charm."

The comment made Fletcher's mind turn once again to Cleo. He finished his coffee. "I think I'll go over some briefs. I have a couple of tough appeals coming up."

"I think I'll just eat these doughnuts," said Ward. "I hate waste."

Fletcher, too, hated waste, especially of time, perceiving inaction as a form of death. Even as a boy, he'd had to keep busy, reading to improve his mind, playing hard to shape his body and working with a demonic intensity to get somewhere—up in the world. Application of his mind and body got him where he wanted to be, got him what he wanted—period.

Yet all his intentions toward Cleo had sputtered and misfired. The failure clung hard; his ego suffered, so he went into his room and sulked, a pastime which in others he considered foolish and unmanly. His feelings were hurt, and he spent the day exploring how it could happen that a woman just met could affect him so.

He decided she was without depth or mystery or promise, acting coy and shrewd and tricky just like every other woman he knew. He uttered an expletive and threw the heavy transcript across the room. It hit the wall and landed with a thud.

Marilyn came to the threshold and glared at him. "Watch your mouth, Fletcher, my children are at an impressionable age."

"Right," he said, holding back any hint of apology.

"You know what, Fletcher. One of these days a woman is going to come along and knock that arrogance right out of you. I'm waiting for the day."

Her comment hit too close to home. He felt about as arrogant as a limp noodle. It was confusing and alarming. He ran his hand through his hair, then smiled up at her. "Think it'll be anytime soon?"

Marilyn gave him the look from beneath her pert lashes that she used on the children and Ward when she brooked no nonsense. "Can't be too soon to suit me. Now, how about getting off your duff and fixing the screen. Ward's all thumbs."

He heaved himself off the bed. "Okay," he agreed, but afterward, he told himself, he'd go for a walk. He needed to meditate, to rethink his existence. The idea startled him. Rethink his existence because a woman stood him up?

It was unthinkable.

He must have brain fever.

CLEO TURNED HER EYES to a break in the treetops, noting the cloudless blue sky. Then she wished she hadn't because she had to wait for a moment beneath the panoply of thick forest for her eyes to adjust once more to the dark green gloom. The straps from her backpack, filled with cameras and lenses, a notepad, a thermos of juice and a bag of trail mix, bit into her shoulders. She shrugged an adjustment and sighed with the reprieve.

Suddenly from nearby, below a thick knot of underbrush came a long-drawn, tremulous series of hisses. She took a step back and squatted, her gaze searching, swinging to and fro until she spied the quarry.

Well camouflaged for nesting ground level, the short-eared owl hen elongated her neck and hissed again. Cleo was elated. Such defense on the owl's part meant that she still had eggs to hatch, or nestlings not yet ready to go out on their own—or both. But Cleo knew she would not get a glimpse of them until their protective mother was calm and feeling unthreatened.

She backed away several yards and under the watchful eye of the owl, began to construct a simple blind. It was easily done with the underbrush and vines and low hanging branches. Cleo did not worry about the noise she made as she set up her camera on its knee-high tripod and dragged up a piece of rotting log on which to lay out the various lenses and the thermos. Though she was raised in the city, experience had taught her that no matter the uproar in an animal's lair, ten minutes of quiet would restore all to normal. Experience had also taught her to focus once with each lens and to use the remote control wire in order to get the best shots. Owls had incredibly keen eyesight so that she knew she was still detectable, but once the blind was constructed, with leaves, twigs and grasses pressed back out of the viewfinder's eye, her hiding place was intact and Cleo did not leave it.

She kept an eye on the nest through lightweight field glasses and snapped pictures with the remote control. The short-eared owl did not hatch all of her eggs at the same time, so one of two owlets in the nest was a fluffy white pouf with dark soulful eyes above its tiny beak. A darling. She knew pictures of it would appeal greatly to the children who read the magazine. Babies of any kind—deer, goat, bear or bird—won hearts, and subscriptions.

As she sat quietly, almost immovable, Cleo became aware of a strange harmony; her heart seemed to beat and pulse to the tune of the crickets singing monotonously in the dew-wet grasses. The sun rose higher, the dew dried. The shadowy blind was no longer comfortable. No breeze stirred; sweat began to trickle down her spine and between her breasts. She drank the juice in the thermos, shifted cramped muscles, and without conscious thought her brain produced images of Fletcher Maitland.

She recalled their conversation of the night before— every word, every nuance in his voice, and wondered if he really had gone to her camper for coffee.

He thought she had nice legs. He liked her hair. He couldn't know how heady those remarks were to her. Her boss thought well of her, but he never went beyond being a professional. After the first rush, Paul hadn't noticed anything beyond his law books and whether or not dinner was on time. Gram, well, high praise from Gram was none at all, which meant she found nothing to criticize.

Cleo rested her chin on her knees and felt a strange sleeping thing rise and turn over inside her. The same sensation had erupted that morning, filling her, enveloping her, surging its way beneath the chaste sheath in which she cloaked her erotic emotions.

When these emotions had overtaken her she had done the cowardly thing—run. From Fletcher, and from the buried longings that made her imagine all the wrong and improper feelings.

What did he think when he saw the note? Had he unplugged the pot? She had only thought of that—of leaving the note—at the last minute. If the pot was unplugged, why, she'd know that he had come.

After another moment or two of introspection, it seemed to Cleo that the most important thing in the world was to check that plug.

She gathered her belongings, packed the camera and the thermos, then shoved the pack out of the blind without disturbing its careful structure. An egg remained in the owl nest. She meant to visit the blind every morning in hopes of getting some shots of the newly hatched chick.

She heard the careless snap of a twig, then another. An animal? Deer? A bear? The nearby Okefenokee Swamp Refuge boasted a population of one-hundred fifty bears. But what did bears know of refuge borders? She pulled the knapsack back into the blind and hunched down, watching as best she could through the vines and leaves.

"I've found just the place," came a small voice.

People. Cleo sighed, and began to shove the knapsack out again.

"I don't want to do this! I told you!" A second voice, a child's, and there was something so plaintive in it that Cleo was reminded of her own childhood. Several yards away two children broke into the small clearing where an old log lay across the patch. Cleo recognized the girl with the huge gray eyes and the whimsical face who had collected Fletcher yesterday morning. Curious now, and with only a slight twinge of guilt for spying upon them, she held to her hidden place.

The boy, sturdier built than the girl, was the one with the plaintive tone. He was grousing, "This is stupid, Katie."

"I know what I'm doing. Pound on that log with your stick. Big Momma says snakes like to sleep under loose bark. I don't want to get snake bit."

Roger tapped along the log with no enthusiasm, dislodging nothing more hazardous than a green lizard. Katie spread a towel over the log, and lay down.

"Okay," she said. "Now pretend I'm dead. You're at the funeral with Mama and Daddy and Uncle Fletcher. No doubt my cousin Lindsey will be in the front row, too. She's such a show-off."

Cleo's jaw dropped. She had a gimlet eye for life's absurdities, but what she was seeing and hearing—the ritualized rehearsal for a child's funeral—was macabre! It had to be a joke of some sort.

"If you're dead, why don't you close your eyes?"

No, Cleo thought. *I don't want to see this. I don't want to . . . Maybe if I run . . .*

"Because you'll sneak off. Don't worry, when I'm really dead, they'll be closed. Now pay attention. Where was I? Okay. Pastor Dopple is going to say all these wonderful things about me, so Mother'll be crying and Daddy'll be takin' care of her. That leaves you. There'll be all these flowers. What you do is go up to one bunch and get a flower, a rose, if there are any—a white one. I'm sure I'll be buried in white, being as I'm little and sin free." Katie lay back, narrowing her eyes to slits. "Okay, get the flower."

"What flower? I ain't got no flower."

She opened one eye wide. "Grab up anything, stupid. Pretend it's a rose."

"I don't like this," moaned Roger, looking revolted.

Cleo empathized with him wholeheartedly.

"You think I like being dead?" said Katie, shrill and scornful.

"I'm goin' to tell Mama what you made me do."

Katie looked as fierce as her thin little face permitted. "You say one word, you snot, and I'll cut you out of my will!"

"Kids don't have wills."

"I'll get one, legal an' everything."

"What're you goin' to leave me?"

"It's not nice to ask that," she admonished primly. "Now let's get on with it." She narrowed her eyes again, stiffened her short length along the log and folded her hands over her abdomen. "Okay. You walk up to my casket and put the rose in my hand."

Roger hung back. "I don't think I can touch a dead person."

"Yes, you can. I'm your sister, you love me."

Roger rolled his eyes skyward.

"After my funeral you won't ever see me again."

Roger yanked his eyes back to earth. "You promise?"

"Unless you don't do this right, then I'll haunt you, Roger. I mean it! Every time you go in the bathroom to play with yourself, I'll be lookin' down from heaven."

Roger's ears turned a deep shade of pink. He stammered and blustered, "You been spying on me again!"

"You forgot to stuff the keyhole with toilet paper." Katie sighed. "I'm getting impatient with you, Roger." To her own ears, Katie sounded just like her mother. It pleased her immensely. "We're goin' to be late for lunch if you don't get the lead out."

He moved forward, one reluctant step after another, plopping a wad of leaves and vines on top of Katie's folded hands. "That's good," she said. "Now lean over the casket and kiss me on—"

"Oh, gross!" Roger turned pale. "I'm goin' to throw up."

"Rog-e-e-e-r . . ."

"No! I'll do the rose, but I ain't kissin' you! That's final! Yuk!"

Katie sat up, raring to protest. She shook the bouquet of weeds at her brother. "You'll do—aggggh! Roger Belvedere Miller! You stupid clod! You made my rose out of poison ivy!"

"I didn't do it on purpose," he wailed, looking properly contrite, but only for an instant and then his feelings won out. He backed into a tree. "Yes, I did do it on purpose! I wish you'd hurry up an' die so we could go home. I'm missin' a whole summer of playin' Little League 'cause of you!"

He pivoted on his sturdy, stumpy legs and went racing into the woods.

"I'll get you for this, Roger!" Katie yelled. "Ooooo, I'll get you good!"

She pulled the towel off the log and began folding it. "I'll get you, all of you!" she said, biting off each of the words and giving them an intolerable edge of bitterness. She glanced about the forest, then looked up. "I have guts!" she shouted. "I have more guts than anybody! I have a fierce will! You can't make me cry, because I won't! I AM NOT DYING UNTIL I'M GOOD 'N' READY!"

The muscles in her face unlocked, going limp, the shout shrinking to a disconsolate sniff, then everything was quiet, except for a slight susurration that was the wind in the treetops.

Katie tucked the folded towel under her arm, and when she turned into the woods, Cleo noticed how pink was the scalp, showing through the thinning hair.

She opened her mouth to call out to the child, then thought better of it. She was herself too shaken to offer comfort. "Dear God," she said thickly, as her stomach tipped and yawed, fishtailing crazily. Cleo was short of breath. She thought she might throw up.

She felt the forest slide away as waves of pity for Katie lapped at her. Cleo's interior voice tried to intrude with a warning, but she brushed it away.

The child's plight stirred old memories, and Cleo looked back through the funnel of the years to one particular summer when she was eleven, seeing her mother and herself as from a great distance....

She had been leaning her ear against her mother's bedroom door, listening to Ellie's weak-sounding voice pleading with Gram. "Mama, there's something wrong with me down there. I know there is. It hurts. I want a doctor.''

"You just want to show yourself, display yourself to a man. It's the red sin in you. That's what it is.''

"I have a fever, Mama. I don't care who looks at me. A woman doctor. Please.''

"I'll make you some tea, and an icebag.''

"Mama! I need a doctor!''

"No! I never displayed myself to a doctor and you won't either. I forbid it.''

The bedroom door was yanked open. Cleo had not heard Gram's slippers swishing across the floor. She straightened with a guilty start. "Gram, I—''

"You were spying. A sneak, that's what you are. Trying to sniff out things that don't concern you.''

"Is Mama sick?''

"Only in her head.''

"But, she said it hurts her.''

"It's her sins that make the pain, not her flesh.''

"If you won't go for the doctor, I will! I'll call an ambulance!''

Gram grabbed her. "You defy me?'' she shrieked, shoving Cleo into Ellie's room. The door slammed and Cleo heard the key turn in the lock.

"Mama?''

"There's nothing you can do, Cleo. Just sit with me.''

"I can go for help, out the window.''

"From a sixth floor walk-up? You have wings, now?'' She patted the bed. "Come here. I want you to promise me something. Promise me, when you can you'll leave Gram, that you'll leave and you'll never come back.''

"You mean, RUN AWAY? Where would I go?''

"When you finish school, that'll be soon enough. But go far. Very far.''

Cleo spent many of those long-ago summer days at Ellie's bedside, not eating, not sleeping. At intervals she
burst into angry tears. She was baffled by what was surely
Death.

Worse, she knew Ellie hadn't wanted to die, and she
wished she could believe Ellie hadn't known she was dying.
But she couldn't hide from herself her mother's last words.
"If I had a choice... It's better for me, Cleo, my life is all
undone anyway. I've never had the strength to fight
Mama. But you do. The times, your youth, the city, are all
in your favor. Get away as soon as you can."

"Could I go to my father?" She had always hoped,
expected to see him; he would come along, swinging
through the door with gaiety and assurance and love, just
in time to change everything for the better.

"No, never. He was a married man, but tender. That's
the most you can ask of a man, Cleo, tenderness. Will you
remember that?"

"I think so. It's not much to remember."

"No, it isn't, is it? But loving someone is all that really
matters. It's a good feeling to be consumed by love. Every
breath you take is alive with anticipation, every touch...."
Her voice was barely holding up; it trailed off, her conversation turning inward, speaking to someone Cleo had
never known.

After a long while Ellie focused on her again. "Don't
hope for too much, Cleo. You'll be happier that way."
Then she had turned on the narrow bed to face the wall.
"Rub my back a little, sweetie. I think I might sleep."

Ellie did sleep then—forever.

At age eleven Cleo learned what only the very old
know—how fragile was life; how dangerous to be consumed by love, how killing to have that love thwarted.
Everything mattered, everything hurt.

After Ellie was buried a strange thing happened. A new Ellie came into Cleo's life, an Ellie she didn't recognize. Suddenly Gram was setting Ellie up as a model. Ellie had manners while Cleo was inept. Ellie had always been a superb student, while Cleo complained about school; Ellie never lost her temper, while Cleo was prone to willful disobedience. Ellie was gracious and respectful to her elders; Ellie would never speak to her mother that way; Ellie was Gram's beloved daughter.

But after Cleo had divorced and returned to Gram, the old Ellie was back, full of sin, tainted. And Cleo had talked to Gram without hearing, touched without feeling, agreed without conviction because it was the only way to make it possible for both of them to go on.

In the end, Cleo had not even been able to keep her promise, for she never got far from Gram. Until Gram herself had died. That couldn't be counted as keeping the promise.

For long minutes after the old images faded, Cleo remained where she was in the present, indifferent to humming insects, the heat inside the blind, sweat dripping in rivulets down her neck, willing herself not to weep.

She knew how that child, Katie, felt. She knew. Baffled, enraged, frustrated. Helpless. Depression seeped into her soul, an aftermath of bereavement...tinged with loss.

Cleo did not know how much time passed. In a dazed fashion she finally slipped the backpack upon her shoulders and set out to return to camp. She knew she needed somebody or something to replace her thoughts of Ellie. Any activity would do, a conversation—about anything with anybody!

She strode through the forest taking long strides, her back straight, her gaze unfocused until she stumbled over a fallen limb. She picked herself up, searching the land-

scape. Had she walked around or over that when she entered the forest? She didn't think so. She pivoted in a slow
circle. The moss-draped trees, the palmetto scrub, the
shape of the landscape had too much of a sameness about
it.

She looked up. The sun was at high noon. She closed her
eyes, picturing her walk in. She had left the camper, taking the path along the river, past Big Momma's house,
which was the camp office. There was a telephone kiosk
and a Coke-dispensing machine on the front porch. The
sight of it in her mind made Cleo aware of her thirst.

Then she had cut across the hard-packed dirt at the
camp entrance, walking on the road verge. She had gone
less than a mile before she discovered a trail among the
trees. A deer trail. She remembered thinking they were
such creatures of habit.

The children had come into the clearing from a different approach. She must have followed them, got turned
around somehow. She was too hot and thirsty to just sit
and wait for the sun to shift. She began to walk again,
more observant, noting landmarks, the fork in a tree, an
oddly shaped limb, a cluster of wild grape vines. Now and
again she stopped, looking behind with a critical gaze, for
the shape of a landscape, trees, bushes or skyline, looked
vastly changed from different approaches. She came upon
the same tree twice.

She couldn't find her way. She was lost.

She began to hurry until she was running.

She ran into a barbed-wire fence, slumping over it, feeling a barb sink into the flesh of her abdomen. She pulled
away, a spurt of blood colored the madras blouse.

Oh, but the fence separated the camp from the Okefenokee Refuge. But which direction? she wondered, succumbing to a wave of panic. Left or right? Then she heard

the faint putt-putt of a motorized skiff. She turned right, which she figured was east and after ten minutes she broke through a wall of matted vines and underbrush. She heard the cry of relief in her throat, wailed back and far flung, as she collapsed in Big Momma Freeman's backyard at the corner of a chicken run.

CHAPTER FOUR

THE ELDERLY WOMAN was hanging out clothes. She whipped around at the squawking of hens, expecting to see the hawk with which she was in constant battle. The dern bird considered her hens his private menu.

"Law!" she exclaimed and hurried to Cleo's side and helped Cleo to her feet, while her eyes grazed the tangled brush. "You sure come through them muskeedines at a clip. A bear after you?" she asked. "Ain't never heard tell of a hant out in daylight."

"No, just my past," said Cleo.

"What'd you say?"

"I meant, I'm fine." She gave the old woman a shaky smile. She felt queasy, aching from her throat all the way down to her stomach.

"You done took sick?" Big Momma asked. "You look all pale, washed out, like some of those rags I was a-hanging."

"The sun got to me," Cleo said, unwilling to reveal the drama she had witnessed between the children and the effect it had on her. The old woman was just the distraction she needed. She let the pack slide from her shoulders, easing it down to the ground, and massaged her shoulders.

"It be hot a'right, and dry. We ain't had a speck of rain in three weeks. Course, the visiting fowkses love that. But the fishing would be a mite better if we had a dab of rain."

"I don't mind a good rain. I like the sound it makes on the roof of my camper."

"You be like my Francine, she allus did like the rain. Dreaming time, she called it. Course, when it rained, I allus wanted her to make bread. Francine be my daughter outen my third mister— Law! You're bleeding!"

Cleo looked down. "I pricked myself on the fence, just a scratch."

"More'n a scratch looks like to me. That there bob wire's rusted, you'll get an infection. You come with me, I got some sulphur. Keeps it on hand, like."

"Thanks, but—"

"No buts, you city fowkses is allus full of buts. It's a wonder the world don't sag with your but'n."

Cleo laughed. "You have a point."

"You et lunch, yet?"

"No, but—"

"You did it again! You can eat with me. I allus like company for meals."

"I couldn't impose on you, Mrs. Freeman."

"You call me Big Momma, I done tole you." They passed the clothes basket and Big Momma scooped out a snowy piece of toweling. "Bleaching and blueing and Argo starch been my Mondays for better'n sixty years, except when it rains, and then it's Tuesdays." She glanced at Cleo's pale face. "Shoulda tole you. When you wash you gotta use blueing, else the tannic acid outen the river turns everything yaller."

The kitchen was small, but neatly kept. Open shelves lined the walls, heavily laden with pots, pans, jars of home-canned foods. There were two stoves, gas and wood burning, side by side. The old silver-gray tabby was curled beneath the wood stove. A huge upright freezer against one wall seemed out of place.

Beneath a deep sink were buckets, folded rags and cans of Comet cleanser. The table was metal, painted white; the cane-bottomed chairs around it had seen a lot of wear.

"You set there." Big Momma pointed to one of the chairs. "Set, and take off your blouse." At the sink she wet the towel and wrung it out.

Cleo unbuttoned the blouse at the site of her injury, but she refused to disrobe.

"You're a mite modest, ain't you? Fer between women."

Cleo's bold proud face concealed something. "I just wouldn't feel comfortable sitting here in my underwear. I'm sorry."

"Nothing to be sorry about. If it's your way, it's your way. Now, let's have a look. Nasty cut, a'right. Peers to me it needs sewing, which I ain't got a mind to do." She began to clean the cut, washing away the clotting blood.

"I have Band-Aids in my camper—" Cleo didn't complete the sentence. She drew a quick breath. For a moment she was in suspension, thinking of Fletcher, their coffee date, broken—with regret now. What a terrible joke on herself if he hadn't come! She felt a violent apprehension. She had to know.

"You're whistling and I ain't even tetched the sulphur to it . . . yet. But I am now. Set tight."

Cleo yelped.

"Stings something fierce, don't it?"

"Worse than iodine," Cleo said after she'd caught her breath. Then she contemplated asking Big Momma about Fletcher, but changed her mind. Saying his name might trigger fate against her.

Big Momma screwed the lid back on the jar of pale yellow powder. "Imagine you're gonna have a scar, sewed or not."

"It won't be the first," answered Cleo. She had scars aplenty, only they weren't visible on the outside.

Big Momma set before Cleo a glass of iced tea, then began to bustle about the kitchen. "We got lima beans, taters and parsley, ground-pepper-cured ham and cornbread—"

"I really ought to be going," said Cleo. "I've taken up enough of your time."

"No, you ain't. You just set. I like looking at you. You remind me of Francine. Your red hair and bein' tall and your liking rain and all. Fair makes my heart flutter." She put a plate laden with food before Cleo.

It smelled wonderful. Trail mix was no substitute for breakfast or lunch. She discovered she was not only thirsty but famished. "Where's Francine now?"

Big Momma shrugged her thin wiry shoulders. "Don't know. She run off. You ever meet a Francine Freeman? No, come to think on it...Francine... Law! What was the name of my third mister?...Smith, that was me first off afore I got married. Then came Jim Bob Jones, my first mister, then came Powder Mullins, then came Abner Houser. That be it. Francine Houser, course Rooster Freeman raised her like his own, afore he died and she run off."

"I've never met a Francine Houser or Freeman," said Cleo. "Did you call the police? Missing persons?"

"Never did. Wouldn'a done no good. Francine could move through the swamp like a shadow. Mix her in with other fowkses and she could dis'pear like wind-blowed smoke—without the smell."

"How long has she been gone?"

"Better'n forty years now. You wants some more cornbread?"

Forty years! Cleo was speechless. Big Momma took her silence for acquiescence and slid another huge slice of golden bread on Cleo's plate.

"Francine was never one for courting. She dreamt of going to the big city and staying." Big Momma cleared her throat. "We had a spec of words and that's when Francine run off. I ain't had word nor note. I'll say this for my Francine, she allus was good at hoarding a grievance. She could do that better'n most fowkses hoard pennies."

Cleo hardly knew what to say, what she was expected to say. "I hope she writes to you, let's you know she's okay."

"She could do that. She learned rightly enough." The small dark eyes glistened. "I speculate when she's settled, I'll get word of some kind."

"Let me help you with these dishes," advanced Cleo, after she'd cleaned off her plate, wanting very much now to make her retreat. "Lunch was marvelous."

"Not today, you be company. Next time, you can be neighborly. Besides, you need to soak that shirt in a basin of cold water, lessen it won't be fit to wear again."

"I will, and thanks again for your help and the meal. I'm not as good a cook, but I'd be happy to have you for lunch sometime."

The desiccated old face brightened. "I'll come. You just have to ask."

Cleo retrieved her pack as she moved off the back porch. She was leaving Big Momma's with a lighter heart than when she'd arrived and with sustenance for body and mind. She was struck again by the friendliness of Southerners, how deftly they involved one in their lives; and the good feeling of companionship lingered.

Her feet flew over the grassy path. A few minutes later she stood staring with quiet joy at the unplugged coffeepot. The cup and saucer were exactly as she had left them, pristine and unused; but he had come. She felt his presence in the camper as one does that of an offstage character in a play. A shiver passed through her, touching every nerve, and the thoughts she had of Fletcher ruled her for a few moments.

The idea of searching him out to apologize for her own discourtesy made her stomach stretch this way and that in queasy undulations. She'd probably manage to spoil everything by saying and doing all the worst possible things.

Cleo glanced at her reflection in the shattered mirror. She looked a wreck. She would shower first, and take a nap to put some distance between the morning's fit of blues and the eagerness and excitement that was beginning to infuse her mind and body.

Suddenly she recaptured the moment when she'd watched him striding away, long and athletic with the easy grace provided by a body tuned to action, resilient and strong. What would it be like to feel those powerful arms around her? she wondered. To experience that hardness inside her own flesh.

Thinking thus, she swallowed a tiny stab of fear. There had been no men in her life since Paul, no man before him either. Men weren't all alike, were they? Gram said . . . but no, she wouldn't think of that now. What if Fletcher . . . Oh, but she was letting her imagination carry her away again. She wet her lips and gathered up towels, soap, clean clothes. After a nap she'd be clear headed and the collection of old ghosts and many small terrors would recede.

This was her milestone year, she reminded herself. She was leaving dangerous ground behind. Positively!

"UNCLE FLETCH, you busy?"

"I'm trying to be," he said, manhandling the screened door to the porch floor.

"I need to talk to you, it's urgent."

"Katie, every time you say urgent— Move that rocker out of the way so I can lay this out flat."

"I mean it this time," she answered while doing his bidding. Then she sat in the rocker, pulled up her legs and rested her chin on her knees. "It's urgent. And personal."

"Personal?" He glanced up at her. "What's that all over you?"

"Calamine lotion. I got an accidental case of poison ivy. It's not bad."

"Don't get too close, that stuff's catching."

"I need something," she said, and the gravity of her words were made more so by the lack of theatrics. She sat quite still, her eyes focused on him.

Fletcher waited for the heavy sigh; it didn't come. He had a sudden feeling of inexplicable dread and foreboding—the kind of feeling he'd get when a trial was going very well for him, and then something unnamed, invisible would seem to clutter his senses and he would know that disaster was about to strike.

"It sounds serious," he said, trying to waylay the inevitable. "Maybe you ought to wait and talk to your mom or dad."

"No, Dad and Roger have gone down to Big Momma's to thump watermelons and Mom's washing clothes. I've been waiting for it to get private, between us." The pulse in her throat was pounding. Her hands, thickly coated with lotion, remained wrapped about her knees. "Uncle Fletch, you know I'm going to die, don't you?"

The inevitable! Fletcher felt his stomach tighten.

"Well, you do, don't you?" Her eyes were huge, the irises dilated, her expression earnest, and yet... Fletcher got a glimpse of the imp behind the solemnity.

"Katie..."

"I know it, too. I heard what the doctor said. My remissions are getting shorter and shorter. And the medicine's not working anymore. When Mom asked him how long I had, he told her to plan an early Christmas for me, very early."

Fletcher felt the sick sensation growing in the pit of his stomach, and he wished he had eaten lunch. It might have filled the hollow place below his ribs. "Don't you think you should talk to Marilyn about this?"

"Mom pretends to me everything is okay. She wants it that way. And since I'm not supposed to know I'm dying, I can't talk to Aunt Mary Ellen either, she'd tell. Daddy goes along believing there's going to be a miracle cure or something."

Fletcher wanted with all his heart to deny the truth of what she was saying. A gesture in futility. He felt suddenly clumsy and inept.

"Well then, what's so urgent?"

"If there was something I wanted real bad and you could give it to me, you would, wouldn't you?"

He held that up to the cold light of logic. "I might, if it was within my province, and it doesn't go against your mother's house rules."

"Mom hasn't made a rule on this, and it has to be a secret, just the same as if I were one of your clients. Y'know what I'm talkin' about? Where you can't tell anybody what I say to you?"

"You mean privileged information."

"It's sacred, isn't it?"

"Sacrosanct," he corrected.

"Sacrosanct. That's what I want. We got a deal or not?"

"All right, but within reason."

"It's reasonable. I want you to help me make out my will."

Fletcher made a sound in his throat.

Katie stiffened. "You're just like Mother and Daddy! You want to pretend I'm not dying. I am! I am! I am!" she said with passion, whispering so that her voice didn't carry beyond the porch. "Nobody will help me, Uncle Fletch. It's not easy to die, not easy at all. I want a will!"

Fletcher cleared his throat of the lump forming there. "I wasn't saying no, you just caught me by surprise." A lassitude weighed down his limbs. "Okay. But you know my specialty is criminal law. We'll have . . . I'll have to check with one of my colleagues—"

"I want it legal, witnessed and everything, like Grandma Baily's."

Above and around the cabin the June wind whispered and rustled and shook leaves. "Legal and witnessed," he agreed.

"Plus sacrosanct," Katie insisted.

"Right."

She leapt to hug Fletcher's neck and kiss his cheek, leaving streaks of calamine pink. "Good, now Mother won't be able to put my things in the attic like she did Grandma's. And my cousin Lindsey won't get her hands on my record collection or my posters. She's been hinting from here to hallelujah about wanting them. I can just see her face when my will is read. She can stomp her feet and pout all she wants and it won't do any good. Will it?"

"No."

Katie looked at him from beneath her lashes. "You're taking me serious, aren't you? You're not just humoring me?"

"I'm taking you seriously young lady and I'm seeing a nasty streak in you that I don't think I like."

She bristled. "You see no such thing! I'm the sweetest little girl who ever lived."

Fletcher didn't know whether to laugh or cry at this child who would never be a bride or have children or grow up. "You are, eh? Who told you so?"

"Nobody, I know it myself. It's not mean to want to protect your most valuable things. Grandma Baily put it in her will that Aunt Mary Ellen couldn't have her good china, and Mom said it was because Aunt Mary Ellen is so clumsy. I'm just being practical like Grandma was."

"I stand corrected," said Fletcher, and Katie looked radiant. *Oh, how lucky we are,* he thought with a morose twinge of irony.

"What do I have to do to get started?"

"Write down what you want or don't want."

"Like a list? Anything?"

"Yes." He felt like crying. He had the look on his face of someone who has seen something frightening and can't get it out of his mind. He felt alone, isolated inside the élan that worked so well in good times, but was no help in times like these. The hand he dragged over his face came away with calamine.

"I know why you look so glum. You're worried you'll have to help me with spelling the words. I'll find somebody else to do that," she added in a grand gesture of generosity. "Unless... You aren't going to charge me, are you? Favors are supposed to be free."

"I wouldn't think of it."

"Good, if I don't spend it before I die—which I might—I'm thinking of leaving some money to Roger to buy that outfielder's glove he wants."

After Katie left to find pen and paper, Fletcher went into the bathroom to wash his face. His reflection glared back at him, drawn and white. Why, he thought, did death have to be so tangible, so solid, so indiscriminate?

He had lost the mood of calm that descended when he had begun to repair the screen but he went back to the task anyway. When he finished he decided on a walk. He needed the fresh air and activity to jar him loose from melancholy.

He strolled upon the path fronting the river. It would take him past Cleo's camper. She might be there by now. He could use the distraction. He had no intention of speaking to her, of course. However, it might be amusing to find out more about her. Where did she come from? What was her family like? Was she married? Separated? Divorced? Why in hell had she stood him up!

CHAPTER FIVE

CLEO INSPECTED her nails.

They were not yet long enough to file. Well, they wouldn't be—not in two days. But her hair was clean and shiny, the red curls hugging her head, she smelled of soap and she wore flattering white slacks with a navy knit pullover. The small wound on her abdomen ached, but the ache was manageable. She knew she looked nice, but refused to glance at her twin selves in the cracked mirror lest she feed on the sin of pride.

She had gone to sleep on the drowsy recall of the poignant threnody the child Katie had wailed toward heaven and awakened on the dream to which she could never put a face. In spite of those broody recollections, she felt refreshed. She was ready to take a stroll through camp to locate Fletcher, to apologize for being such a clod.

Exuberant one minute, terrified the next, she couldn't make herself take that first step out of her allotted campsite.

Twice she strode to the edge of her camp and stared down the path that wound through the park. Each time she retreated, finding some small thing that yet needed doing. A pair of folding camp chairs was still in the trunk of the car. She removed them. She washed the madras blouse, then had to string a clothesline on which to hang it.

For a while she sat under the awning in one of the chairs watching a group of youngsters take turns diving from the cypress into the deep dark hole in the river. She searched among them for Roger and Katie, but the distance was too far for recognition.

In the end she knew she was defeated. She could not go searching for Fletcher. It was too brazen a move. Too forward. She had verged on letting herself be guided by a heady romantic notion, building a fantasy around Fletcher Maitland.

She ought to know better. Just because she felt warm all over each time he came to mind was no reason to go chasing after a man. She had to find a zone between reality and illusion lest her behavior sink into impropriety. Besides, all he had to do was look into her eyes and she would fly apart.

However, the thought of cooping herself up in the camper for the remainder of the afternoon held no appeal. She moved her typewriter out of doors to the picnic table beneath the checkered light and shade, giving one last thought to Fletcher—she hoped he would come by on his own.

At first she stopped typing when there were loud shouts and catcalling among the children. Gradually, as she became engrossed in detail, the voices, alive and joyful, faded outside the clattering of the keys. Soon, her concentration was wholly upon the article she was writing.

She was not aware of Fletcher's presence until he spoke.

"I halfway expected to find you packed and hauled out of here this afternoon," he accused, standing over her, attractive in khaki slacks and blue chambray shirt, sleeves rolled to his elbows. He was indisputably male, sexually vital—and angry.

Cleo started, a flush of pink rising to camouflage the thin blue veins pulsing in her temples. A hot cloud grazed her eyelids. Exactly what she had hoped would happen had happened. How could he have divined her plea? Her voice failed her and air would not go down her lungs. She made a slight gesture with her hands, remembered her nails and shoved them out of sight on her lap.

"I—no. Why should I leave? I've only arrived."

Fletcher gave her an icy stare, trying to ignore the fact that her lightly fringed eyes seemed to take up her whole face. "You stood me up this morning. On purpose. You didn't—"

"You're mad at me."

"Clever of you to notice," he said, feeding his frustrations over Katie on Cleo's dismay. He knew it wasn't fair, but he couldn't stop himself.

She felt his eyes on her face. If he kept them there much longer she was afraid she would start to tremble. "I'm sorry. It was a rude thing to do. You have every right to be angry." How could she tell him that she was never very good at man-woman relationships, that she didn't think she was lovable, that she never knew quite the right thing to say or do once past introductions. "Would you like to sit down?"

Fletcher's bruised ego was clamoring for attention. Resting his elbows on the wooden table, he folded one hand over the other, and locked his gaze on Cleo. A fire burned behind her eyes, aflame with inner turmoil. Had he caused that? His spirits began to lift.

In a small pool of silence he realized she was waiting for him to continue the conversation. He wondered what would happen if he bluntly told her he wanted to bed her, that he couldn't get her out of his mind.

Uncertain of what she'd respond to, he decided to remain in the safe area of backgrounds. "It's occurred to me that I don't know who you are, where you're from, when you're leaving to go back . . . or to whom."

"Chicago. I hope I'm parked for the summer. And you do know who I am, you know my name."

"And this?" He tapped the typewriter with a fingertip.

"I write articles for a children's science magazine."

"Freelance?"

"Half-salary. I mean, I do field studies in the summer, take photos, things like that..." Oh, boy. She wasn't making any sense.

He looked at her intently, seeing again that constructed barrier of self. Her aura of sexuality fascinated him. He was certain that she was unaware of it, but it was there in the tilt of her head, the full breasts, the slender waist that flared into rounded hips. Only somewhere on her face— was it in the haunted look in her large amber eyes?—reflected a sensually unfulfilled life.

He had a sudden image of himself plunging into her, ingniting her smoldering sexuality, making it blaze to engulf them both. On another level, not at all sexual, he was aware of how adroitly she was avoiding the personal side of his questions. "Your family?" he asked.

"There's just me."

"Boyfriend?" He couldn't help it.

"No."

She was free. For him. The knowledge made his heart behave oddly. "Knowing your name and that you're all alone—those facts don't tell me much about *you*. Where you were born, who were your parents, what were you doing when you were five?" He discovered he wanted to know everything. What she liked to eat for breakfast, what made her laugh, cry. He watched her expression fill with alarm. Why in hell was she so frightened?

"When I was five?" Cleo asked weakly, her laugh shaky.

"And not the least...in case you planned to skirt the question, what made you stand me up?" His voice was melodious, richly promising. The more quietly he spoke the more aware Cleo was of his power.

"I don't know—panic?" she added in a small voice.

"Impossible." But he knew it was the truth, and she was trying to hide it beneath a veneer of nonchalance. He laughed, wishing her features revealed more than they did. He suddenly felt expansive, generous to the point of forgiveness. "Will you have dinner with me?"

"I beg your pardon?"

"That's the very reason why. To beg my pardon. Otherwise, I'll never forgive you for standing me up this morning. And over dinner I'll tell you all about Fletcher F. Maitland, accidental author."

There was a sudden great commotion beneath Cleo's ribs. Break bread? Become friends? No, he wanted more. He was lustily intense, giving off distinct sexual signals. Her mind raced ahead. Lovers? For a day? A week? Then what? At summer's end she wouldn't be able to live with herself.

She hadn't been able to keep a husband with her body and Paul was far less a man than the sexual corsair before her now. She knew enough about herself to understand how fragile was her female psyche. She couldn't bear another rejection. Anyway, she didn't want anything to happen, only for the situation to remain in excited suspension.

"I can't," she said, "but let me make some coffee...."

A second refusal? Fletcher couldn't countenance it. His ego flared. "No thanks, it's dinner or nothing."

Avoiding his eyes, Cleo straightened a stack of notes at her elbow. "Then...I guess it's nothing."

Fletcher was having trouble. Women pursued him, draped themselves on him, waited for his calls. They adored him, catered to him, sent him gifts and asked to do his laundry. When he was in a bad mood they moved around him as if the least word or gesture would cause a seismic shift. It was implausible to him that Cleo couldn't sense that. He felt pressure building behind his eyes.

"You don't give an inch, do you? I thought you were...but you're not, you're the most arrogant, the most stubborn woman I've ever met!"

Cleo visibly recoiled. "That's not true! I'm not at all arrogant—"

"Is that so? What do you think you are? Beautiful? Kind? Intelligent? Sensitive?" His tone tilted toward irony, with perhaps a touch of reproach on his own behalf.

With fire burning her cheeks, and caught up in the images of her he'd spurned, Cleo looked away. The sun was setting, the heavens streaked pinks and purples, dusk hovered and Fletcher's shadow lay elongated upon the sandy earth. Her gaze drifted back to his; she looked at his mouth and lost her composure.

"I don't know what I am. I've just sort of made myself up as I went along. I know I'm not beautiful. I do hope I'm intelligent, and sensitive. I can tell you're more angry now than when you arrived...but I sense you don't want to stay angry with me. Are you standing on principle by any chance? Is it because of your book?"

"My book doesn't have anything to do with this," he said, thwarted by an inadequacy of words that always before had come to him quickly, smoothly. For an instant he saw himself flailing uselessly around in the courtroom like a first-year law student.

"Please, change your mind?" she said. "Let's start all over. Have coffee with me in the morning. Eight o'clock. I'll be here. And then you can tell me all about your book." She spoke brightly, trying to salvage the unsalvageable.

Fletcher looked at her throat, slender and tanned against the navy knit. He had been so certain that she would capitulate. With an abrupt movement he got to his feet. "I can't. I have things to do—fishing. Another time."

A cool polite statement, lacking future promise. For an instant Cleo imagined him taking her out, holding her hand, their heads bent together, whispering; her inner voice reminded her this was fantasy. I know it is, she silently replied to it, and matched Fletcher's tone with a sinking heart. "Another time..." He meant never. "I...well, good night..."

"You, too."

She watched his back until he disappeared in the shadows, then her gaze strayed to the river. Invisible to her were the ancient forces that pulled it, tugging at it, driving it toward its meeting with the great Gulf of Mexico. One last glimmer of sunlight flickered upon its coppery surface, then faded on the current. Ancient, primitive forces tugged at her, too, warring within her. She felt them, felt fragmented, felt her devils closing in.

Cleo! Go after him!

I can't.

Why not?

I'm scared.

CHAPTER SIX

THE CABIN HAD AT EACH SIDE a door that led into a hall that circumvented the huge front room and allowed one a measure of privacy, and separate entrances to bedrooms. In no mood for companionship, Fletcher used the side entrance. The door slammed on his heels. His mild expletive brought Marilyn to the upper reaches of the hall.

"Fletcher! I wondered where you got to. Could you start up the grill for me? Ward took the kids fishing, and if the coals aren't..." Her voice trailed off as Fletcher came out of the darkened hall into the lighted living area. He was wearing a scowl that meant war was imminent. "Never mind," she said. "I'll do it myself."

"I'll do it. Where's the charcoal?"

"What's with you, Fletcher? Three nights ago you stalk in here in a huff, pack up without a word and run off to Atlanta. Then, at two o'clock this morning you're back, banging on the door to be let in. What's put you in such a bad mood?"

"I'm not in a bad mood."

"You are, damn it. It's written all over your face. Katie said you two have a secret project? Is it anything to do with...?"

"I'll need charcoal starter, too," Fletcher said, trying to sidestep her query.

Hysteria was an ever-present backdrop in Marilyn these days. She maintained a careful distance from her own emotions since Katie had been diagnosed—and overcompensated by watching everything close to her for shifts in moods, demanding a happy front.

Marilyn dried her hands on her apron. "Everything's on the porch." She followed him out. "Please, what's going on, Fletcher? What did Katie say?"

He gave her a depreciating grin, one that suggested Katie had only some childish prank on her mind. "It's a private matter."

"Private from me? I'm her mother!"

"The little twit put me on my word of honor."

Marilyn refused to be deflected. "Honor? What does honor count now?"

"It counts to Katie, and to me. I love her too, y'know. Besides, she likes having secrets. It makes her feel important, special."

"But, I want to know what she's thinking!"

Fletcher picked up the can of starter, the bag of charcoal. "Then ask her," he said, feeling a flash of pique, regretting it at once. More gently he said, "She would like to talk with you, Marilyn. She has so many questions."

Marilyn's face crumbled. "I want to, but...if it's about...I can't, I just can't. I'd fall apart. I feel like I'm held together with a weak rubber band as it is. Anyway, what could I say to her? She's bright. She'd know if I was lying. Besides, I'm not sure what I believe in anymore." She looked up. The black ceiling of sky flowed with a million stars. "If everything's all right with Katie, why're you so gloomy looking? Is a case going badly?" She held open the screened door for him.

"No."

"No," she mimicked. "I know you, Fletcher, and something's out of whack. Is it Ward? He's not holding together so good either, is he?"

"It has nothing to do with Ward."

"Then it is a person. Who?"

"I got stood up—a coffee date," he added, though he had not intended to say any such thing.

He could tell the unexpectedness of his reply caught Marilyn in mid-thought; he could see her wrestling with a picture of a woman—any woman!—refusing him. She had been waiting for him to go down for the count, feverish and cursing.

Years before, when she was taking his measure along with Ward's, she'd accused him of being a repressed romantic. Accused him of being a man who recognized how sex appeal, even more than sex itself, became power, saying it was a binding magnetism. She swore he cultivated his sexual charisma, using it inside the courtroom and without. "No wonder women throw themselves at you," she'd often said. "You practically beg them to!" Fletcher expelled a chagrined sigh. At least Marilyn's mind had shifted from Katie.

"Stood up? By a woman? Here in Big Momma's camp?" Disbelief was etched so deeply in her tone, Fletcher had to laugh.

"Right on all three counts."

"I don't believe it!"

"It happened. You can stop grinning. Into each life a little rain must—"

"But, who? When? Where is this paragon of a woman who can resist you?"

"Parked in number eleven at the end of the path." He deposited the charcoal and can of starter on the picnic table near the grill. "Go do your gloating somewhere else. And while you're at it, turn on the outside lights, will you?"

CLEO HESITATED on the narrow lane that wound through the camp.

But three days of thinking about Fletcher, three nights of midnight madness, lying awake hoping he would knock on her camper had driven her to seek him out. She was fast losing the unaccustomed derring-do that was pushing her to this utterly absurd thing.

Of course he could be gone—back to whatever life he lived. She would never see him again. In which case she would go on with her own life that flowed along drably, tolerating the loneliness lying in the corners of her existence. She didn't understand this pull he had over her; she had no standard to measure it by. But it kept her feet moving.

So far she had strolled past two cabins that were empty, two that were occupied. The children sitting on the stoops were not Katie and Roger. She deduced that since Katie called Fletcher uncle, he must be sharing quarters.

Approaching a third cabin that was occupied—two vehicles were parked at its side, inside lights were on—her courage flagged. She'd never be able to go up to the door and inquire for Fletcher.

The cabin yard was suddenly illuminated, the light spilling out onto the lane capturing her in mid-stride. A small sound of surprise erupted from her.

From several yards away Fletcher looked up and saw her, arrested in movement like a startled rabbit. Well! He felt his heart skipping, then throbbing. "Out for a stroll?" he called, aiming for sarcasm, missing it because of the marvel of discovering her there.

Cleo tried to think—if she said yes, she'd have to keep moving, past the cabin, past Fletcher... Oh, damn! Her throat was closing up. "No. I mean—" Her feet felt like lead. Lost on both ends. Oh, help! she pleaded silently, watching Fletcher close the distance between them in several long strides.

"You're not out for a stroll?"

In front of the cracked mirror she had practiced and practiced what to say. Now every single one of those words escaped her.

"About that dinner invitation..." She faltered, mortified. Suppose he said, "Forget it!"

"What about it?"

"I thought... if we're still friends, after..." She was wound as tightly as a spring, babbling, making things worse. "Is it still open?"

Now she'd made a fool of herself. Oh, it would haunt her and haunt her, like so many other times she'd been foolish first, regretful later.

Her body swayed slightly. She looked as if she were about to take flight. Fletcher sensed she was terrified. Of him? After she had so neatly put him in his place? It was beyond his understanding. Even more perplexing, he had a growing awareness of a reservoir of innocence about her, isolated in some sort of élan that was all exterior and strongly sexual—to him, at least. Maybe she didn't realize what signals she sent out. He had the most overpowering urge to put his arms around her. "It's open," he said briskly. "How about tonight? Will you join us?"

"Us?" Oh, wonderful reprieve. Now if her knees would just stop knocking.

"Family friends. We're here together. Grilled pork chops and I don't know what else Marilyn has in store for us."

"Wouldn't I be intruding on such short notice? I was thinking..." fantasizing just the two of us, a candlelit dinner, soft music...

"Fletcher? Do we have company?" Marilyn called out from the porch.

"Yes, we do." He put his hand on the small of Cleo's back, propelling her toward the cabin. "Come out and meet Cleo Anderson. I've invited her to dinner."

Marilyn stepped into the yard. To Fletcher's everlasting relief and Marilyn's credit, she hid her surprise.

"Welcome," she said, smiling, her gaze darting to Fletcher, then back to Cleo, who was grappling with distraction because Fletcher's hand was burning its imprint into her back. Stepping out of his reach, she accepted Marilyn's outthrust hand.

Katie's mother, thought Cleo, noting family similarities in the gray eyes, dark hair and small frame. Knowing what she did, Cleo wondered how Marilyn coped, how she managed even to smile. "If I'm intruding, or your dinner is already planned, we could make it another time," she said. Cleo wasn't at all hungry. Being near Fletcher fed her spirit. Anything more tangible was beyond consumption.

"There's plenty and we'll grill trout, too, if Ward and the kids have caught any. They should be back any minute."

"If I can help you, I'll stay. I hate sitting while someone else is working." If she was made to sit still and make trivial conversation, she'd burst.

"You can help me turn the chops," Fletcher said.

"It only takes one to do that."

"Practical girl," said Marilyn. "If you don't have an aversion to peeling potatoes, you've got yourself a job." As she led the way into the cabin, Marilyn asked, "Are you by any chance in number eleven?" When Cleo answered in the affirmative, Marilyn shot a glance over her shoulder to Fletcher. Aha! The mysterious paragon, her look seemed to say.

It cost Fletcher a huge chunk of his pride to make several trips into the kitchen during the next fifteen minutes—for celery spice, for a platter, for onion salt. He managed to brush against Cleo only once. She had stepped out of his way as if it had been unintentional, forcing out of him a muttered apology. He caught snatches of conversation. They were discussing the best insect repellants, tanning lotions, fabric, gussets—what in hell were gussets? He wondered if Cleo had asked even a single question about himself.

There were ten minutes of pandemonium when Ward returned with Katie and Roger and a string of trout. Cleo was introduced around and warned not to shake hands with the children. "Poison ivy—somehow," said Marilyn.

It was a bad moment for Cleo, for the morning spent in the forest came rushing back to her.

"You're the one Uncle Fletch went to see in the middle of the night," said Katie, her gray eyes suddenly lightened by the impishness of her grin.

"What's this?" questioned Marilyn, looking from Fletcher to Cleo, whose face was glowing pinkly.

"I didn't let him in," Cleo said, her dignity shredded.

"I didn't ask to get in," Fletcher countered, hating to admit it.

"Who's going to clean the fish?" asked Ward, and as an aside to Fletcher, "Remember I saved your neck, this time."

"Clean them yourself and at the outside sink," ordered Marilyn. She herded her offspring into the hall. "C'mon you two, bath time before mealtime." And, over her shoulder to Cleo, "Dishes are in the cabinet over the sink, if you'd like to set the table."

"Out of the mouth of babes," Fletcher said, when they were alone.

"That's all right, no harm done." Cleo gave him a slight smile; it was, Fletcher realized, full of self-awareness and just as completely lacking in it. She turned to the cabinet and began taking down plates.

Fletcher got glasses, opened chilled white wine, and soft drinks for the children. He glanced at her as he poured the wine. "What made you change your mind? And don't skitter away like I've got some unnamed social disease."

"Do I do that? Skitter, I mean."

"I get the feeling you're in flight all the time." He handed her a glass of wine. "I also noticed you're adroit at not answering questions. I have a client or two like that."

"Client? You're not a full-time writer?" But she knew what his answer would be. There was that special inflection on "client," whence all monies and fame came. Paul had talked and talked of . . . she let the thought trail away.

"I'm a criminal attorney. I told you I wasn't a writer."

"I should've guessed, your glibness with words…" She was past him, her face smooth and uninterested, while her stomach turned into a leaden rock. An attorney. Like Paul. Fate had misused her!

She carried dishes and silverware to the round wooden table, then counted out napkins. She shouldn't stay here, she thought. She had to make some excuse.

"I get the impression that you've had a bad experience with an attorney."

She looked at him, tall, attractive, vital, lounging against the counter—the dark eyes fixed on her face with a bright intensity.

"Because I have," she answered.

"What was it?"

"None of your business."

"Oh now, that's cold. I deduce you came out on the short end." Come on, he thought. Talk to me, open up.

"I came out, period."

He was reading her face, her body language; her reaction was that of a woman scorned. Perhaps used. Certainly divorced. A salvaged dignity. Now wasn't the time and the place to get into it. He refilled her wineglass and took it to her.

"I don't want it," she told him. "I seldom drink. It goes to my head." She was already feeling light and untethered, anchored only by remembered despair and present uncertainty.

"I'll make sure you get home, and safely. Cleo... give me a chance?" His smile was golden, pleading. He wanted so to touch her, put his hand under her chin, make her look at him, really look. He found himself willing to show her his vulnerabilities, tell her things about himself that he'd never revealed to anyone. He felt like he was in a tight corner. He had to say the right thing.

"I didn't mean to touch on a subject that makes you unhappy. You've been on my mind and I find I like you very much." Fletcher listened to himself in amazement. How easily that came! And, he meant it!

In an instant Cleo's head came up. "Why? Why do you like me? We're different. You're far more sophisticated and you know you're attractive."

He grinned. "Opposites attract, don't they? You're no slouch yourself. I do have a reputation for flawless taste where women are concerned."

She looked startled. It was as if he had flung her a challenge, daring her to deny to him that she was attractive, taunting her to deny his own appeal—if she could. In the diffused light of shaded lamps her amber eyes flashed, her chin went up revealing a vein pulsing in the soft hollow of her throat.

"I'll concede your taste in women," she heard herself saying. Somewhere deep within she was shocked at her own audacity. But he made her feel so seductive. She was responding to him in a primeval way.

Fletcher laughed, the tension in his body unraveled. "A two-sided rapier thrust! I'm undone."

Cleo gave him a reluctant smile. "You deserved it."

"What did he deserve?" asked Marilyn, emerging from the narrow hall. Her face was flushed, her hair damp from bath steam. "Never mind, don't tell me. Just pour me a glass of that wine." She sank on the sofa, depleted. "Vacations are so restful!" Then apropos of nothing, she said, "I miss my aerobics class, my coffee klatches, my—" A dry sob tore from her throat. "I can't handle it! I just can't! It's beyond enduring!"

Cleo stood frozen at the display of emotion. Fletcher moved to Marilyn's side at once and sat next to her. "What's happened, what can't you handle?"

"Look," she choked, unclenching her hand. Thick strands of damp hair clung to her palm. "Every day she loses more. The medicine makes her sick, makes her hair fall out. She's going so bald. I can't—" Fletcher scooped the hair from her palm and disposed of it.

"What can I do to help?" Cleo whispered catching his eye. He shook his head, nothing.

Marilyn wiped at her eyes. "I'm sorry, Cleo, I'm ruining your evening. This is a family matter. I should have kept it private."

"Don't worry about that—please." Cleo felt helpless; she was helpless, and the helplessness brought to the surface emotions better kept buried.

Roger and Katie burst into the room, then stopped short. They were clad in pajamas, freshly shampooed hair slicked back, their hands dabbed with calamine. "What's the matter, Mom?" asked Roger. "You cryin'?"

"No. Fletcher told us one of his obscene jokes. Made me laugh so hard my eyes watered."

Katie looked skeptical. "We didn't hear you laughing."

"Well, I did," she sniffed. "Go tell your dad we're ready to eat." She moved off the sofa. "Cleo, you sit there, next to Fletcher..." Her eyes bespoke another silent apology. Cleo smiled through her turmoil, and was once again made aware of Fletcher's commanding presence as he touched her arm and guided her to the table. Her thoughts shouted at her, echoing and contradicting each other.

Ward and Fletcher carried most of the conversation during dinner. Ward was an insurance broker, designing corporate group packages then bringing in the best insurance carrier. He was a mathematical whiz and for Cleo's benefit did number puzzles until Marilyn called him a show-off.

Katie and Roger argued over who caught the biggest fish. Marilyn chastised them with the reminder that company was present. The food was tasty. Ever aware of Fletcher's close proximity, Cleo managed only to swallow small bites. She was grateful when coffee was served, signaling the end of the meal.

"What do you do when you're not out camping?" It was Ward Miller asking, and Cleo, lost in her own reflections, at first didn't catch that he was speaking to her.

"Cleo?" Fletcher slid his hand along the back of her chair, touching her on her shoulder.

"Oh! Sorry. I write for a children's science magazine."

Katie and Roger perked up. "Which one?"

"*Bees 'n' Things*," Cleo told them.

"Hey!" said Katie. "We get it in school. You write that?"

"Not all of it, just the wildlife articles and the question and answer column."

Katie's eyes narrowed to slits. "So you're the one!"

"One what?"

"When I was in the fourth grade we had a science project. Mine was lizards. I wrote and asked did lizards have eyelashes and you never answered me!"

"Katie! That's not nice," warned Marilyn. "Besides Cleo might not have been working at the magazine then. That was two years ago."

"Yes, I was, but I don't recall your letter, Katie. I'm sure I would have remembered it."

"Maybe you didn't know the answer and you threw it away."

"I hope I didn't. Letters do go astray sometimes."

"I got the answer by myself anyway. Lizards don't have eyelashes. I caught one and looked at it under a magnifying glass."

"Good for you. That's just what I would have done."

"Really?"

"Really. You have a scientific mind. I have a bushel of letters with me. Maybe you'd like to read some of them and see if you can help me answer them."

"I'll help!" exclaimed Roger.

"She's not asking you, stupid," said Katie.

"Mom! She called me stupid."

"Well, it's the truth. Mom says for me not to lie."

"Nerd!" Roger sputtered.

"If there's going to be any name calling around here, I'll do it," announced their father.

Marilyn sighed and began to clear the table. "If only someone had warned me..."

Fletcher pushed back from the table. "Come on, Cleo, I'll walk you home."

Home? The evening was over? "I won't just eat and run. I should help with the dishes."

"No," said Marilyn. "You've done more than your share already. Besides, I wash, Ward dries."

"Since when?" he asked, his coffee cup clattering against the table.

"Since I just said so."

"If we don't make our escape," Fletcher whispered in Cleo's ear, "we'll be caught in the cross fire."

She bid a quick good-night as he steered her firmly out the door. Katie was fast on their heels.

"Oh, no you don't, back in the house," Fletcher ordered.

"I just want to have a word with Miss Anderson. A private word."

"No."

"Yes, let her," Cleo intervened, and to Katie said, "We don't have to stand on formality, do we? You can call me Cleo."

Fletcher moved off, waiting for Cleo on the path.

"I was just thinking that if you're a writer, you can spell pretty good, can't you?"

"Pretty good," agreed Cleo. "Why, do you need help with some school work?"

"I'm not in summer school. But I'm doing something personal and I need help spelling the words. It's sacrosanct though. You couldn't tell anybody."

"Sacrosanct?"

"Right. That means you have to keep your mouth shut."

"I think I can manage to do that, if you're certain you want my help. You don't think your mother would—"

"No! It's for her, in a way—"

A testimonial of some sort, thought Cleo. The child wanted to leave something of herself behind to be remembered by. It was sweet, and sad. "I'll be glad to help then. I'm at number eleven." A mosquito buzzed; Cleo brushed it away.

"Katie!"

"I'm coming, Mom. Tomorrow?" she said to Cleo.

"In the afternoon, that's when I type up my notes."

"I'll help you answer letters, too," Katie said in parting.

"What'd the little twit have up her sleeve?" asked Fletcher as Cleo joined him on the path.

"I'm on my word of honor not to tell."

"And, you're honorable."

Cleo looked at him in the moonlight. "Very much so."

There was something in her tone. Fletcher knew he'd been given a signal, a warning. He was going to have to go more slowly than he'd thought. But how taken he was with her, the way her long shapely legs matched his stride, the piquant look of her profile.

The moon's path was interrupted here and there by towering trees. The night seemed gentle and beautiful and perfect, the camp a place without anxiety or unhappiness. And yet it wasn't. Life surged in the shadows, animals scuttled out of harm's way or into it. And the cabin they had just left was filled with undercurrents of tension, turmoil and sadness. Cleo felt distanced from it, yet a part of it, and bereft.

"You handled things back there quite well," Fletcher said as if, uncannily, he had read her thoughts.

"I felt like the odd man out. What's wrong with Katie?"

"Bone cancer. A marrow transplant failed earlier this year. It was a last hope."

They were past Big Momma's house and on the river path before Cleo spoke again.

"How long has she been sick?"

"Two years."

"I wish there was something I could do to help."

"You helped tonight."

"I didn't do anything."

"You didn't back away from Marilyn when she had that touch of hysteria. If you had left she would've felt worse. Her friends tell her she's brave, so she thinks she has to be, all the time. And, Katie seems enthralled with you," as I am, he thought. "She'll be on your doorstep to look at those letters." He moved closer to her and paused. "The wine didn't go to your head after all."

"No."

"Then I don't have an excuse to tuck your arm in mine, so I'll just brazen it out and do it anyway."

The crispness of his shirt sleeve, the ropy muscles gone taut in his arm sent a shiver through Cleo. It felt so right, so fine to have him so near. "This is crazy," she said softly. "I've only just met you and your friends and—"

"And you're already a part of our lives. Stranger things have happened."

"Not to me."

"Because you usually don't take risks."

Cleo stopped abruptly. "Why do you say that? You don't know me. You don't know what I will or won't do."

Fletcher thought he did. He liked to know what people were after, what they believed, what they stood for. He found Cleo forthright, open, honest and her personality was clearly defined—yet, at times he found in her a disturbing reticence.

"You're playing it very safe with me," he said, his voice dark and intimate, seductive with those lazy interior syllables that were so like an actual caress. Cleo felt fear rising in her throat; it warred with desire that permeated all else. She slipped her arm from his. He caught her hand, clasping it with her own, holding fast as he tugged her in step again. "See what I mean?"

"No!"

Her reserve was at full tilt again. Uncertain what she'd respond to, Fletcher decided to talk about his background and began speaking.

He was thirty-eight years old, he told her, the only son of a sharecropper. When the farm on which he'd been born had gone wholly mechanized, his father, Willis, had moved the family to Atlanta where he found work as a mechanic with that city's transportation department.

His mother, Mattie, had been an imposing, iron-willed woman, somewhat of a nag. In the city, Mattie was soon accustomed to the luxury of running water, a roof that didn't leak and canned foods right off the grocer's shelf. She wanted more and more. On the salary he earned, his father was unable to satisfy her cravings, yet Mattie would not let Willis strike out on his own as a mechanic, for which he had a rare talent.

Fletcher was seventeen when Mattie died, he said, and then suddenly there was tranquility in his home. Dust collected in corners, under beds, dishes went unwashed for days, but his father began to laugh again. His spunk was gone, but not his good nature.

Fletcher had loved his mother, yet he couldn't help but notice how her absence altered his father. Where women

were concerned, the difference influenced him pro-
foundly.

"That's why you never married?" asked Cleo.

"That, or I haven't yet met the woman who could sway
me. Now, how about a few words about Cleo Anderson?"

"I graduated from the College of Du Page in Glen El-
lyn, Illinois," she said.

Fletcher laughed. "Could you spare a few more words
than that?"

"My mother died when I was eleven."

"Who raised you?"

"My grandmother."

"What about that terrible attorney?"

"My ex-husband."

"Ouch!"

"You have the same glibness of tongue."

"From now on, I'll stutter."

Cleo laughed, but as they reached the edge of her
campsite, the laughter died in her throat.

Fletcher squeezed her hand. "You're scared to death I'm
going to kiss you good-night."

"Why should I be afraid of that?" He was casting a
spell, helped by the moonlight, the cool splash of the river,
the susurration of a gentle wind that sent moss swaying as
if to nature's melody.

"You might find that you like it . . . and me."

"I doubt it. I mean—I do like you, but only as a
friend."

"Let's put it to the test, shall we, friend?"

He pulled her close and began caressing her taut face,
smoothing the frown at her forehead with a fingertip. Cleo
stiffened with resistance, but her bones seemed to soften
at his touch. She tried feebly to push him away.

"Lovely friend," he murmured.

"Don't," she protested.

"All this talking and talking...it doesn't mean anything. Let me show you what's real," he said, and stopped her mouth with his, nibbling on her lips until they began to swell with heated passion, until...she let them part to catch her breath, and he thrust his tongue into her mouth.

When it touched hers, demanding response, Cleo was electrified. Her brain screamed, bad! but her own tongue leapt to join Fletcher's and a throbbing took hold of her deep interior self.

Fingers that had caressed her face were on her back, kneading flesh, setting it aflame, and ever so skillfully pressing her loins to his so that she felt—couldn't help but feel—the growing hardness between his legs. For one long lovely sensual moment she strained to him and then a lucid, hovering panic reached out to her.

"Let me go!" She struggled away from him, yet the instant she was out of his arms she felt she had denied herself something essential. "You shouldn't have...we shouldn't have..." She didn't want to look at him now or even have any more conversation. Her heart was pounding, the strength of her own emotions a fearful weight.

Fletcher paused at the underlying desperation in her tone. "You wanted that as much as I did, don't deny it."

"I said we could be friends!"

He looked at her face, pale and trembling in the moonlight. "Cleo... We're adults here. You're acting like a fifteen-year-old on a first date."

"I'm not...not loose! You assumed... You took liberties. I don't ever want to see you again." Oh, but she did; she was so horribly mixed up.

Liberties! It was such an old-fashioned term, Fletcher almost laughed, but Cleo was so serious, he choked it back. "If liberties were taken, we took them with each other. You kissed me back, you responded to me." Swiftly he reached out and brought her body to him, his hands guiding her hips to his for an instant. "That didn't happen all by itself, Cleo."

She jerked away as if burned. "It can!" Faintness, accusation, unbelief made her voice waver.

Fletcher took a deep steadying breath. "Yes, sometimes, but this isn't one of those times. Our bodies came together, our lips..." He ran his hand through his hair. "I can't believe we're arguing about this."

She edged toward her door. "I have to go in now. Thank you for dinner." Her inner voice was guiding her, telling her what she should do, what she should not do—to keep the devils away.

Too late Fletcher caught her movement. "Wait!"

"No." She slipped inside the camper; he heard the latch catch. No lights went on, no sound came forth.

"Cleo, I know you can hear me. I don't know why you're so skittish, but you're making me think some terrible dark things. We're going to talk about them. I'll get to the bottom of you sooner or later. You've stirred me up and I'm not easily put off." He banged once on the door to make certain he had her attention. "And this is the last time I ever talk to you through this damned door! If you ever shut it in my face again, I'll snatch it off its hinges." He paused, listening hard, hearing nothing. "Good night, friend."

Cleo sat on the bed in the dark, shaking. She couldn't explain what was happening to her. She had just let him... She had wanted to be in his arms more than she had ever wanted anything in her life. She still wanted…she rubbed the palms of her hands down her legs as though to erase the sensation of having touched him.

She'd have to leave tomorrow, she thought. She'd have to hitch up and leave.

That's my Cleo, always running from the good things in life, jeered the small voice.

Oh, go away, it's your fault I made a fool of myself tonight.

Not me, Cleo dear, I was rooting for you. For a minute there I even thought you'd forgotten Gram and all her preaching.

I never forget Gram.

More's the pity. You don't really expect Fletcher to tolerate her mad old ways do you?

I don't expect anything! Oh, I feel so wanton, moaned Cleo. There was a demanding hunger in her and it kept mounting and mounting. Every waking thought of Fletcher made her wretched, every dream had his body entwined with her own.

As the hours dragged, sleep dulled the anguish, but it never completely vanished.

FLETCHER PAUSED on the path overlooking the river, his mouth tightening as he reflected upon Cleo. He seethed with a sharp anger that she had turned from him, escaped him. He could still taste her on his lips, could still feel the shapely length of her pressed to him. He was bone hard, aching with the need for release.

For some reason she was fighting her own nature; she exuded sensuality. All the signals were there, radiating from her—the tilt of her head, the small intake of breath, the discernible quiver in her full lower lip. A man was supposed to resist that? Yet she turned out to be a complete contradiction of all his expectations. Hell, he didn't need to wait for her to come around. He could have any woman he wanted.

Still thoughtful, he left the path, moving onto the lane that fronted the cabins. Any woman. Only Cleo posed some kind of challenge. Any woman wouldn't do. He wanted her. He'd keep her at arm's length while he orchestrated her seduction. A touch here, a look there, soft words. In the end she would cast off that odd barrier, offer herself to him.

Liberties, indeed. He knew just the liberties to take, to use... he was enchanted with the vision. He grew hard again. Damn!

Illogically his anger returned. Did Cleo think she only had to coo, talk in that throaty voice, bat her lashes and he would fall at her feet?

His steps slowed, a thought struck—above the eyes and in the pit of his stomach and in his thighs. Maybe he was falling... No way! Poets made too much of love. He was just bored and had been too long without a woman. Cleo happened to be in the right place at the right time.

He went in the side door of the cabin and to his room, undressing in the dark. His thoughts traveled to his parents, especially his mother with that inevitable hint of a whine in her voice. He mentally viewed the random couples whom he knew.

He was back on track now.

Somewhat eased he lay down upon the cool sheets, believing his own counsel, though the belief did little to relieve the ache in his groin.

At some point during the night he sat up and swung his legs over the side of the bed. He was hooked. He didn't know how she had done it. He was hooked and miserable and happy. He wasn't himself at all.

CHAPTER SEVEN

DEW DAMPENED Cleo's tennis shoes. It was early and she'd had the showers to herself, which was just as well. She was in no mood for polite conversation.

She was in a state of flux. If she meant to leave, she should batten everything down, hitch up the camper and check out of the park; she should say goodbye to Big Momma and move on—after all, her work required no particular place, only nature.

The silver-gray tabby joined her on the path, brushing up against her leg. Cleo stopped and scratched the cat's ears—another small gesture of procrastination.

Did she have no destiny to fulfill? she wondered. To go backward was to enter the dark archway of her past, to go forward...she could see no forward, no future of substance.

All she could see, feel, was Fletcher's lips on hers, his searching mouth, his hands on her waist, fueling a desire that was staggering in its intensity.

Quick behind the growing desire came the demons swarming about her. She stumbled through them in the corridors of her mind, cordoning them off with slender threads of hope.

If she abandoned the opportunity before her now, then what? She was bankrupt of good memories to take with her into old age. Fletcher was unforgettable; he would make a good memory.

So, stay! ordered her innermost voice. *What have you got to lose?*

Only myself, my heart, she answered.

The park came alive with a sudden flow of traffic toward the river. People poured out of cabins and campers as if some great news had been carried on the summer wind. Roger and Katie ran past. Katie skidded to a halt. "Bears!" she whispered. "Across the river."

Watching Katie race to catch up with Roger, Cleo had an attack of conscience. She had promised to help Katie with spelling, promised to involve the child in her own work. It would be a terrible thing to disappoint such a child. She had been thinking of herself, being selfish. She could help Katie today, then leave tomorrow, she told herself.

The knot of bear watchers was sitting on the river bank in front of her own campsite. A female and two cubs were cavorting on the opposite bank. Cleo hurried to set up a camera on a tripod. No one spoke above a whisper. The children put hands over mouths to muffle laughter at the cubs' antics; the adults, like Cleo, snapped pictures.

Within fifteen minutes the crowd had grown to such a size that the volume of whispers rose. The shaggy female glanced at her audience, then ambled from the river; she swatted at her offspring to get their attention and disappeared into the underbrush, the cubs reluctant followers.

Katie was sitting alone on the sandy bank. Cleo adjusted the lens and snapped several frames of the child.

"Is the coffee made?"

"Fletcher! You startled me." Cleo's eyes flashed through thick golden lashes, her lips parted; she faltered and became clumsy in dismantling the tripod.

"Here, let me do that." His voice sounded odd, clipped, as if his life had been broken into and he was at some temporary loss as to how to repair it.

Of course, Cleo thought, he was remembering last night and how badly she had behaved. It was a wonder that he approached her at all today.

"I'm sure it is. I set it to perking before I went to the bathhouse. Are you certain you want to have a cup with me?"

"Not having coffee is how we got off on the wrong foot, don't you think? I thought we ought to back up and start again."

"But we can't undo—" Cleo began, her voice strained with the idea of new beginnings and the sensation of warmth in her thighs at having Fletcher so near.

"I'm willing if you are," he said.

A hand touched Cleo's arm. "What time this afternoon?"

She looked down into Katie's expectant face. "How does three o'clock sound?"

"Could you make it right after lunch, instead?"

"No, she can't," said Fletcher. "You take a nap after lunch."

"I hate taking naps! I'm eleven years old. Mom just wants me to sleep my life away."

"That's not it, Katie, and you're being rude to Cleo. She said three o'clock."

Katie expelled a giant sigh. "I'll be on time."

"Good. Now scoot. Your mother had breakfast almost ready when I left."

"Aren't you coming?"

He looked to Cleo, contemplative, meeting her eyes. "No, I think I'm invited for breakfast with Cleo."

Something passed between them, and it was as if Cleo were saying, "Breakfast—yes, but that other thing you want—it's out of the question."

Katie left. Cleo looked warily at Fletcher. "I can offer you sausages and scrambled eggs, but you'll have to sit outside. There's not room for two—"

They ate at the picnic table, sitting opposite each other, primitive forces wreaking havoc with their appetites. Cleo shifted food about on her plate. Fletcher pushed eggs around on his, only a few bites ever reaching his mouth. "You're a good cook," he said.

"Thank you," she answered, wondering how he could tell.

"About last night—" he began.

"I'm thinking about leaving tomorrow," she said, watching his face; he didn't seem surprised.

"I halfway expected you to try to leave this morning."

"Try? You were going to stop me?"

He took a sip of coffee. "I let the air out of your tires last night."

She laughed, a small sound of disbelief. "You didn't..."

"You have this avoidance complex, skittish. I pointed it out, remember? I think we ought to at least explore what's going on between us—"

Cleo leapt up and hurried around the side of the camper. Fletcher was fast on her heels. Sure enough. There was her beat-up old Chevrolet, its two front tires flat. She stared at the car, stricken. "You did! I can't—"

"I haven't done anything so childish since I hid the chain off Ward's bicycle when we were twelve—the precise reason escapes me now."

"My tires will be ruined!"

"I'll pump them up again. Big Momma keeps an air pump around here somewhere."

Cleo turned on him, fury making her eyes glisten. "Go get it! You're too much, too pushy, too . . . everything!"

"You're too subject to fits and flights of fancy, mostly flights. I just don't want you to leave before we talk."

"You want more than talk."

For a beat, Fletcher's composure cracked, then he replied, "If you mean sex, yes, I want you, but I can get sex anytime. I want to know about you, I want to see if something's there, something different."

For a brief moment Cleo had the sensation of hanging in space. Her body was light, weightless, her throat closing on the thought, *What if there isn't?*

"You're displaying an underhanded kind of arrogance," she said. "What makes you think— What about my feelings?"

"If we're not on the same track, why, we'll be friends, just as you said in the beginning."

Awful! This was awful. He was skewering her with her own words. "Put the air back in my tires."

"Walk with me to pick up the mail first. When we drop it off at the office, I'll get the pump. Fair enough?"

"I don't think it's fair at all."

"But, you'll do it."

She stood there for a moment, in shirt and shorts, knowing her hair needed brushing, feeling trapped and looking inward at her life. "I'll walk with you to the mailbox," she said.

It was a rural box, on the highway, a mile from camp; it was down the same road that she had veered off from into the forest the day she discovered the owls. A lifetime ago.

They walked side by side, without touching, as if some great proprieties must be observed at any cost. To Cleo's way of thinking, it was Fletcher's show. She wasn't about to start him off. Silence was her protection.

"You said your mother died and your grandmother raised you," he began. "Was she ample lap and apple pie?"

The sky was blue, the sun rising. Cleo meditated a moment before she answered. "Gram was religious and dignified. Her apple pies were delicious."

"You never curled up into her lap?"

"No."

"What about your dad?"

"I—I never met him."

"Your grandfather?"

"Died before I was born."

"I see."

It was too much, too soon for Cleo. "You see! What do you see? I know what you're doing. You're treating me as if I were on the witness stand."

"I'm just trying to get a handle on you."

"Like a teacup?"

He stepped in front of her, grasped her shoulders and shook her, not ungently, as if he wanted her to understand without words. He saw her eyes grow wide and fill with alarm.

"Cleo. Listen to me. Four nights ago I went back to Atlanta. I roamed my house. I couldn't sleep. I went to work and couldn't concentrate. I went into the courtroom and couldn't perform. I couldn't eat. All I did was think of you. I couldn't get you out of my mind. I turned my practice over to my associates so I could come back here. I've never done that! Never left the helm, never given up control. Do you understand what I'm saying?" He became conscious of her warm flesh beneath his fingers, the length of her bare legs, the shape of her mouth. "My God! I could make love to you right now, standing up—" He dropped his hands from her shoulders. "But I'm not touching you."

Dazed, Cleo backed away and stumbled down the road. The light caught her hair and it blazed. Fletcher moved to her side, staying there, in step.

"I've seen you less than a half-dozen times. I've had no more than a handful of conversations with you. And yet . . ." He spread his hands in a helpless gesture. "I have to know what it means."

Her face turned ashen. When she could manage it she said, "I don't know what it means. Don't expect me to."

"Just tell me about yourself . . . everything."

"No!"

"Are you hiding something? Are you running from something? I can help."

"Save your lawyer skills for your clients. I don't need them." She was trying to be sensible in the face of what he'd told her. Being sensible meant compressing her heart, keeping it from expanding and thudding in her ears.

They came to the mailbox; he took the mail from it—magazines, a newspaper, an electric bill, rolling them into a tube and carrying them that way, slapping his leg with the bundle now and again in silent exclamation of his thoughts.

Because she was watching him out of the corner of her eye, she saw when he glanced at her, too, as if reconnoitering the enemy. She could even tell when he decided to press on, for the muscle in his jaw jerked once before he spoke.

"You never met your dad. Why?"

All right, she decided. He wanted to know. She would give him knowledge. Adrenaline coursed through her body. "Because I was illegitimate."

He paused in stride, looking at her. "How does that make you feel?"

"It doesn't make me feel anything."

"You're not a very good liar, Cleo. Your neck is pink."

A summer wind was blowing; she lifted her face to it. "When I was a little girl, I hated it because I had no father like the other kids. Now . . . well, now it's just fact."

"You never tried to find him, find out?"

Time dripped in minutes before she answered. "I am who I am, what I made myself. He can't change that. It doesn't seem important now. My mother told me he was a married man."

"That must have been sad for your mother."

"Yes."

The wind snapped at his dark hair. "How old are you?"

"You're relentless, aren't you?"

"When I have to be."

"Thirty. So, what does that tell you?"

"That you were born in an era when it was considered terrible to have a child out of wedlock. How'd your grandmother take it?"

Cleo fixed her eyes on a thing distant. To look closer was to see her devils closing in. "She didn't like it."

"Did she like you?"

"Stop! Please!"

"I can't. I wish I could but I can't."

He was causing her pain, hating it, but driven by a need that was all consuming. He wasn't sure what he was driving at, what bit would put it all in place for him. A gut feeling was all he had. It happened to him often enough when he interrogated a client. A feeling at the back of his mind that made him pursue shadows until they solidified. Cleo's expression was tense. He was close to something.

"What was your grandmother's name?"

"Ida Anderson."

"Did Ida Anderson like her granddaughter?"

The interior voice that lived in her brain shouted a warning. *Trick!* it said. Cleo's emotion was a live thing, in movement like running water. She shook her head, silencing the voice. "In her own way. She didn't have it easy. When grampa died he left her with little more than a set of china and a daughter to raise. She worked as a cleaning lady. That didn't leave a lot of time for lap sitting."

"Sounds to me like you're making excuses for her," said Fletcher.

"I'm not making excuses," she protested. "Gram's dead now, so..."

He had a hundred other questions, but her profile was rigid. He had touched a raw nerve and could almost see Cleo shrinking inside herself. He wondered where inside her psyche she took herself to make life tolerable.

"Wanna hear a knock-knock joke?" he asked, to change the subject and cover what he was thinking.

Reprieve! Cleo made a sound in her throat, part laugh, part sob. "Inquisition's over?"

"You ought to see me in the courtroom." He couldn't help himself; he slid his arm about her waist and pulled her back from a chasm. "That's where I really shine."

"Braggart," she said, aware of every bone, muscle and tendon in the arm that held her. He wanted to know everything about her, wanted to make love to her. The idea of it crowded into her already over-full brain. "Have you found out all that you want to know?"

"You're not a nag, that's good news."

"That's all?"

"I don't think you're ready to hear what else I know or think."

"You're being condescending."

F<small>OUR</small> <small>HOURS OF RAKING GRASS</small> was too much for Cleo. Not the physical exertion, though it was hot and she sweated profusely, but for her hands. Within two hours huge blisters had raised up on the soft flesh below her thumbs.

Being near Fletcher in so ordinary of circumstances made her feel sick and exuberant. Sick because of the need and want building within, exuberant because the work kept her mind free, the bad spirits mute and invisible.

Her task involved trailing behind Fletcher, raking what he mowed. She had ample opportunity to observe him. More and more she liked what she saw of him.

He had tied a band of cloth around his head to keep sweat from his eyes. When his shirt became soaked, he took it off and she could see the muscles rippling in his back. Cleo held her breath and tightened her grip on the rake. A strong man, she thought, in more ways than one.

He stopped beside her as he mowed down a row while she raked up. "Don't rake that low spot until the wind's ad a chance at it. I stirred up a passel of mosquitos."

"Thanks for the warning." *How natural this all seems,* thought as she watched him continue on behind the er. They were talking, working together as if they'd n each other for years. Talking as if the walk to the x had not happened. She was disarmed.

a moment she allowed herself a touch of self- —Fletcher had a way with women; he admitted it. rking his way on her. Had she been thinking of the context of friendship she would be wholly she was thinking along the lines of more than o was he.

believe for a minute that they'd end up er it was would just end—period.

"Okay," he said, offended. "Here it is. I think you're a woman for whom passion is as natural as breathing. There isn't a trace of coyness in your seduction. Yet in the midst of it—and I'm talking about last night, you pulled back."

She jerked out of his embracing arm. "I didn't seduce you! I didn't even try!"

"See, I told you you weren't ready."

"Let me tell you what I know about you! See if you're ready for this! You wouldn't know morality if it slapped you in the face. I backed away last night because you were going too far. We've only just met. Good girls don't—" she heard herself and clamped her mouth closed.

"Good girls don't what?" So there it was, he thought, the boundary he had to cross.

"You just want one thing." Her face was flushed and hot looking.

In the distance the sun scintillated, waved and shone on the road surface like pools of mirrored water.

"You want it, too."

"I do not!" she said thickly, forcing the words out. Her long legs carried her away from him, her very soul seemed to gasp at his audacity.

He increased his stride, staying with her. "You want me, Cleo. And I want you. Life is not artfully arranged like some masterpiece that hangs in a museum, though I think there's something to be gained by studying it. You look at a painting and wonder at the complexity of it, wonder at the story behind it. What provoked the artist to make that first stroke with his brush. How many layers of paint it took to create the picture."

"I'm not interested in a lesson on art appreciation."

"I'm talking about you," he said. "Just letting you know you bewitch me."

Cleo stopped and closed her eyes. "That's the lawyer in you talking." But she knew it wasn't so. Her mouth went dry trying for the courage to tell him he bewitched her, too.

"Big Momma's coming to meet us," he said. "We can get back to this later."

"I could've writ the mail and sent it to myself faster 'n it took you to haul it," the old woman accused. She unrolled the papers, the magazines, shaking them out. "'Lectric bill," she said. "Nothing from Francine. Reckon she still ain't over her mad spell. Waal, you all come along. I got a pitcher of tea made. You're looking like you could use it."

Big Momma led them around to her front porch. A boy of eighteen or so was there, sitting on the stoop. His name was Wesley and he smiled shyly at Cleo when she was introduced.

Fletcher clapped him on the back. "You've grown a foot since I saw you last, Wes. You cutting grass today?"

"Nope. Just came by to tell Big Momma I can't. There's some big forest fires in Florida and the lumber companies are asking for help. I'm going."

"Wouldn't hurt for us to get a speck of rain, either. It's so dry hereabouts I can smell it," said Big Momma, returning with the huge glasses in which she served tea. Cleo accepted one with thanks.

"The swamps wouldn't burn, would they?" she asked.

"Sure they would. When they ain't wet, they're dry and burn like tinder. I've seen it."

Wes said goodbye. They all watched him get into his truck and drive off. "Hope he don't get hurt," muttered Big Momma as she sat down.

"He can take care of himself," said Fletcher.

"My grass can't," she said slyly. "Reckon I'll have to put out a call for volunteers."

Fletcher winced.

Big Momma talked over his head to Cleo who was sitting on the lower step. "Used to be there was a young man come here just a begging for work around this place so as to get a cabin discounted. I felt pity for the poor thing and gave him a speck of work. Over the years he went and got rich and haughty, too good to get his hands dirty now— some dern fowkses got memories shorter 'n a two inch twig."

"I think she's talking about you, Fletcher," said Cleo. She was still wire-taut, heady with old and new emotions. Fletcher looked at her, and when their eyes met she didn't look away. It was an invitation of sorts, not open, but not primly closed either. It was the best she could do.

"She's a guilt-maneuvering old hag," he answered with affection. His smile took them both in, but Cleo felt it was just for her.

"That's settled," said Big Momma, the wrinkles old face drawing and folding back on themselves faction. "And don't forget to cut close down and the washrooms. This dry spell's got all heading for water, and you can't see 'e Don't want nobody to get snakebit." S pillow-padded rocker. "Cleo, you w

"I can't today—"

"She's going to help me," s

"I've never cut a blade o

"First time for everyth her to her feet. "You brigade."

"I promised Katie-

"I heard you. Three c four hours away."

She looked down the even row of mounded grass the mower had spewed out and took up raking again.

Overhead, pine warblers chittered, gray squirrels leapt from limb to limb following her progress, chastising when she came too close to hidden stores. Cleo laughed at their antics, chattering right back, but by a mental law of gravitation, her mind kept returning to Fletcher.

Each time the wheelbarrow was filled with clippings, Fletcher stopped mowing and trundled it down to a mulch pit near the chicken run. Cleo walked beside him. The sun was past its zenith though still bearing down. She dabbed at a rivulet of sweat on her neck with her shirt tail.

"I hate to tell you this," she said, "but I'm ready for a shower."

"Me, too. How're you at scrubbing backs?"

"No experience at all," she answered, keeping it light for she felt balanced on a narrow ledge; one slip and she'd be lost forever.

"Ah! but you're a fast learner. Look at all the grass you've raked and you've never done that before either. Which I might add, I find astonishing. Thank goodness for grass. It kept me in pocket money when I was a kid."

"There wasn't a blade of grass on 55th Street where I was raised. Concrete, front, side and alley."

"You were married." There was just the vaguest edge to his voice.

"There's a connection between grass and having been married?"

"In a roundabout way. Didn't you ever scrub your husband's back?"

"No."

He dumped the grass then leaned the wheelbarrow against a shed. "Seems to me I missed something."

"I won't answer any more of your questions. You've probed quite enough for one day." She smiled to take the sting out, to pretend his earlier questions and her answers had been of no importance.

His returning smile was wicked, enticing. "No, I haven't, but the defense never lets the opposition know its strategy."

"I'm the defense," she told him.

"Great! We're both on the same side."

"I'm glad you think so. Now, I'm heading for the showers."

"I have a better idea. What about a swim?"

"Aren't you forgetting something?"

"Am I?"

"The air in my tires."

He paused, a skillful pause born of years of study, and how to make silence work for him in the face of recalcitrant clients and stubborn prosecutors. "Do I have your word of honor you won't take off on me?"

"For today, anyway."

"Poor old tires," he cooed silkily. "Having to stay flat like that. The rims are probably cutting into the rubber."

"That's not fair! You promised—you said walk with you to get the mail...next you have me raking grass. You're getting a lot of mileage out of those damned tires and they aren't even moving!"

"Your word of honor first," he demanded. "Ward and I are going night fishing. There's a place we can put the boat in the river about twenty miles from here. A good trout hole. I don't want to be worrying that you've taken a hike while I'm—"

She wasn't going anywhere, but she had to save face. "A hike!" she blustered.

Fletcher just stood there, silent, stoic.

"Oh, all right!"

"Good. I'll meet you at the river in fifteen minutes. Go suit up."

Stripping naked and suiting up was just what Cleo couldn't make herself do with Fletcher two feet on the other side of the wall of the camper. She could hear the swish of the air as he pumped the device with his foot.

She went to the bathhouse instead, rinsing off before she tugged on her modest one-piece swimsuit. The scratch on her abdomen was almost healed, an angry red line in the creamy flesh. Then she dallied, brushing her hair, oiling her body, massaging extra into her hands. She didn't want to arrive at the river before Fletcher did.

Leaving her discarded clothes on a shelf to retrieve later, she stepped from the bathhouse. She felt uneasy strolling through the park in her swimsuit, though everyone else did it, old and young. She draped a towel about her neck, covering her bare shoulders, and modesty prevailed, at least in her own mind.

Fletcher was leaning against an old pine, watching for her. While she was still several yards from him, her steps faltered. A gust of hot wind lifted the towel from her shoulders, whipping it to the new-mown grass where it lay in the dappled sunlight.

She wanted to vanish and not see Fletcher's dark eyes drinking her in—as if never in his life had he seen a woman in a swimsuit. She tried to avoid meeting his eyes until she heard him whisper, "You're more beautiful than I imagined."

She had to look at him then. The swim trunks he wore were well-fashioned and molded to his thighs. The maleness of him drew her gaze there. She wanted to stare and stare and stare.

That was the wickedness in her. That was what made all the air in her lungs disappear suddenly.

He had not taken his eyes from her, either. She liked that he hadn't and she liked what her imagination was doing, wicked or not. She felt the sun on her body, felt an inner heat rise to meet it. An old voice intruded, creating more conflict within her. *Ellie's made you into what she was— evil, lustful like the whores of Babylon.*

Cleo unlocked her gaze from Fletcher's and raced into the river, leaving shame behind. But the river was no place to hide. Nowhere was it more than waist deep, except the diving hole and that looked black and ominous. An alligator cave, she had been told. Though Big Momma swore there hadn't been an alligator in this part of the Suwannee in years.

She lowered herself to her knees, letting the copper-colored water embrace her, turning to face the shore in time to see Fletcher make a shallow dive and glide along the surface to her side.

"Is it too cold for you?" he asked, maneuvering the length of his body so that he, too, was on his knees, though the river came only up to his chest. The fine dark hairs on it glistened with droplets.

"No, it's wonderful. There's a current on the bottom, I can feel it pulling the sand out from me." The river water stung the blisters on her palms. A small hurt, though, and easily borne, worth the pain to be near Fletcher.

"You mean like pulling the rug out?"

The allegory was not lost on Cleo. "Do you never stop probing?"

He appeared to mull that over. "I'm just curious how I affect you."

"Why don't you just ask?"

"Could I? Straight out and get a direct answer?"

"Of course."

His eyes narrowed so that she couldn't see into their depths. "Tell me."

She tried to laugh. "You confuse me."

He threw up his hands, splattering water. "You're trying to outwit me."

"Somebody needs to. You've had it all your way up to now, haven't you?"

He treaded water. "Not entirely. I get stumped now and then. I'm stumped now."

Cleo inhaled deeply. "How do I affect you?" she asked bravely.

He took in her amber eyes, the red curls—wet, the sun giving them golden tints, the high cheekbones that made her look sophisticated and the freckles that made her look like a child. "You already know. I can't eat, sleep or think."

"I gave you an answer, you gave me a riddle." She stretched out on her back, moving her arms just enough to keep afloat.

"You're the riddle. There's an odd mixture of elements in you, Cleo. The sensual, which is the way you look at me with those wide golden brown eyes of yours. Then there's the coolness, the way you move and look away as if to negate the sexuality. You make me wonder if you're aware of the mixed signals you send out. My riddle is guessing which signal to respond to." He knew which signal he wanted to respond to, which one he would succumb to in the end. He just didn't know how far to go, how fast. For the most important question he had no answer. Would their coming together be the beginning of an end? Or the Beginning?

"Mixed signals?" Cleo stopped her lazy paddling, felt her heart plunge into a deep well of darkness. She wanted to cry out that she didn't know herself. She had a sick craving within her; it spread like a wind-driven fire from her stomach throughout her body. Fletcher had seen it! Recognized it and its thin veneer of respectability.

She wanted to be invisible. She let her body—that betrayer of soul—sink below the surface. If she could just stay on the bottom, drift with the current . . . demons began to nibble at her shoulders. She opened her eyes. Minnows.

Air bubbles spewed about her, not her own, Fletcher's. His hands were reaching for her, encircling her waist, dragging her to the surface. "What in the hell were you thinking—"

"Nothing. Minnows were nibbling on me. You didn't have to yank at me like that."

He cursed himself. He'd seen her fragility, suspected its source, and stupidly he'd put voice to her own fears. He felt a twinge of uncertainty, a rare sensation for him.

There was her flesh beneath his hands, pliable. She was brushing water from her eyes, smoothing her hair back; the lifting of her arms made her breasts rise above the top of her suit. Uncertainty fled.

"Let's go towel off," he said, "and find some shade." He let go her hips and took her hand.

Cleo allowed the contact without protest, thinking, Please God, don't let him think too terribly of me.

He doesn't think terribly of you, he likes you.

But he knows my dark side now.

So? Everybody has a dark side.

What do you know? You say one thing one time and another thing another time.

That's what makes life interesting.

Cleo sat on the grass, using her towel to dry her hair. Fletcher sat on his, mulling over his thoughts. Women wanted to change him and he had vowed never to be changed, yet here he was, changing. He could feel the metamorphosis, the shedding of his cynical self, all because of a chance meeting with Cleo. What would that do to him in the courtroom?

In the bedroom?

He glanced at Cleo, her profile pained and rigid. She seemed to obliterate his sensibility and reason.

He could feel loneliness pouring out of him and good warm feelings pouring in. "Are you all right, now?"

"It just scared me when those fish started biting me."

"You're probably the most delicious item they've had on their menu in years."

"They were babies. They hadn't lived years."

"Why don't you look at me?"

"You're doing enough looking for the both of us." In the distance shimmery heat auras rose from the river. Across it a great blue heron settled on the diving tree. Cleo kept her gaze on the bird.

He grinned. "I thought I saw that golden brown eye swiveling my way."

"If you're fishing for compliments . . . you know you're good-looking."

"Beauty is in the eye of the beholder. For all I know you might think I look like a warty old frog."

The rigidity was gone now and he could see the trace of a smile at the edge of her mouth. "You're lovely when you smile, did you know that?"

Her heart fluttered once. She inspected her nails. She had shaped them, put clear polish on them. "You have a nice smile, too."

Fletcher lay back, crooking his elbow over his eyes. "I know what you want, Cleo."

It was safe to look at him now, when he wasn't watching her do it. "I didn't know you could read minds."

"I can read yours."

"You could make a lot of money telling fortunes."

He lifted onto his elbow and his dark eyes burned into her. "I'll court you, but there's going to come a time when courting, just being together, like this, won't be enough."

There was no need to ask what he meant. Wild spurts of excitement and dread warmed her flesh, making cheeks turn bright pink. She turbaned the towel around her head and stood up. "I have to get back to my place now. I'm starved."

His hand shot out, grabbing her ankle. "I'm starved, too."

She moistened her lips. "I'm talking about chicken salad."

"So long as you know I'm not." There it was, said. His hand moved up the smoothness of her calf then stopped. "I'll see you tomorrow."

It was an upward struggle for Cleo to answer him. "Morning or afternoon?"

"For dinner. I'll pick up a couple of steaks in Fargo. We'll throw them on your grill. How does that sound?"

Like you're giving me time to ponder all you've said, like you've handed me an ultimatum. "Like a pleasant way to pass the evening," she said, turning, and walked rapidly back to her camper.

CHAPTER EIGHT

"AM I TOO EARLY?" Katie stood in the shade of the awning, peering into the door.

Laying aside the sandwich she had picked up, which had already been in the shadow of her mouth, Cleo beckoned her in. Katie squeezed past to the table. Small though she was, she didn't just sit. She dropped down, sprawled and bivouacked on the seat.

"This is neat," she said, appraising the interior of the camper. "It's like a playhouse or a turtle shell, having your house on your back."

"I was just having a sandwich. Would you like one, or a soft drink?"

"I could handle a Coke."

"Coming right up."

Cleo moved the typewriter to make room for plate and glasses and the bulky cloth satchel Katie was hugging to her chest, then she sat opposite the youngster. "So tell me, what's this spelling project you've got going?"

Katie sipped her Coke, then her lips parted in a toothy smile that was at odds with the serious glint in her eyes. "First, I ought to tell you something about myself."

"You don't have to," said Cleo, at once dismayed, suspecting what was coming. She felt cornered. She had already weathered an onslaught of emotions that day and didn't know how much more she could absorb. She discovered Katie's sensitive face mirroring her own dismay so that she felt compelled to add, "But if you think it's necessary..."

"It's like this," said Katie, dropping all pretenses. "I'm sick, real sick. *Dreadfully* sick," she embellished for Cleo's benefit. "But you don't have to worry. It's not catching. I'm not talking about poison ivy. That's cleared up."

Cleo knew she was being watched for her reaction, for a display of pity, and that the pity would be rejected.

The Sundays she had volunteered in the children's ward of the hospital back home filled her mind. The smells, the false cheerfulness of nurses and parents, the brave and sometimes frightened faces of the children raced into her mind's eye. Those children who were brave wanted to be honored for that, those frightened begged comforting. She had felt inadequate then and she felt inadequate now. Was there ever a right thing to say in such circumstances? She knew, too, that she couldn't mention the scene she had witnessed in the forest.

"Fletcher told me that you were ill, Katie. I wish it wasn't so."

The pinched little face relaxed. "I wish it wasn't so, too. The problem is, I'm going to die sooner than I expected, and I've got to make a will."

Cleo floundered. That wasn't at all what she had expected. "A will...?"

At Cleo's tone Katie went on the defensive; her eyes narrowed, her chin thrust out. "You said you'd help, you're not going to back out?"

"No, but I had it in mind that..." She made a helpless gesture with her hands. "I don't know what I had in mind. I don't know the first thing about wills, though."

"Oh, we don't have to," Katie replied airily. "Uncle Fletcher is gonna make it legal. I just have to write down what I want."

"Wouldn't it . . . wouldn't it be better to have someone in your family help you? A will is such a personal matter."

"I can't get Mom to help because she feels bad already. Y'know what I mean?"

Cleo nodded, allowing that she did. Katie went on anyway.

"I'm her only little girl and I won't ever grow up and go to college or have a husband or babies. Roger'll have to be the one to give her grandchildren now." She took another sip of Coke. "Of course, they prob'ly won't be much . . . poor pitiful things."

"You've thought it all out, then," said Cleo, fascinated, yet repelled by the élan with which Katie spoke of death, thinking, some hurl themselves against life. Still others lie down and let life have its way over them. With a sudden clarity she realized that her own mother was one of the latter. She could see that now. Strange, it should take a small dying child to make her realize it. Strange—or was it fate?

"If you mean about the spelling," Katie was saying. "I have thought it out. Dad's secretary does all his spelling. Roger can't spell, neither can Big Momma. My aunt Mary Ellen would tell my mom, and Uncle Fletcher is too busy."

"But, I'm a stranger. . . ." Cleo could think of no other protest.

"That's okay. I like you. So does Big Momma. So does Uncle Fletcher," she added slyly.

Cleo left that bait alone, pretending that her heart was not in transit and examined the palms of her hands. The skin below her thumbs was raw where the blisters had broken. "I like you, too," she said finally.

Katie fingered the satchel. "Do you know any dead people? I mean, personally."

Denial was on Cleo's tongue, but denial took a lot of energy and all of Cleo's energies had been diverted, used up in the hours of raking, the time spent with Fletcher. "My mother and my grandmother," she said.

"Great!" Katie produced a dog-eared notepad. "When I get to heaven, I'll say hello to them for you." She glanced up, warily hesitant. "They are in heaven, aren't they?"

"I . . . I believe so," said Cleo, moved in her soul, and putting her best face on in a situation which she would never have imagined in a thousand years.

"My grandma Baily died already, too. She's prob'ly already met your mother and grandmother. Unless...do they smoke or dip snuff? Grandma Baily won't have anything to do with people who have vile habits like that."

Cleo looked out the door where the sunlight played in many strange ways, falling through the foliage. "They didn't smoke or dip snuff." She heard her interior voice coming close, trying to put words in her mouth. She chased it away.

"Can you write in cursive?" Katie passed the notepad to Cleo. "I can read cursive or printing. You can add their names to my list. Heaven's such a big place, if I don't have names, I'll never find anybody."

"You're more practical than I would be in your situation," returned Cleo, wondering where she was finding the wherewithal to hold up her side of their conversation.

"Well, going to heaven isn't like going to the movies or to camp," Katie chirped. "You have to *plan*. I think things out scientifically," she added, recalling that Cleo had said she had a scientific mind. "Ida Anderson and Elenora Anderson," she read. "Which is which?"

"Elenora was my mother."

Katie added "Cleo's mom" beside the name, then smiled up at Cleo, her gray eyes bright with invitation.

"You can come to my funeral if you like. All my friends will be there. The music will be pretty good—" her voice dropped, anchored with indulgent generosity. "Reverend Dopple is so boring, but I have to let him do it or his feelings would be hurt. Be sure to bring lots of Kleenex. Everybody will be crying because it'll be so sad, and I'll be so beautiful."

Cleo sat immovable. "I feel sad already."

Katie's expression filled with amazement. "Why? I'm not dead yet."

"Katie..." Cleo had an odd uncomfortable feeling. "Have you talked with anyone about death, somebody who knows? This is so overwhelming..."

The thin little shoulders drooped. "The truth is, nobody likes to talk about little kids dying. Mom won't, Daddy thinks I'm not going to die, Roger wishes I'd hurry up and get it over with—"

"What about your Reverend Dop—?" Katie didn't let her finish.

"I tried. He said I'd make a cute little angel and then he called Mom, she started crying, then when Daddy came home they had a fight." She looked straight at Cleo, her brow furrowing. "Besides, I'd never make it as an angel. They have to be too good."

Cleo dropped her chin into her hands and laughed. It felt good in her throat. "I'd hate having to make it as an angel myself."

But you did spend thirty years auditioning for Gram's approval, injected her other voice.

That's not the same thing, replied Cleo, trying to shake the interior dialogue.

It's close, though, said the voice, getting in the last word before Cleo shut it out.

"Grandma Baily knew she was dying," Katie said around a heavy sigh. "I asked her how she was doing it. She said she was making the best of it."

"That's what you're doing, isn't it, making the best of it?"

"It's kind of like homework—you know you've gotta do it even if you don't want to. I guess you're telling me you don't want to talk about dying, right?"

Cleo swallowed. "It's a big responsibility. I may say the wrong thing. I do that a lot." She could see the child withdrawing, see hope shriveling. "Oh, Katie . . . I'll listen, but I don't know much. I don't know if I can help you."

"You can spell, you said—"

"That, I can do," Cleo said, feeling consumed and thinking, Oh, but you want so much more—love, hope, empathy, gaiety. Where would she find it for the child, Cleo wondered, when she couldn't find it for herself. "As I recall, the deal was—you'd help me answer letters in exchange."

Katie eyed the typewriter. "Would you teach me to type, too?"

"One thing at a time. Goodness!"

"Okay, but let's do the spelling first." She dragged out of her satchel a long yellow pad. "I snitched this from Uncle Fletcher. You like him, don't you?"

"What words do you need help with?" Cleo asked.

"He won't talk about you, either," purred Katie.

Cleo let that float by, leaving Fletcher within the outskirts of her mind. She had more on her emotional plate this minute than she could digest in a month of Sundays. It came to her that Katie's realities were not so far from her own realities. Each of them recognized her personal albatross, but went on with life anyway, compensating the best she knew how, whatever wind blew.

A gray squirrel peeked over the step, catching her eye. She tore off a crust from her sandwich and tossed it. "Little beggar," she said, watching it inspect the bread, discovering she could still smile. Then she returned her attention to Katie. "What words are you having trouble with?"

"How I'm starting is; A great tragedy has befallen me. So, how do you spell tragedy and befallen?"

"Very dramatic," said Cleo, shaking her head. "You're going to break some hearts."

Katie giggled. "Yeah, my cousin Lindsey's who wants all my posters. She's thirteen. You'll meet her. She's coming this weekend with Aunt Mary Ellen and Uncle Joe. You won't be able to stand her."

"Why not?"

"Mostly because she just got breasts." Katie leaned forward, expression intense, betraying her envy. "She's so proud, she'd grow an extra pair on her back if she could."

Cleo had a sudden urge to clear her throat. "Want some more Coke?" she asked.

Katie refused to be distracted, declining with a shake of her head. "I don't know how she went and got any before me. If there's one thing in the world I want before I die, it's breasts."

"Maybe yours will grow," offered Cleo lamely since it seemed that was the only hope left to Katie.

"They'd have to swell up before this weekend to do me any good."

"Don't be so downhearted. A figure isn't everything. You have brains and wit and big gray eyes. That counts for something."

"I've always had those," Katie replied archly. "What I want is a miracle. How old were you when you got breasts?"

It was a subject Cleo did not want to explore. Talking of her own puberty, the attempt to suppress it, was like pulling threads from an old tapestry that was worn and much shredded from wear. The old tapestry couldn't bear it and neither could she. "I don't remember, but I was older than your cousin Lindsey."

Katie flung her head back and closed her eyes. Cleo thought the behavior was theatrics, reaction to her answer, but Katie's face went gray before her eyes, then she noticed Katie's fingers clutching the table edge; they were bloodless.

"Katie! What's happening?"

"Give me a sec," she whispered, sucking in air.

"I'll go get your mom."

"No! Wait," came out an anguished whisper. "It's only my legs. Sometimes my shins hurt." She opened her eyes revealing their pain-filled depths.

"I think I should—" Cleo started, but Katie stayed her with a suggestion.

"If I could just stretch out on your bed a minute, the pain'll go. It always does."

Against her better judgment, Cleo lifted Katie away from the table and placed her on the bed where the child lay immovable, a little pale monument. "What if I rubbed your legs? Would that help?"

"Not much. But cold towels do."

Cleo plugged the sink, ran some water and dumped in a tray of ice. When she began to wring out towels she discovered her hands trembling. Katie flinched when she wrapped the towels about the thin legs. "I'll be fine in a minute," she promised.

"You can't do this by yourself, Katie. I'm not sure I want to be involved in a conspiracy behind your mother's back. She—"

"You don't understand. She can't take it. She's not strong like I am. She can't accept it. It hurts her. I can't stand to see her hurt. I want her to remember me happy. Y'see, Grandma Baily didn't look too good at the end. She sort of shriveled, and Mom said she didn't think she'd ever get those last days out of her mind so she could remember the good."

Cleo sat on the bed and took the small—and dirty—bare feet onto her lap. "You can't be brave for everybody." She understood now why Katie was endeavoring to make everything—even her death, beautiful. "Are the towels helping?"

"Yes."

"The truth? You don't have to be brave for me."

"In that case, do you have any aspirins?"

"I do, but—"

"They stay down better than my medicine."

Cleo got the aspirins, having trouble with the stopper because the wringing out of the towels had made the blisters on her hands begin to sting and ache again. Katie insisted on inspecting the broken skin.

"Better not let Big Momma see, she'll put sulpher on it, and it stings like the devil."

"You talking about me behind my back again?" asked the old woman poking her head in the door.

Cleo spun about. "Mrs. Freeman!"

"You sound like lightning done struck you, Cleo. How come I was Big Momma this morning and now I'm Mrs. Freeman again?"

"You startled it out of me."

"Waal, I brung you a thank you for raking," she said, thrusting a cloth-wrapped plate at Cleo. "Fudge cake."

In one fell swoop Big Momma eyed Katie, the towels on her legs, inspected the shelves, the cracked mirror, the tiny stove, the table and storage beneath the bed. "She come to you for sympathy, I reckon," she said, speaking to Cleo but nodding toward Katie.

Cleo smiled her thanks for the cake. "An attack of some sort. I was just trying to make her comfortable."

"You ain't faking?" the old woman shot at Katie.

"No, I really hurt this time."

"Been taking your medicine?"

"I take it, but it doesn't take to me." This wrung a snort from Big Momma.

There was room for one to stand comfortably in the camper, not two, and Cleo felt the closeness. She offered the old woman a seat at the table.

"Reckon I can set a spell, been working my bones thin today, cleaning cabins."

"I can make some coffee, or I have soft drinks," said Cleo, remembering her manners. Big Momma agreed to a Coke, and while sipping it, watched, beady-eyed, as Cleo dipped and wrung the towels again.

"Fletcher's done took to you, ain't he?" she said, once Cleo was sitting on the bed again.

Cleo's heart quickened. "We're just friends."

"That's the best way to start in my estimation," avowed Big Momma. "Rooster Freeman and me was friends nigh on twenty years afore we—" she cut a glance toward Katie. "Your eyes is closed but I can see your ears wiggling, Miss."

"I know all about sex," Katie said primly.

"From slipping up on fowkses and spying on 'em, I suppose."

"From books. Big Momma, how old were you when you got breasts?"

"Law! Kathleen Ann Miller you agitate me more'n Francine did and that ain't no stretch. You need a set-to with lye soap, cure that tongue of your'n."

"I was just asking . . ."

"You're gonna ask your way into hell and damnation if you ain't careful."

"I'm going straight to heaven and you know it."

"Meanwhile, I ain't got to put up with you."

"But, you're still sewing on my dress, aren't you? Big Momma's making my burying dress," Katie told Cleo. "But we have to keep it a secret from Mom."

Cleo winced.

Big Momma got up and touched Cleo's arm. "Ain't nothing you can do about Katie's mind working the way it does. She's got it in her head to light her own candle. It don't surprise me one whit. She allus was strong headed. No doubt she's elected you for some job or other. She'll sneak it on you, like she did me."

"Cleo's helping me do my will."

For a heartbeat Big Momma looked puzzled. "Law! And you ain't rightly walked the face of the earth yet. I got to get on back to the house and ponder on that. I thank you for the cola," she said to Cleo. "And you keep to Fletcher. It allus did pain me that he ain't found a partner. Allus expected him to show up here one day with a bride in tow. Never did 'spect him to find one right here on the river."

"I just met him," Cleo said. "We're just friends."

"He likes Cleo," said Katie.

"I knowed it when I come up on him letting the air out of her tires," said Big Momma.

Cleo saw her protests spreading in large circles, like chaff before the wind.

"Do enjoy that cake, Cleo," said Big Momma in parting. "It was Francine's favorite."

"I will." She followed Big Momma out and flopped down on the stoop. Wind made the awning creak, fish crows squabbled among themselves. Cleo went inside herself where there was no pattern to her thoughts. They were fragments, twisted, old and new spinning together.

Let me show you what's real. I'm starved, too. How'd your grandmother take it? Busy work! Can you spell tragedy?

"I feel all right now," said Katie.

Cleo looked back over her shoulder. Out of the corner of her eye she saw the shadow of her face in the old cracked mirror. Her twin selves looked tranquil; it was unnerving.

"I'll walk you home," she said.

THE BOAT, trailing with the river current, tugged at its anchor. The air was moist, retaining some of the heat of the day, except in pockets of cooler air where mist drifted. Somewhere close by a horse nickered. Herons nested atop moss-covered trees that lined the sloping banks. The trees themselves, spread out and drooping, made earth and water appear eerie and menacing. It was a timeless scene and Fletcher lingered over it until his mind took off on Cleo again.

Only one corner of his being remained open to the star-brightened external world. It was that corner that felt the sway of the current, that knew he ignored fish taking bait, that was aware of Ward's epithets, muttered low because Roger had given out an hour ago and was curled asleep in the bow.

Body and spirit, he was focused upon Cleo. He missed being near her and was suffering a howling emptiness. A dozen times he had opened his mouth to suggest calling it a night. But the fish were biting and he had no easy excuse as an exit.

"Do you mind a comment from the floor?" Ward asked.

Fletcher tore himself out of his turbulent reverie. "No, go ahead."

"It doesn't hurt."

"What doesn't?"

"Falling in love."

Fletcher experienced a spasm of apprehension, a growing knot where an empty stomach had been. "Who's falling in love?"

"You are. All the symptoms are there. You can't eat, you've gone absentminded. I've been watching you trying to put rules to it. I can see it in your eyes. There aren't any rules. You can't do love like you do law. And you can't explain it, either. It just happens. I thought I ought to tell you."

Fletcher almost laughed. All that without once mentioning Cleo's name, as if it had to be skirted, left unsaid so as not to make her real. But in his mind she was so real he could feel her, taste her, smell her.

"All right," he said. "You've told me."

Ward made a sound in his throat. "You don't sound enlightened."

"I'm enlightened."

They fished some minutes in silence. Ward cleared his throat. "I know you wrote that book tongue in cheek," he said, "but you revealed more about what makes you tick than you know."

"Now who's being analytical?"

"Well, it says something about you, doesn't it, when you see women, on principle—as out to stop your fun."

"Ward..." Fletcher said, making the name a warning.

"I'm on the wrong track?"

"Right."

"Mosquitoes are getting vicious. Think we ought to stay or go on back to camp?"

"It's up to you."

"I'd just as soon stay." He dug around in the cooler. "Still some beer left. You want one and something to eat? I brought a couple cans of sardines."

"For crying out loud, Ward. Sardines. Why didn't you pack up those ham sandwiches?"

"What's wrong with sardines?"

"We lived on them for two years running, remember?"

"I kind of liked those years," said Ward. "The sardines, the cans of cold beans. The biggest problem in those days was when the key broke and we had to dig 'em out with a pocketknife..." Ward's voice trailed away. He seemed to have crawled into himself and blocked out the rest of the world. In the starlight Fletcher saw his silhouette slump.

"You want to talk about it?" he invited, knowing he couldn't change Ward's life, or undo what was happening. But the shift would distract Ward from him, from Cleo, and he had a very deep and primitive feeling about Cleo. He wasn't ready to share that with anyone.

"I wish Katie weren't dying."

Fletcher frowned at the crushed resignation in his friend's voice. Ward had always been the stalwart optimist to his own cynicism. But now wasn't the time to remind him. "That's the first time I've heard you admit that she is."

Ward reeled in and recast the line, which sang as it peeled off the spinner.

"Did you know Katie's got Big Momma making her shroud? And she asked me yesterday how much money was in her college fund and was it really hers. So I've got an idea what she's up to with you." He shuddered and expelled a long breath. "Marilyn needs somebody or somewhere to direct her anger and frustration. I'm making myself it. As long as she can . . . makes me look like an ass to everybody, doesn't it?"

To Fletcher the shadows along the shore seemed deeper and darker than before and sinister in some unfathomable way. "A good ass," he said, knowing that was what Ward needed to hear.

One of the reels began to whir. "Hey! I think we got a big one," cried Ward excitedly. Fletcher caught the undertone. The light brouhaha was to cover the ache in his friend's throat.

"Better reel it in," he said. "Could be an old shoe."

"Hah! If it is, it's trying to swim all the way to Florida."

Ten minutes later the fish was landed, a huge old catfish. Ward tossed it in the cooler, then began baiting his line again. "What I said earlier, about falling in love and all—"

"I admit it."

Ward ran the hook through his thumb. "Hot damn! Look what you went and made me do."

Fletcher commiserated. "Look what you went and made me do." In love. Spoken aloud and no taking it back. A thick, hot, sick pressure filled his chest.

The old catfish squirmed and flopped around in the cooler. Fletcher commiserated with it, too. Then, for an instant his heart skipped a beat, his loins began to tingle,

and he sat there in the boat with his eyes closed thinking of
Cleo. A fish took his bait and ran with it.

"You gonna reel that fish in or not?" asked Ward.

"Reel it," answered Fletcher. He'd reel in Cleo, too, he
thought. Yet, he wasn't blind to the hurdles he must overcome. Somehow. He recalled the reticence that leapt into
her eyes every time he got close or touched her body with
his own. He wondered at the source of that. Her upbring-
ing? Or her marriage that had gone sour?

He netted the fish and recast, hook baitless. He'd have
to discover whatever it was that held Cleo's sensuous self
in check, and exorcise it. But the idea evoked a darker
shape. He suspected without being told, he'd get one
chance, no reserving the right to cross-examine. Better
make it a humdinger the first time, he told himself.

AGAINST HER WILL, Cleo's thoughts drifted. She thought
of Fletcher. She kept remembering the feel of his strong
fingers clasped about her ankle, the look in his eyes, the
threat...no, the assurance in his voice that had stirred
something in her that refused to return to its former
quiescent state.

She tried to concentrate on sleep and on the mental article she was writing, forcing her thoughts away from
Fletcher...

Yet deep inside where salvation lay, she wanted what he
wanted. Just admitting it to herself let loose the fear and
shame, making her throat go tight.

Oh, how she had fooled herself. It had been her demure, straight-laced ways that had attracted Paul. She
knew that these were surface things, put there by Gram. In
marriage she had expected to blossom to become a whole
woman. Instead she had shriveled. Paul had shouted and

sneered and turned away. Sex was his duty, he'd said. Cleo
was not to enjoy it. Good girls didn't.

But sex was out there—in books, in movies, on television. It was right here in camp vibrating between herself
and Fletcher. She felt the old kernel of dread swelling
alongside the craving for Fletcher.

Her interior voice hung around hour after sleepless
hour, coaxing, making a nuisance of itself. *Go on, do it
once outside of marriage, Cleo. Who's to know?*

Me.

*May I remind you that you're thirty years old? Don't
you think you're acting a bit silly?*

If only someone could rearrange my life, thought Cleo.

Pull your own strings, you idiot!

Maybe she would, Cleo internalized. That's just what
she would do... it made sense. Maybe. She puffed up her
pillow and turned her face into it and planned the most
perfect dinner, seeing herself smiling into Fletcher's eyes,
seeing herself saying yes. Seeing herself fearless, without
shame.

See how easy that was, Cleo? You feel good, admit it.

Oh, that's what you call this sensation? I thought it was
terror.

CHAPTER NINE

"I'M GLAD TO KNOW I'm not the only little kid that can't spell," said Katie, scowling at another letter. "This one's from a second grader."

Cleo answered absently. It was late into the afternoon and she wanted to begin getting ready for the dinner date with Fletcher, however she didn't have the heart to send Katie home.

Since right after lunch they had been working outside at the picnic table. The camp had settled into calm. Checkout was at noon, and after a flurry of departures no children swam and only one lone fisherman had taken a boat out.

Earlier, Big Momma had scurried past carrying an armload of linen to one of the empty cabins. She had called a greeting saying she had no time to dally.

Now it seemed that even the birds and squirrels had retreated, as if they'd decided to wait and beg tidbits from new arrivals.

"Hey!" said Katie, excitedly. "Here's one I know the answer to... finally! It asks, do sharks have ears. They don't, do they?"

"Nope."

"That makes up for me not knowing why the sky is blue... Uh-oh, here comes the biggest pest in the world." She narrowed her eyes at her brother. "What do you want, Roger?"

"Mom says for you to come home right now. You didn't take your medicine or your nap."

"You told!"

"I did not!"

"I'll be there in a minute."

"I'm supposed to wait." He edged up to the picnic table. "You doin' letters?" He wasn't asking Cleo directly, but his hint was too broad to miss.

"We were," she said, making good use of the interruption. "We've finished for today. Why don't you come with Katie next time?"

"He won't last, he can't sit still for five minutes," said Katie, sounding injured. "Besides, he can't read."

"I can read. I'm as smart as you!"

"It's only fair to let him try." Cleo smiled at them. "You run along now." She had a salad to make, a dressing to mix, plus she couldn't decide about vegetables to the steaks Fletcher promised. Pork 'n' beans or canned corn. The bag of charcoal and starter were still in the trunk of her car, needing to be retrieved and set out by the grill. "I'll put these things away. And, Katie...next time, make sure you've had your nap and your medicine before you race over here. The letters will keep. I don't want you getting sick on me—" She almost added, again, but stopped before she betrayed that to Roger, who would no doubt carry the information back to his mother.

Katie looked crestfallen. By now Cleo knew this for the artifice it was. Katie seemed to have an inborn skill at getting her own way. "Now, scoot," she said sternly. "Your mother's waiting."

"Okay," said Katie, raising a small and not very successful smile.

Cleo was tempted to relent, offering ten more minutes, but she did want to look her very best tonight, which meant she had yet to iron her wraparound skirt and the fine knit top she'd wear with it. "I'll see you tomorrow—both of you," she added pointedly for Roger's benefit.

Like reluctant puppets, feet dragging, arms hanging, the children moved off.

The old silver-gray tabby followed Cleo into the camper and lay down on the seat, curling her tail as if she were gathering her skirts about herself in a demure and lady-like fashion. The cat was company of a sort so she let it stay. Talking to it as she accomplished each task kept Cleo's thoughts outward.

Two hours later, as if sensing she was no longer welcome, the cat made a grand exit and Cleo went to stand on the grassy knoll leading down to the river. The breeze was stronger there, cool against her flushed face. And just by turning ever so slightly westward she wouldn't miss the instant Fletcher turned onto the river path down by the boat pier.

She saw when he stepped onto the path, the whole of him seeming to take up the landscape. She tried to take her eyes away, to look at the sky, at the trees across the river or to look down as she smoothed her skirt, but she could not move her gaze. Hesitantly, she went to meet him, dignity dictating a leisurely pace.

"A nice evening for a cookout," he said as she fell into step with him. "A cool wind to keep away mosquitoes and no clouds. We'll see stars tonight." He held up two paper sacks. "Strip sirloins and a bottle of red wine."

"Marvelous. I haven't started the grill, though." The wonder of it all, her voice sounded normal.

"The grill's my lookout. Speaking of looking..." His gaze swept over her, noting the taut skin over her cheekbones, the brightness of her eyes, the way the knit delineated her breasts. He saw, too, her reaction to his appraisal; a pink flush climbing her neck. "You look especially nice."

She brushed a wind-blown curl from her face. "Thank you."

"I wouldn't mind if you returned the compliment seeing as I drove all the way into Homerville to get a haircut."

"You do...look nice." He was wearing loafers without socks, tan slacks rolled up to his calves and a collarless shirt that emphasized the strong tendons in his neck. He smelled good, too, of soap and after-shave.

"Well, I'm glad that torturous bit of pretention is out of the way."

"You're playing with me. I suppose that was a display of the drawing room wit you're so proud of?"

"Not a very good example?"

"No."

"How'd you know I had any?"

"Marilyn mentioned it."

"You mean you haven't noticed on your own? That's a blow. Here I was thinking I'm charming and desirable and—"

"Start the grill, why don't you?" she said, taking the steak and wine from him.

"I brought you a present."

Cleo's fingers tightened on the neck of the wine bottle. "You did?"

"Yes." He reached into his back pocket and withdrew a copy of his book.

"Autographed, I suppose?" The sarcasm was slight, but it pressed down on each word.

"You're not seeing it in the right light, Cleo. You don't have to like what it says."

"Then why—?"

"It brought us together. If I hadn't written it, and Clara and Beverly hadn't... Why, I might never have known you were even in camp. I shudder to think..." He watched her eyes grow wide, begin to fill with turmoil. "Well, never mind for now. Did you make a salad?"

Cleo blinked. "Yes, it's in the fridge, and I thought... I have a cloth for the picnic table and some candles..."

"Sounds romantic."

"I didn't mean romantic. That's absurd." She said it lightly to hide the depth of her feelings. Oh, yes! She wanted romance, love, to be loved.

He tossed the book away and swept her into his arms, not a satisfying sweep because she brought the steaks and wine into play to keep her length from his. "Admit it, Cleo, you want a romantic atmosphere."

"I just want everything to be nice."

"Give a little. Say, romantic."

She gave him silence. She had no choice. There was a cataclysmic upheaval somewhere near her thighs. She couldn't speak and pay attention to that at the same time.

"Okay. We'll just stand here like this." He locked his fingers behind her back, applying a mild pressure so that they were both aware of the cold from the steaks, the shape of the bottle biting into their abdomens. "Romance is what makes the world go round. Everybody needs a little romance in his life. I need it, you need..." He looked at her, grinning playfully. "I've got romance. Guess where it's settling."

"Turn me loose, Fletcher, or—" She thought she ought to back that up with an attempt to move out of his arms, however her body wasn't about to do what her practical brain dictated. Not while his voice was caressing her, making her feel so special, and his maleness enclosed her in its aura.

"If you're threatening to scream, I'll scream louder and drown you out."

Cleo sniffed, managing disdain without moving an inch. "You're making a scene."

"No one's around. I guess it's our own play. If anybody was watching we'd get bad reviews. Be sweet...say romance."

A delicious warmth was spreading throughout Cleo's body and down along her legs. She could hear in her own ears the muffled, insistent beat of her heart. "Don't be silly!"

"Come on, say it with a smile. No, better yet, give me a sultry look. Lids at half-mast, a little fire in those golden eyes."

"You're crazy!"

"Sultry," he commanded, tightening his arms.

"The steaks are leaking."

He leapt back, glancing at her blouse, his pants. "Clean as a whistle! You're off the hook this time, *friend*. Now that I know about your sly nature, I won't be caught out a second time."

The lovely feeling ebbed, leaving Cleo a trifle weak. "I'll go season the steaks," she said.

"They're probably medium rare already."

She turned back. "You have a vulgar mouth, Fletcher Maitland."

"It's called sexual innuendo." *And, I mean to teach you the difference between vulgarity and good sex, my sweet.*

Her cheeks flamed, but as soon as she faced away from him, a slow smile tilted the corners of her mouth. She liked having romance and sexual innuendo in her life. For sure they would complement the steaks. Then he might not notice he was eating pork 'n' beans.

"Cleo!" he called a moment later. "Are you saving that wine for Christmas, or what?"

"It's coming!" Darn! He wasn't giving her a minute to herself to sort things out, to plan... She poured the wine and took several large sips. It sloshed into her stomach with untrustworthy warmth.

Plan and execute a defense against his charm. That's what you mean isn't it, Cleo?

Get out of here! I can manage this myself.

Tsk, tsk. Aren't we the edgy one? Better watch out, my dear, you may be a loose woman before the night is done.

WHILE SITTING ACROSS from Fletcher at dinner Cleo kept discovering airy hollow places within herself. Steak and salad and beans came nowhere near filling them.

Romantic atmosphere? It surrounded them in spades, thought Cleo happily. Her every sense was heightened. She was aware of the fragrance of the citronella candles flickering in their yellow globes, the sway of moss above their heads, the distant slam of car doors punctuating their conversation. All about them shadows were deep and elongated, some of them pushed into obscurity by the wedge of light spilling from the open camper door. At the picnic table she and Fletcher were in their own world, a dimension of two.

Fletcher spoke of his life on the farm in his early youth, the exciting move into the city, his paper routes, yard work, his first bicycle. Cleo had never owned a bike, never learned to ride one.

"I don't believe it!" he exclaimed. "Everybody can ride a bike."

"I was big on hoola-hoops," said Cleo. "I was quite good." At least, she had been until Gram caught sight of the gyrations and claimed the hoop was the devil's invention.

Fletcher laughed. "That's not the same thing." He paused, thoughtful. "I can see right now, you need educating on more than one subject. Hell! You need educating on all the fun things in life."

"I had fun. It was just a different kind than what you had." She stood and gathered together the plates and utensils. "I'll just put these in the sink and bring the coffee."

Fletcher watched her as she moved, felt the blood course through his veins and his pulses quicken. His patience was wearing thin, frustration building up in him. In a courtroom he'd know precisely when the prey had mellowed, when he could close in for the kill. With Cleo he had the feeling that she might yet elude him. Control was everything now, he knew.

He had listened to Cleo closely, sorting the odd fact and arcane bit of information. She reminded him of clients who came into his office and talked all around a subject, unaware that what they didn't say gave him more insight into a situation than what they did say. Cleo talked some about her mother, a little about her marriage, but was altogether reticent about her grandmother.

The puritanical old woman who had raised Cleo ate into his thoughts. He couldn't expect to undo a lifetime of austerity within a couple of weeks. But time was of the essence. He couldn't leave his law practice in the hands of others forever. Too much was at stake.

"Is that frown you're wearing because of me?"

"My thoughts ran away with me for a minute." He took a tentative sip of coffee. And then his brow creased a little bit more. "Tell me, how're you getting along with Katie?"

"She's a darling." Cleo smiled. "You may have a problem with her will though. She's got an awful lot of 'ifs' in it. As in, Roger can have my money if I don't spend it first. Lindsey can have my Madonna posters if she sits in the back pew at my funeral. Oh!" Cleo was suddenly contrite. "She's got me doing it. She invited me to her funeral as if inviting me to a . . . a party!"

Fletcher reached out and covered her hand with his own. "She's found a way to handle what's happening to her. She wants to be in control as long as she can."

"She's done that. I don't see how Marilyn and Ward..." Her voice trailed off.

"It's tough on all of us."

When Cleo looked at him, he was smiling gently at her, a warm light kindling his dark eyes. "What're you smiling at?"

"You. Us. I like you, Cleo, more than any woman I've ever known. I feel good when I'm with you. My heart even beats faster. You wouldn't believe what other parts of me do." His smile went from gentle to a devilish grin.

She tried to withdraw her hand from beneath his, but he tightened his grip. "It's getting late," she observed as if she had a thousand and one things that needed doing when in truth, she was beginning to feel that unless Fletcher was there beside her, nothing was worthwhile.

"Nine o'clock is late? How about a stroll around the camp?" She nodded. He pulled her to her feet and they were several yards along the lane when a car turned in and caught them in its beams.

A man hung his head out of the car. "Well, well, if it ain't the counselor."

Fletcher groaned.

The car moved forward, stopping when it was abreast of them. A couple was in the car and the man leaned back against the seat with a knowing smile. "Who's your lady there, Fletcher?"

Cleo hung back, but Fletcher pulled her forward. "Cleo, meet Horace Applewhite and his wife, Magda." Cleo bent down slightly and exchanged hellos. It was too dark inside the car to make out features, but she had the impression of a big man and a small woman.

"What provoked you to tear yourself away from all the criminals lurking in the streets of Atlanta, Horace?"

"Why, you did my friend. I've got a bit of news for you."

"You couldn't leave it with my office? I don't like that gleeful tone of your voice. It bodes ill."

Horace said to Cleo, "Marilyn said you're at number eleven. That's next to the last from the end of the road, right? I'll just go park."

"Our evening's shot," said Fletcher glumly.

HORACE APPLEWHITE was a huge man with a strong jaw, intelligent blue eyes lit with a teasing gleam and a cleft in his chin. His wife, Magda, was lovely. Slender, raven-haired with the most translucent skin Cleo had ever seen, her face a mingling of delicate bones and firm muscles, smooth on the surface and finely shaped. The light spilling from the camper had given Cleo a good look at them.

While her husband wrestled a cooler out of the trunk of their car, she approached Cleo with an appraising eye and open curiosity. After a long moment she said, "I knew it!"

"Knew what?" Cleo was undone at having been so keenly gone over by another woman.

"That it had to be a woman. I thought at first it might be Katie was worse . . . the reason Fletcher turned over his practice. Everybody in his office is in a real twit. By that I mean thrilled. Fletcher usually saves the most difficult cases for himself. Now his junior partners are having their chance. But I called Big Momma and she said Katie was no worse, no better.''

"You and Horace are some of the regulars?''

Cleo was keeping half her attention on Horace who was making himself at home. The cooler was on the picnic table now; he was hauling beer out, passing one to Fletcher.

"Pretty much. Horace went to school with Fletcher and Ward. You might say that between Horace and Fletcher there's a long-standing friendly enmity. That's a warning so you won't go ape when the shouting begins.''

"Cleo, come over here,'' Fletcher called, dragging up her lawn chairs. "You're on my list, Magda, so don't go filling Cleo's head with nonsense.''

She laughed. "Ah! The protective male scouting his territorial rights.''

Cleo sidled up to Fletcher. "What is going on?'' she whispered.

"None of that,'' said Horace. "I can hear a pin drop at forty feet.''

"You don't know?'' Magda said, ready to tell. "My darling husband here, was one of the recipients of Fletcher's little missal. You've heard of that, I presume? I have a friend who's an editor at a small press. He brought Fletcher's book out.''

"Because you sent it to him,'' countered Fletcher.

"Because he offered you ten percent royalties, you mean. Appealed to your greedy nature.''

"I used the money to set up a free legal aid fund for indigents.''

"Criminals, you mean.'' Horace aimed his beer toward Cleo. "I go out on the street and risk my neck to catch the baddies, then your friend here, gets them off.''

"I only insist on evidence, gathered properly, law-fully."

"Hah! The way you protect criminals, you'd think they were an endangered species."

"It's the law that's endangered! If we bypass it for one, we'll do it for all, then what of the innocent that get trapped? They'll fall through the cracks—"

"Stop it!" shouted Magda. "Don't you two start just yet." She spied the grill, coals still glowing. "Say, do you mind if I throw a couple of steaks on that? We haven't eaten. Horace got this bee in his brain that we had to start out as soon as he got off from work—"

"Aunt Magda! Aunt Magda!" Katie came racing into the clearing and threw herself at the woman. "Mom and Dad will be here in a minute. Did you bring your tarot cards? Will you read for me?" Katie spoke breathlessly over Magda's shoulder to Cleo. "Aunt Magda has Gypsy blood. She can tell the future!"

Magda untangled Katie's arms from her neck. "The future I foretell this instant is I'd better get some food in Horace. When his stomach starts grumbling it sounds like an earthquake.

"Oh, please. . . ."

"I will not be manipulated by a skinny eleven-year-old," said Magda. "Get off my lap. First I put the steaks on the grill, then the cards, after which you must go off to bed."

"I promise," said Katie sweetly and exchanged Magda's lap for Cleo's. "Aunt Magda will read for you, too. She can tell you *everything*!"

"Another time, perhaps," Cleo said quickly. Too quickly, she thought, shivering. She wasn't sure she wanted to know her future now. She felt she was rapidly losing the tenuous grip she had on the situation . . . affair? Dare she think that word with Fletcher?

She smoothed Katie's flyaway hair, what little there was of it and felt the little body trembling with excitement. She had to consciously put away thoughts of pity. Katie had so much and yet so little ... so many dreams and wishes, so little time ... and such endless hope.

Horace excused himself with an apology. "Beer goes right through me on an empty stomach."

"Doesn't look empty from where I sit," needled Fletcher.

"Don't get nasty, pal. This is an iron stomach."

"Beam broke in the middle though."

"You ain't gettin' the last word. I got it. But I'm saving it for later, so you just whisper sweet nothings in your lady's ear while I tend to nature."

"Wanna hear a few sweet nothings?" Fletcher teased after the giant lumbered off.

"Can I listen?" asked Katie. "Are you going to talk sexy?"

"No and no," said Cleo with haste.

Fletcher smiled wanly. "I'm sorry everybody's just sort of plopped down in your space...."

"Cleo doesn't mind, do you?" put in Katie.

"Why don't you go hide in the bushes like you usually do?" Fletcher admonished.

"Because I've got permission." She hung an arm around Cleo's neck, looking smug.

"I don't think you're going to win this one, Fletcher. And, I don't mind the company. I like meeting your friends."

Liked meeting them because now she could put off having to face the shameful things, the discreditable impulses that rose to the surface when alone with him. If he suggested bed now she didn't think she could say no. And one did have to approach sin logically. She needed time to make it the right thing to do.

She lifted her eyes to find Fletcher studying her as though seeing her for the first time.

Caught, he faltered for the fraction of a second. "You're beautiful when you laugh, Cleo."

She dropped her gaze and broke the contact. Katie squirmed in her lap.

"That was a sweet nothing, right? I wish somebody would fall in love with me." She wrapped her next words around a huge sigh. "If I had breasts I know somebody would."

Cleo jerked to her feet, and almost sent Katie sprawling. "I'll just go see if Magda needs any help. I think there's some salad left."

"Cleo . . . wait . . ." Fletcher looked after her for a long time, and then he turned to Katie. "I ought to yank your tongue out with a piece of string."

Katie puffed up. "Why? What'd I do?"

"Your subject matter is not always appropriate for mixed company and you know it. Cleo is shy. You embarrassed her."

"How can a grown-up be shy?"

"Because of the way they were raised."

"How was Cleo raised?"

"Not to talk about body parts in mixed company."

"Oh." Katie stared balefully at him. "You think she's mad at me?"

"Probably not, but she ought to be."

"You're mad at me, though."

"I'm on the leading edge of it."

"I don't want to sit here and talk to you anyway," she said sniffing. "I'm going to get my fortune read."

Why, you little snip of proud flesh, Fletcher thought, watching her stump off to the camper. He noticed that her left leg seemed to drag. Hurrying, she compensated by going up higher on her right foot. Damn and damn again! He pressed his fingers to his temples.

He felt all churned up. The whole evening had gone awry. Hour upon hour was what he needed with Cleo to loosen her up, to get through to her, to dissolve that barrier that shot up at the mention of anything sexual.

He had always managed control of his body, but now he began to wonder if it could take the onslaught of raw emotion that exploded within it every time he got close to Cleo. Once aroused he was used to getting satisfied. Now he was like a time bomb, ticking and dangerous, capable of exploding at any moment.

The thought made his mouth dry. He opened another can of beer and took a long swallow. For the first time in his life he envied every married man on earth.

CLEO SAT CROSS-LEGGED on her bed, sipping champagne out of a cup and watching Magda tell Katie's fortune. The champagne was Magda's. When she had offered the other woman some of Fletcher's red wine, Magda had refused with a graceful wave of her arm that set her bracelets to tinkling. She didn't like beer and if one was to drink wine, why only the sweetest bubbly would do. So out of the cooler the bottle was produced and opened by Horace, and now Cleo felt just the slightest bit tipsy.

The sound of the men's voices drifted on the wind. Sometimes a low murmuring, now a shout, or a mocking curse punctuating the air. They argued history, morals, social law, old cases. Ward had joined them after popping his head in the camper with the message Marilyn would be along as soon as she showered. Katie was ordered home, but given a five-minute reprieve so that Magda could finish her fortune.

"Uh-oh," said Magda, tapping the Chariot. "This card keeps coming up. It means aggression. You fixing to have a fight with somebody?"

Impatience radiated off Katie in waves. "My mom, if you don't hurry up."

Magda laughed and aimed a comment to Cleo. "Somebody needs to tell this kid that destiny cannot be hurried." She shuffled again and laid out the cards. "Here we go again. Now the World card. A journey. You're going on a trip, and soon."

Katie scowled. "The only trip I'm planning is to heaven. I hope it's not *that* soon."

Magda froze, immobile for long seconds. Watching, Cleo knew the shock she was experiencing, and when Magda glanced quickly her way, she could offer only silence and woe.

"This is a very short journey," Magda said finally. "I think tomorrow. It looks like a canoe trip."

"No!" gasped Katie, delighted.

"Yes, and I see an early start. So early you won't be able to keep your eyes open if you don't take your tush home right this minute."

"Oh, Aunt Magda . . . please? One more shuffle? I'll be thinking what it is I want most in the world."

"One more card." Magda turned it over. The Star. "Ah, hope!"

"Nothing more definite?" Katie pleaded.

"Hope is always definite." Magda stacked the cards. "Now, off with you." She gave Katie a hug and a swat on the behind to help her on her way, and afterward looked over at Cleo. "I can't believe she said that. A trip to heaven! What does Marilyn say?"

"Marilyn doesn't know. Katie has the idea that her mother can't handle—"

"I think she's right. Marilyn has always been high-strung about some things. She was a basket case when her mother died. I guess Katie picked up on it." She shook her head. "Geez!" She began to put away the cards. "I'd better check those steaks."

"How long have you been doing tarot?" asked Cleo.

"Years and years. You like a fortune?"

Cleo wanted it very much. "No. I really don't believe in any of that."

"Ah, a skeptic." Magda smiled, her gaze roving to the cracked mirror.

"I didn't break it," Cleo said.

"But, you're worried about the bad luck of it anyway?"

"Maybe, just a little."

There was no more said because Horace bellowed for food and they went to join the men. Then Marilyn arrived, more champagne was poured, and the conversation drifted to the forest fires so much in the news and the proposed canoe trip to the Suwannee Canal inside the Okefenokee Swamp.

"Have you and Cleo decided to go?" Marilyn asked Fletcher.

"We have other plans for tomorrow."

The champagne had loosened Cleo's tongue and her reticence. "We do? What?"

"You'll know tomorrow."

Magda patted Cleo's arm. "He means he'll improvise. He wants you to himself. Isn't that right, Fletcher?"

The wine was speaking to Cleo in a thousand tongues. "No, he must mean lunch or something."

"It's the 'or something' you better watch out for!" boomed Horace, giving Fletcher a friendly leer. Then he sobered. "Damn! I almost forgot, counselor. I bring you tidings and warnings."

"About what?" Fletcher kept an eye on Cleo. He longed to give shape to the thoughts crowding his mind. He was elated that Cleo was accepted by his friends, and that she accepted them. He felt a manful pride, having her there in the chair beside him. Beside him—he realized that's where he wanted her for the rest of his life.

"B.B. Bostwick. Con man, habitual criminal. Racks up old ladies for their savings."

"He was up for sentencing yesterday. I turned that over to Jacobs."

"That's the joker. He escaped from the deputy when he was being moved from the court house to the county jail for processing to the state prison. He's out to get you."

Fletcher jerked, alert. He sat straighter in his chair. "What the hell! You waited—"

"What's this? No love for a client?"

"Would he come here?" Marilyn asked, worried.

Fletcher grimaced. "I hope not. But—"

"The guy's a schizo, ain't he, counselor? He's capable of anything."

"Shut up, Horace. You're scaring me." Marilyn leaned toward Fletcher. "Why? Why would one of your own clients come after you? You're one of the best trial lawyers in the state."

"You have to know how the criminal mind works. They think a good attorney can get them off. I never promise that. I only promise a fair trial and if we don't get it, appeals all the way to the Supreme Court." He noticed the stricken look on Cleo's face and reached for her hand, enclosing it in his. "The police'll catch him, if they haven't already. There's nothing to worry about. I'll call Jacobs first thing in the morning. When did this happen, Horace?''

''Just after the noon recess yesterday.'' Horace opened another beer. ''Sheriff's office said he must've had help. He was being escorted down the hallway along with some other prisoners, he was last in line—''

''Manacled?''

''No, just handcuffed.''

''And?''

''When the deputy started counting the prisoners into the van, he was short one B.B. Bostwick. Speculation is, he just faded into the lunch crowd.''

''Wearing handcuffs?''

''Well, a witness reported seeing a handcuffed man being put into a late-model Ford. Who knows a plain-clothes detective from a regular citizen? These guys put on an act. Truth to tell, if I saw a well-dressed man hurrying a handcuffed prisoner out of a courtroom, I wouldn't question it either, unless it happened to be a case I'd worked.''

Marilyn shivered. ''It's spooky and here we are way out in nowhere, no phones in the cabins...'' She stood abruptly. ''The kids are by themselves. Let's go, Ward.''

''You're getting panicky all out of proportion,'' soothed Fletcher. ''Bostwick is probably on the other side of the country by now. He's a con man—''

''With a violent streak,'' said Horace.

Magda pinched him on the arm.

''Ouch! What was that for?''

''A runaway tongue.''

Ward heaved himself off the picnic bench. ''We need to turn in anyway if we're to get an early start. I've reserved the canoes for eight.''

Magda began to gather the plates she and Horace had used. Fletcher stopped her. "Cleo and I'll do that."

"My, my, you have gone domestic, but I won't belabor it for now. Horace and I had better hit the sack ourselves. I still have to unpack. We're in cabin seven, next door to Ward and Marilyn, by the way. Dinner is on us tomorrow night, okay?" She included Cleo with a wave of her hand.

"We accept," Fletcher said.

"We do?" The words came slow and slurred. Cleo looked around, startled, unsure the words had come from her.

Magda laughed. "You better put this gal to bed, Fletcher. Champagne's not her cup of tea."

"I'm fine—really." Cleo began to clean the picnic table. Now that she was on her feet she did feel awfully like she was floating. She tried focusing her mind on that terrible man who was after Fletcher, but concentration eluded her, as did the dishes that—for goodness sake—refused to stay stacked.

"They've gone," said Fletcher. He picked up beer cans, tossing them into the garbage.

"Good."

"Good?"

"I mean—did I say good-night?" She looked at him, contrite. He was glowering at her.

"Look here, Cleo, why don't we just leave these dishes for morning. You need to be off your feet." He put his arm around her, propelling her toward the camper.

"I don't have to be off... I can't even feel my feet."

"That's just what I mean."

"Fletcher? Did I tell you that you smell nice? Your after-shave is so sexy...you're sexy too, the sexiest man I ever met. Paul wasn't at all sexy—" She stumbled going up the one step. "Oh! 'Scuse me. My head is so...so bubbly."

"You're drunk." He got her to sit on the bed, legs dangling.

"I'm not at all drunk, maybe a bit woozy, though."

"Same thing. Let's just get your shoes off."

She watched him undo the straps. His hands at her ankles reminded her.... "Fletcher." Her voice sounded distant, disembodied; their eyes met. Her mouth had gone too dry to say anything else. Instead she put her hand on his shoulder, then lightly trailed her fingertips up his neck.

Very, very slowly, Fletcher put aside her sandals and stood up. He shook his head. "Not tonight," he said softly. "It's not how I want you."

Adrenaline shot through Cleo with a sobering effect. *No!* She wanted to die. She swallowed down the pain in her throat. "I'm ... I'm sorry."

"Cleo, darling, there's nothing to be sorry for. I'm not refusing the invitation, just taking a rain check." He fluffed the pillow and pushed her gently back on the bed. Then he brushed her lips with his fingers, moving them across her cheek, down her neck, trailing feather-light over her breast.

Cleo experienced a fleeting urge to resist, to slap his hand, but the urge was mere reflex, lost in her wine-drugged brain.

He expelled a raspy sigh. "I could almost change my mind...." He bent over then and kissed her lightly on the lips. "Don't trust myself any more than this," he murmured when he drew away.

"Fletcher," she whispered.

She saw him flinch. "Please! Don't say another word. I've got in my mind how it should be between us, Cleo. I know how it *has* to be."

"You'd better go," she said flatly.

He moved back, staring at her intently for a heartbeat. He was painfully aware of his raw desire to lie down atop her and make love to her until dawn. "You're being a bit of a tart right now, only hearing what you want to hear. You're not listening to what I'm saying."

How could she? Cleo wondered, when less polite parts of her were screaming for release. "I've heard every word. You don't want me."

"I want you." And if he didn't leave in the next instant, he'd take her, consequences be damned. "What I don't want is remnants of Paul and your grandmother in bed with us. Now, you think that one over, tell me in the morning if I'm wrong. Then, I'll take that rain check."

The demons suddenly surged about Cleo and she had no wherewithal to chase them away. She sat up, her face tense. "Get out!" she shouted. "Just . . . get . . . out." From somewhere deep in her brain the laughing started.

He sure told you, didn't he, Cleo? I couldn't have said it better myself.

She heard Fletcher's "Good night, don't forget to lock up" just barely through the muddle in her head.

Wobbly, she held onto the bed, the stove, the table as she snapped the latch. Before she turned out the light she caught her twin reflection in the cracked mirror. There are two of me again! She moaned. Visible sin on one side, and she didn't know what the other was, but it was worse, so much worse.

The laughter came again, mocking and sneering. *Want me to tell?*

Oh, leave me alone! she screamed silently, and was suddenly crushingly tired. She had made such a fool of herself! Sprawling across the bed, she wept until she felt like an empty shell that had once contained life, but was now hollow and echoing the past.

Once, just before dawn she awakened with a single lucid thought. She must leave Georgia . . . return to Chicago where she had an apartment, a job, acquaintances—*things*. Return to nothing, that's what. She felt a small sense of panic. She was thirty years old. Thirty years old and alone! It didn't bear thinking about, not anymore. She pounded on her pillow and turned her face into it. Another hour of sleep, she told herself, then she'd be entirely clear headed.

CHAPTER TEN

CLEO EMERGED from the shower shack with her robe and towel slung over one arm and personal tote on the other. She was clean, but not as refreshed as she had hoped. Wine-induced sleep, thoughts and dreams had left her disoriented. Stepping onto the back path that led to her campsite, she came face to face with Fletcher. Her heart sank. The last person in the world she wanted to see!

Last night she had acted so stupidly, exposing herself like that. He must be horribly embarrassed, probably pitying her, wondering how to let her down tactfully without hurting her feelings.

She glanced briefly at him. He looked a little strung out himself.

"By any chance do you have a kind word for a lonely lawyer this morning?"

She felt an anxious stirring inside, a tension that held her body in its grip. "No."

Averting her face, she kept on walking.

"You got coffee made?"

"No," she tossed over her shoulder, presenting him with her profile.

"You packed yet?" He laughed at her startled expression and tapped his temple. "It aches, but it's still working. You don't think that after I've gone and fallen in love, and seen my life go topsy-turvy, that I'm going to let you run off and hide, do you?"

A little something clicked in Cleo's brain. A quickening.

She was aware of a barricade rising, the past looming, squeezing into the moment; Gram, dead, yet alive in her brain, arms folded, accusing. Paul gone out of her daily life for years now, though leaving her filled with self-doubts. But the awareness was only a momentary diversion.

Of course, she hadn't heard Fletcher right. She replayed his words in her mind. It sounded like ... *gone and fallen in love*. The words refused to sink in, to make sense. She looked at her feet, mildly surprised to find them moving forward in an ordinary way as if having a mind of their own and a destination to reach.

"Heads up!" Fletcher shouted.

The command came seconds too late. Cleo shifted her gaze, but her momentum carried her into a huge old pine.

"Whoops!" He caught up, reached to steady her. "For a minute there I thought I wasn't going to get any reaction out of you. Hold still while I see how much damage you've done."

"I'm fine," she said vaguely.

"Scraped your forehead." Gently he brushed away some pine bark, then pulled a handkerchief from his pocket and dabbed at the scratch. "You'll be okay." He was grinning.

"Fletcher," she said, voice small, inaudible, so that he was compelled to watch her lips form the words. "What did you say a minute ago?"

"That I didn't think I was going to get—"

"Before that." The voice came stronger now, accompanied by a slight gesticulation of her hand.

"About having coffee made?"

She shook her head, a flicker of agitation leaping into her eyes. "After that."

"Oh, you mean about being in love with you?"

Cleo leaned against the tree. Oh, wonderful solid tree— rough brown bark at her back, an anchor to reality while her heart tried beating its way past her ribs, all the way out of her body. "I thought that's what you said...."

Love meant so many things—companionship, laughter, pain, Sunday mornings. *Sex.* Oh, God!

The sight of her face melted him. He laughed softly. "It hit me like that, too." He pressed his mouth close to hers for a moment before drawing her into the curve of his arm with a proprietary air. "Come on, I'll walk you back to your place. I was just on my way to Big Momma's to call Jacobs."

"Did everybody get off to the state park okay this morning?" Impossible that she could carry such an inane conversation on the outside when inside was total chaos. She felt quite flushed.

"Yes, if you call nursing hangovers okay, and kids racing around like maniacs at 6:00 a.m." He gave her a happy, albeit calculating look. "You'll be all right for a few minutes?"

"Of course," she said hoarsely. She would be, too, if she could just sit down. Common sense said her legs were long and tanned and strong, but she knew for a fact her bones were falling away at the joints. Only the borrowed strength of Fletcher's arm kept her from toppling. He deposited her on the picnic bench at her campsite and traced the shape of her lips with his finger a lingering second before he left.

Cleo watched him go, convinced all her dreams were about to come true. Love, he had said. But she wasn't worthy of love.

She made do with the way she looked because...
because she looked that way, was all. And, she knew she
was mixed up about sex. Gram had started her on the road
to confusion, and Paul had capped it. No matter how
much she tried, the confusion got in her way.

This was her milestone year. That was a given. She
didn't want to grow old alone. That, too was a given.
But...

But, nothing! mocked the inner voice. *Here's another
given for you, Cleo dear: There are sixty-two single men
for every one hundred single women between the ages of
thirty and thirty-four. You have a chance at one of those
men. You're always talking about Fate. It's looking you in
the face. Put that in your milestone pipe and smoke it.*

Fletcher hasn't mentioned marriage.

*You heard what he said, falling in love has knocked his
socks off. Give the guy a chance. Just keep on... hang on
to your good-girl image out of guilt and a misplaced sense
of morality and see what it gets you...*

Respect, that's what.

*Respect! Hah! Think more along the lines of a cold and
lonely bed, no children of your own, wrinkles at forty that
aren't dear to anyone.*

Cleo pulled herself together, only managing it by telling
herself not to think until her head was in a better place. She
put away her robe, made her bed, and washed dishes from
the night before.

"All I got was the answering machine," said Fletcher
when he returned. "Jacobs's probably spending the
weekend at his place on Lake Lanier. Did you make coffee?"

She nodded, forcing her eyes to focus on his hands as he
reached around her to pour himself a cup. They were
strong hands with long lean fingers. Loving her meant,

must mean, that he wanted to touch her forever with those hands. She inhaled deeply to pull oxygen into her lungs.

"I guess I'll just have to take the bull by the horns," he told her, his eyes taking on that intent penetrating lawyer's look.

"What bull?" she asked, laboring under the distraction of her thoughts, his hands and a shortness of breath.

He tilted the cup, draining it into the sink, pouring out the clear hot water.

"Oh! I must've forgotten to—"

"Yes." His strength dominated her preoccupation. "Come on, let's go down to the cabin. Nobody's there and we need the room."

Cleo's hand fluttered to her throat. "Room for what?"

"What do you say we start out with coffee and conversation. I'll make the coffee and you make the conversation. There's so much about you I want to know. Afterward, we'll just let nature take its course."

"Nature?" Panic rose like a separate entity having a voice of its own, shaping words. Mortified, Cleo heard them clatter off her tongue. "Fletcher! Wait. About last night. That was the champagne talking, not me." Not the real me.

"Good, because I don't want to talk to champagne. I want to talk to you." He pulled her out the door, closed it behind them. "It's time for a little modest realism, darling. There's more to love than storybook phantasm. I'm getting used to the enchantment. I want to make sure there's something left, something to build on when that goes."

"That's convoluted lawyer's talk," she snapped, sounding like a weak rubber band. She was firmly in his grasp, unable to retreat.

Overhead the morning sun was lighting the sky, birds chirped, wind blew. Up ahead an elderly couple sat on the boat dock, fishing with cane poles. Cleo was sure she was still in bed, dreaming. She'd wake up any minute.

"Except that you know what I'm talking about."

"I don't," she lied.

"Well, we have that little matter of a rain check to settle."

Cleo experienced a tremor, almost a shiver, as if reality had touched her for the first time. She glanced at him, eyes wide, face pale, the spatter of freckles across her cheeks standing out in stark relief. "I never agreed—" But she had, with looks, caresses, kisses. Oh! she thought, why am I fighting?

He stopped suddenly, yanking her into a savage embrace, pressing his full length against her, the desperate hunger for her awesome, a consuming greed. "You feel the chemistry between us, Cleo? Do you feel it?"

What she felt was the taut straining hardness between his legs. She felt too, sensations surging up, filling her, writhing their way, escaping from beneath the celibate sheath in which she had hidden her erotic emotions. "Yes," she said, because denial would be useless.

"Yes, what?" Fingers splayed, his hands were sliding down her spine. It seemed to Cleo those fingers were kneading the erotic flames, fueling them.

"Don't—"

"Yes, what?" he repeated, tight-lipped, determined to draw from her this truth, needing to hear it, terrified that he could so easily lose her to that chaste other world in which she secured her emotions.

"I feel the chemistry," she admitted in a voice so fragile, so faint, he had to again watch her lips shape words to be certain he had heard them.

He withdrew his arms, and took her hand. When they were abreast of the old couple fishing on the pier, Cleo averted her face, for the old woman was smiling at her, a special smile reserved universally for lovers by alert observers.

At the cabin Fletcher opened the screened door, thrusting her on through, not ungently, though he held onto her hand until they were standing on the threshold to his bedroom. It was in disarray, the bed unmade, a briefcase spilling its contents over a dresser; on the floor, a suitcase was open; under the bed a single discarded sock reposed, mateless.

"It's not the most romantic room in the world," he said. "But this is where it's going to happen for us."

She jerked her hand from his. "No!"

"Yes." He blocked her retreat with his body. "Cleo, you're the most sensuous woman I've ever met. You just won't loosen up. I'm hoping that together..."

"You just want to go to bed with me!"

"I want to marry you."

All Cleo's senses were muffled. She held her breath. She was independent, self-supporting, on her own—everything she was supposed to be. A man, a stranger, really, whom she hadn't known barely two weeks ago, wanted to marry her. He had somehow ingratiated himself into her every thought, made himself into a cocoon that surrounded her. He loved her. He said so. She loved him back. Inside her, pirouetted a tiny figure of hope.

"When?" she blurted.

Fletcher laughed. "I don't know when. That depends on you."

He guided her back to the living room. Cleo collapsed on the sofa, feet curled beneath her and watched Fletcher do ordinary tasks at the sink; he rinsed out the coffeepot, measured the grounds, plugged in the pot and took down mugs.

"Is this some sort of silly game we're playing?" she asked.

"Silly?" He looked at her gravely. "Cleo, it's been my experience that when a person goes through a bad time, they have to talk it out, get it in perspective. It happens all the time to victims of wife abuse, child abuse or crime."

"But, I'm not a victim of anything!"

"In my field I see a lot of marriages go down the tubes because people don't or can't communicate with each other. So, I think we ought to talk. Especially about your attitude toward sex. It disturbs me. It disturbs you, too. I don't have to be a psychoanalyst to see that."

Cleo's face flamed. "I just don't believe in sex outside of marriage."

"Because good girls don't?"

"Yes!"

"You're not a girl, Cleo. You're a woman, with wants, needs, urges."

"I don't deny that."

"But you deny yourself satisfaction."

"I don't go around jumping into bed with every man I meet, if that's what you mean."

"Since I'm in love with you, I'm glad to hear that, but I already knew you didn't."

"I don't have to stay here and listen to this! It's... it's too clinical."

Fletcher leaned more heavily against the counter at which he'd been standing, waiting for the coffee to perk. "You don't have to stay."

There was something so ominous in his soft words. Cleo looked sharply at him. "And, if I go?"

How far could she be pushed? Fletcher wondered. How badly did she want him? He saw Cleo in his arms, her eyes half closed, her mouth, her body warm and pulsating beneath his. He had an inkling then, of how man lives on hope, how he twists it, prays for it, aches for it. "I like sex, Cleo. I don't want a wife who huddles behind a closet door to undress. I want to see you naked. I want to know every inch of you. I want you to want me the same way. If we can't talk about it like the adults we are..." He shrugged, gesturing with his hands spread wide. "Another point..." He knew he sounded as if he were in the courtroom, giving his final summation in front of a jury. But he likened Cleo to a jury of one and this was a case he meant to win. "I'm thirty-eight years old. I only want to go through this once, it's too nerve-wracking. I can't eat, sleep or concentrate, except on you. I understand what's meant by romantic thralldom now, but that goes with familiarity and when it does I want to be on solid ground. I want a marriage that will last."

He's giving you an ultimatum, Cleo. If you don't want to spend the rest of your life alone, you'd better do the smart thing for once in your life and stay put.

Cleo was becalmed, limbs leaden; for a few seconds she even thought her heart had stopped beating. She looked at Fletcher. Really looked, seeing things she hadn't noticed before—a tiny scar that cut through one dark eyebrow, the small mole on his left arm, but mostly she looked into his eyes, those windows to the soul. In those windows she saw pride, compassion, hope and...was that fear? Perhaps that she would walk out of his life? Needing something solid to cling to, she gripped the sofa arm while she thumbed her nose at the demons swirling about her.

Maybe—oh, just maybe—she could talk it all out. And if so—if it would make things really change—make the demons fly away—she was willing to endure.

"I want to stay," she said.

Fletcher looked at her gently, but all the gentle looks in the world couldn't penetrate the terror, real or imagined he saw in Cleo's expression. "Tell me about when you were a little girl, about your mother, your grandmother..." He poured their coffees, discovering his hands were trembling.

"You're acting like it's true confessions. My life wasn't . . . isn't like that at all!" She was the center of his attention, unprepared, terrified of her new status, of being loved, of how easily love could disappear. The dream without a face flashed through her mind.

He took her hands and wrapped them about the mug, enclosing them with his own, allowing her to feel his strength, to know it was there for her. "Tell me how it was, then." His voice was filled with a quiet intensity Cleo had never heard in it before.

But still she wavered, for to dredge up all the old hurts, old fears, some of which were with her yet, was not easy. They were troubles worn to fit like an old pair of shoes; they pinched now and again, but she wasn't certain she was ready to relinquish them for something new; unknown.

He bent and kissed her brow, savoring for a moment the smooth flesh beneath his lips, knowing if he ever needed a clear head, it was now. If ever he needed a delicate hand, a good sense of balance... "I love you, Cleo."

Her mouth went dry. "I've never really talked about those years to anyone."

"It's time you did, and got an objective view. Let's take our coffee and go sit on the porch in the rocking chairs. I want to hear about your first day in school."

Cleo laughed, exhaling relief. School! That was easy. "Oh! I hated it! My dress was too long, my arms too thin and I was a head taller than anyone else in class." She looked down into her cup, seeing another world—blackboards and chalk, bells, the clatter of plates in cafeterias. Suddenly her past was on the move, marching forward, a private revolution, breaking out like a breath held too long. "First grade was when I learned the other kids had fathers and I didn't . . . I used to make believe I was an orphan."

The words were almost lost because she was speaking to herself rather than Fletcher, traveling off somewhere without him. Time, which could not be measured in the ticking away of the hours and minutes and seconds, slipped away in starts and stops of half sentences, of incidents recalled, bits and pieces of life's debris spoken aloud at Fletcher's urgings: What happened then? What did you do? What did Gram say? Until the whole bleak picture emerged.

As she spoke, her memories ignited so vividly she forgot Fletcher's presence, but he saw every nuance of her remembering face. He saw tenderness, regret, sadness, fear and the brightness of unshed tears.

Finally she looked over at him, not smiling. "Was that enough for an objective viewpoint?"

He more readily understood her now; in the purest of clarity, he saw she needed to be loved unreservedly. Loved for, not in spite of, her flaws and imperfections. "You know what I think? That I've latched on to a brave strong woman."

"Brave? Me?" Cleo didn't think so. She had reacted to Gram's perpetual reproach to herself for having been born out of wedlock. The truth was, she had spent her life too agitated with demons and worry to see that. Too busy trying to keep herself safe. Hardly the sort of person one would call brave or fearless or strong.

"You fought the devils off, didn't you? All by your lonesome? Do you still look under your bed before you go to sleep?"

"Of course not."

A white lie, he thought. "You know what else I see...suspect? That your grandmother was a sensuous woman herself and afraid of it, or perhaps angry that she didn't have an outlet after her husband died or left."

"He died."

"But you only have her word for that, Cleo. Women in her era spent a lot of time living up to their neighbor's expectations of them. My own mother was that way. Then your mother had an illicit affair. To your grandmother sex was the root of all the evils in her life. Sex to many women in her generation was a thing only tolerated because of wifely duties. Imagine how she must have felt if she discovered it was a thing she liked, wanted. I can see her thinking she had to save you from that, especially after she thought she'd failed with your mother."

"That would take more imagination than I have."

"When it comes to yourself, you're a skeptic. Why do you think she shifted her passion to religion, becoming a fanatic? I'm surprised she didn't balk at your marriage."

"I didn't tell her until after the fact. There was nothing she could do." Cleo gave an embarrassed laugh. "She got her two cents in after we broke up."

All had not been resolved, Fletcher knew. Cleo had passed over her former marriage and dodged most of his questions in that quarter. He cursed himself for not having the guts to pursue them. Little stabs of jealousy had stopped him.

He watched the late-morning sun find a path through foliage, sprinkling the mulch-covered ground with lacy patterns. Then for a minute he looked at Cleo without saying anything, cataloguing the surface of her, lining it up with all that she had revealed and had kept sheltered in her being. There was far more depth in her than he had suspected. He saw again that odd mixture of strength and fragility, the appealing manner in the way she hoisted her chin. He felt she was his in spirit now. He wanted more, he wanted all of her. The thought made him giddy, and because he had to touch her, he put out his hand and laced his fingers in hers. "How do you feel?"

"A little drained," she said, leaning her head back on the rocker.

"A little drained," he repeated, looking at her throat, the length of her neck that was so compellingly vulnerable. "How about in love?"

Her voice was unsteady, a whisper. "Yes."

"Think you could undress in front of me?"

In broad daylight? Cleo's entire self repulsed that idea. "No!"

A mischievous expression flitted across his features. "Could you watch me undress?"

"No!" To see him naked! His body wanting her. The picture of it took shape in her mind while a furious flame began to lick at her thighs. "Well . . . maybe."

"Maybe . . ." He laughed, caressing her with his gaze, understanding it was up to him to find exactly the right moment, that all the preliminaries must be orderly and observed. A situation that was plainly taxing his control beyond measure. "I have news for you, sweetheart. If the goose won't, the gander sure ain't." He stood up suddenly, desperately in need of an activity to replace the one he most desired. "Let's make some sandwiches, and put a few beers in the cooler and go for a boat ride, down the river a couple of miles. We'll take one of the putt-putts."

Cleo was agreeable. She needed to put some space between the telling and...whatever was to come anyway. "I'd like to take my camera...."

"Go get it."

"We have made progress! You're trusting me out of your sight, when there's air in my tires?"

Fletcher took up her teasing tone. "In lawyerese it's called personal recognizance. If you don't show up to meet your obligation, then you forfeit the trust bestowed." Looking at her, the bantering went out of his voice.

Cleo inhaled. "I'll be right back."

"The docks...ten minutes," he said and went to throw together some sliced ham and bread. Six or so miles down river was a small island that had once held a house before a long-ago flood had swiped it off its pilings. Now there was only a rickety pier left to mark the site. A good place for a picnic, Fletcher mused. And perhaps, a good place, too, to satisfy another kind of appetite. The bedroom could come later. He seized upon the salacious thought, whistling as he filled the cooler.

CLEO SAT on the bow and focused the camera on Fletcher. He was wearing a stone-colored desert hat at a jaunty angle. He refused to be coaxed into flipping the brim back to get the shadow off his face.

"I hate having my picture taken."

She gave him a look of mild rebuke. "Every face tells a story. I want to record yours, not just your unshaven jaw."

"Oh, yeah, a story? What does this face tell you?"

"That you're stubborn. Look up there, Fletcher, what kind of bird is that?"

He tilted his face and she got a picture.

"That was sneaky."

"I think it's going to come out all chin and Adam's apple." She lowered the camera and drew her sunglasses down over her eyes from their perch atop her head.

Blue skies towered overhead; hot sunshine beat down. From the banks of the river came the bittersweet smell of pitch and dry pine twigs. Cleo watched the riverbanks, equating with them a tranquillity that permeated her being, though she had an unsettling feeling that the tranquillity was only on the surface. She had a sense of expectation as if a curtain were about to rise on the second act of a bold and unrehearsed play, for in spite of his teasing, his gay mood, she noted in Fletcher an aura of tightly reined animal energy.

Sweat began to bead on her lip. She wiped it away with a fingertip. "Is there some place in particular we're going?"

"What makes you think that?" said Fletcher over the low hum of the motor that left a lacy wake spreading out behind the small skiff.

"Now I know we are. You answered my question with a question."

He veered off to the right, taking them closer to shore. "Look there."

The mother bear and her cubs were wallowing in a shallow pool. Cleo raised her camera. "Slow down!" she called and snapped several frames before they motored past into a narrow inlet.

Cypress, black gum and bay lined the inlet, moss-laden limbs meeting far above their heads to create a cathedral-like calm. The unexpected shade was glorious.

"Wonderful!" Cleo exclaimed as the boat swept deeper into the lush dewy coolness.

Fletcher cut the motor, but kept his hand on the tiller as the current, swifter in the deep trough between riverbank and island, carried them farther into the green gloom. Without the sharp sunlight the copper-colored river appeared black.

He coaxed the skiff nearer the island, which was little more than a spit of land, held together by the roots of sawgrass, palmettos and a few giant cypress and poplar, but the trees, along with the underbrush, hid them well from other boaters that might be traveling downriver.

The skiff bumped into pilings. Nesting catbirds fluttered into the air. Cleo jerked. "Why didn't you warn me?"

"Next time sit so you can watch where we're going. Throw a rope over that stump."

"What is this place?"

"My secret swimming hole." He hauled the cooler, a blanket and towels onto the pier, which was missing more boards than he recalled. "Wouldn't you know," he said, squinting and looking up, "the only spot on this side of the island with a break in the trees." The sun beamed down on the boards.

Cleo was still dealing with "swimming hole." "You didn't say anything about swimming," she said with righteous indignation. "I didn't bring my suit."

"Swim in your shorts," or naked, he thought, manhandling the boat so that it wouldn't interfere with diving off the pier.

"These are my best pair of white shorts. The river stains everything yellow."

His answer was a mixture of delight and derision. "I forgot."

"Phooey, you did! You planned this . . ." Planned it all out to get her off guard, after she was feeling so safe. He

Her gaze shifted, taking him all in, dwelling on his lap for a microsecond. Still she wasn't smiling, but sober, her throat feeling suddenly swollen. "I wanted those things done to me, too."

Fletcher had been speechless only once before in his life. When a prosecutor had put a witness on the stand to rebuke his client, the defendant, and the prosecutor's witness then proceeded to confess his guilt to the crime for which Fletcher's client had been charged. The entire court had gone quiet, then bedlam struck. Fletcher couldn't believe his luck then and he was having trouble believing it now. His eyes glazed over a little.

"Are you shocked?"

"No..." He didn't want to say the bastard's name. "That your husband... It's beyond me how he could keep his hands off you."

"It might help if you knew... after we married, he and Gram got along well. It was odd... she was always on his side."

"I'm on your side, darling, our side..." His voice went husky and trailed off.

"So..." Cleo said. She wanted Fletcher badly, but she could see from his expression that he needed a few minutes to absorb what she had said, the meaning of it. Her body screamed for movement, to stretch its limbs. She eyed the cool green canopy above the water. "I think I'll take that swim now."

"You're kidding..."

"No." She stood up, began to disrobe—blouse, shorts, then... both hands going in back of herself to unfasten her brassier.

"You're going to just..." This was too much! She was naked now, her back to him. His eyes followed the line of the curve in the small of her back before flaring

had made a point of saying the bed was where it was going to happen, so she could put off the thrumming in her heart, but now it started up again. "You swim, I'll just sit here on the blanket and watch." In the sun. She could feel sweat beginning to trickle down between her breasts.

Fletcher removed his hat, then his shirt, folding it with great care, forcing Cleo by his deliberate movements to watch him, perhaps to dwell on his body, their physical differences. His sex was coming alive with a spirited heat. Watching Cleo out of the corner of his eye, he took off his shorts. Well, at least now, he had her undivided attention, covert though it was.

She didn't want to look at Fletcher, knew she shouldn't, but couldn't help herself. She was captivated by this new naked view of him, the lean and healthy lines of his body, muscular and tanned. When he kicked off his shorts her lips parted in a telltale gasp.

"Don't get your hopes up," he said matter-of-factly. "The water's cold. The second I hit, my old dingus is gonna die."

Caught, Cleo buried her face in her hands. "Exhibitionist!"

He stepped out of his sandals. The boards were too hot on the soles of his feet to dally. He moved to the edge of the pier and dove with a great splash.

Shame and pleasure warred within Cleo. Her new self argued with the old. Fletcher had a point about Gram. She could see it clearly now. Of course. How foolish she'd been all these years. Gram had pressed her fears upon young Cleo, overwhelming her at an impressionable age.

When she had married Paul she had expected those fears Gram had laid on her to evaporate, but she'd had the unlucky fate to marry a man who felt threatened by a sexually aggressive woman. He had inflated the shame, the guilt she felt. Oh, she could see it all now.

Sweat poured from her in runnels. For a few seconds she watched it bead and run in rivulets down her arms and legs, a cleansing sweat, she thought, ridding her of the worry that she wasn't like other women.

She felt all at once lighter, free from the weight of her fears, renewed with energy. She wanted to tell Fletcher about it, but as he angled over to the pier she was overcome by a sudden shyness, daunted by this deeper knowledge of herself and what it meant. Where it would lead.

He rested his arms on the pier and his chin on his arms, glaring at her in weighted silence. Stubborn wench, he thought, wondering what had made him think the river and the island would make it happen naturally. He hauled himself up and went to sit beside her, knees bent to observe a modicum of modesty—hers.

"How's the water?" She kept her gaze riveted on a swaying piece of moss across the inlet.

"Just right." He watched her dab at sweat on her face, her arms, while keeping her eyes downcast. Eagerness and wanting were coursing through his veins. But he wanted their first time to be special. For her, for himself. Love, he thought. Love and sex. He wanted both. He wanted it all. "It'll be good between us, Cleo."

She looked at his face then, her eyes huge, revealing an inner turmoil. "I think so, too. Oh, Fletcher...I feel like I'm about to burst..." She drew her knees up, grasping them with her arms, the towel dangling from her fingers. Once bitten... She sighed. Fletcher was much more man, much stronger than Paul had been, yet a man was a man. Suppose he, too, wanted to dominate her? Wanted her coy, demure, pretending to be something she wasn't. She didn't think so, but she had to know. She felt an odd strength

suffusing her. The shyness went. "Suppose I want to do something that...you don't. Suppose it's wrong? What would you think?"

"I can't think of anything you'd want that would be wrong for us to do. Give me an example."

The vein in the hollow of her neck began to throb and pulse. "An example?" The silence was so long Fletcher was almost driven to break it. "Suppose I wanted to touch you...down there?"

His heart began to hammer, in tune with the insistent throbbing in his groin. He was prepared for anything, everything, but he knew any sudden move, any pressure on his part might destroy this tentative mood. "I hope you do."

Her eyelids fluttered. "Suppose I wanted to..." she swallowed the last of the sentence.

"I didn't hear you."

"Maybe kiss your nipples."

The hammering began to roar in his ears. R_ passed across his face, more eloquent than langu_

She averted her face. "Those are things I_ do...before. Paul said—"

"I'd like to kill him!" Fletcher groaned, se_ clarity now. Raised in a household where _ til marriage, then Cleo had picked th_ marry, a man who felt threatened _ vances. God, but the newspapers were_ the courts.

"But, what would you think o_

He lowered his legs, exposin_ ted fiercely from the tangle of_ damp from the river. "Wo_ can't wait?"

at the swell of her hips. The view was exquisite and he was in agony. "Cleo! Look at me . . . at this." His hand flailed in the area of his lap.

She turned, just enough to put the length of her profile—rounded breasts, seeming almost too much for her slender torso, upturned thrusting pink nipples, the slight concave of her stomach, and her long, long, legs. Fletcher found himself holding his breath.

"You have an admirable dingus, Fletcher. But I'm all hot and sweaty. I want a swim . . ." she smiled at him, adding in a husky voice, " . . . first."

She moved to the edge of the pier and dove, causing hardly a ripple in the water.

He stared right into the sun, as if to burn out the vision of what he had seen. But it continued to flicker in front of his mind's eye. After a moment, he followed her into the river.

"You're saying yes to everything, aren't you," he said when she came up for air, brushing hair and streaming water from her face.

She laughed, and kicked off to float on her back, shamelessly flaunting her nakedness. "Is that what it sounded like to you?"

Her eyes were bright, her smile inviting. Fletcher slipped his hand under the water, letting it trail over her breasts, her ribs, her abdomen. "That's what it sounded like, looks like. . . . Do you like me doing this?"

"If you keep it up, I'll drown." Her voice was shaking, the teasing in it swallowed up by the erotic sensations pooling in her feminine core.

"I know a practical solution."

"You're thinking about keeping your hands to yourself?"

He pushed her toward the pier. "That's so far from what I'm thinking, it's not even funny."

He pulled himself up on the old boards then gave her a hand up. "This is the practical solution I had in mind," he said as his mouth urgently sought hers, his tongue finding entry and thrusting deep. Hot blood spurted into his manhood. Engorged, it throbbed against Cleo's thighs, seeking entry into her with the same urgency as had his tongue.

His hands explored her—everywhere. Cupping the untanned flesh of her breasts, brushing her softly tumescent nipples, hesitating at the small scar between them, sliding over her hips until he felt a rapid heavy trembling move through her entire body.

"My legs aren't going to hold me up much longer," she said, her voice an echo from some distant place.

He lowered them both to the boards, the harsh feel of them barely registering in Cleo's mind, their heat the heat of her own body so that she could not discern which was which. She knew only that she wanted to do all of the things that had been forbidden to her. She lifted her eyes, meeting his, inquiry written into her heavily lashed look.

"Whatever you want," he said, his voice husky, even while he wondered if he could bear the pleasure of it. He was aroused by her lips moving over his, her tongue searching the interior of his mouth, as her hands went gliding over his shoulders, down his back. His hunger for her now was vast, white-hot, searing.

She turned her face into his chest, feeling it—wiry hair, texture of skin—with her face until her lips discovered his taut brown nipples, astonished at their softness. Tentatively she licked one, then the other. Fletcher moaned as a sensation roared down his spine in steep descent, finding its quarry. He was certain he could not bear the excruciating pleasure of it. Cleo's lips closed over his nipple, her tongue exploring, then she sucked. A primitive sound erupted from his throat.

As if that were a cue, her hands began to drift, taking instinctive measure of his arms, his shoulders, his chest, his abdomen, drifting...until he felt her fingertips, first tracing lightly then encircling his sex. He felt some primeval thing rising in him, trying to gouge out his insides, and he gave a low ragged cry. "Enough!"

Cleo withdrew at once, her expression wary. "You said I could..." A fragmented tone, riddled with hurt, betrayal.

"You can." He tried regulating his gasping breath. "But, darling, a man can only take so much before...I almost..." He grinned shakily and rose up on his elbow. Finding the perch hard on his funnybone, he dragged up a towel and made a pad. "Let's just see how much of it you can take before hollering uncle." He trailed his hand up her thigh until his fingers danced lightly in her silken triangle. The pleasure was piercing, tremendous. Cleo gasped.

"See what I mean?" he said throatily, becoming enthralled with what he was doing, with her response, so that a part of his mind that clung to reality told him he was still lost. He bent his head letting his tongue make moist swirling motions across her nipples, then he gathered one into his mouth.

Cleo wanted to say yes, she could see what he meant, but when she tried to speak her mouth went into a trembling spasm and only whimpers of pleasure emerged. His fingers moved on her, feather-light, so that her hips responded of their own willful accord, arching to meet him in an ancient rhythm.

The sun beat down upon her closed eyelids and behind them came bursts of kaleidoscopic colors that pulsated in

rhythm with her heartbeat. She tried to concentrate on the
colors, to distract her from what Fletcher's tongue was
doing, where his hands were meeting her flesh, but her
brain could not be dragged from recording the erotic torment in the pleasure centers of her body.

The pleasure heightened in a deep richening tempo. She
murmured half sentences, called his name joyously. Her
voice reminded Fletcher of her lips and he went to them,
feeling them swell beneath his own as he caught them in his
teeth. Making a little noise in her throat, Cleo dug her
fingers into his back.

Her legs arched open, an invitation, and he let her lead
him. She smelled sweet, tasted sweet, tasted of herself, of
the river. He mounted her. Engorged, wild with desire, he
thrust into her, gasping at the warmth and moistness, the
smooth silken feel of her flesh that sheathed him.

Then she was moaning, her ankles locked at his waist
and no man could resist that...no man, he told himself as
her hips thrust upward and he drove deeper, letting his
body find its own rocking savage rhythm.

Every muscle in Cleo pulled taut with instinctive
knowledge that the explosion was near, trying to antici-
pate it, contracting and releasing Fletcher's swollen sex. He
begged her in a broken voice not to do that. She pressed
her palms against his chest, feeling the thudding of his
heart. She tried to tell him that she had never come so far,
had never felt such pleasure, that stopping was beyond her,
but her words got lost, garbled. She was so near a pinna-
cle...so near, yet the feeling hid, mysteriously wedged in
her flesh somewhere. She tightened her legs about Fletcher,
cried softly for him to press her harder. He rose higher,
thrust deeper and the wedge, thus pummeled, disinte-
grated.

Her hands roved over the rippling movements of the muscles of his damp, powerful back, the moist tip of her tongue crept into his mouth, demanding and wild with all the pent-up longing. The feeling began . . . a sudden cascading release, washing over her, resonating very strongly along every nerve she possessed, fading slowly in undulating shuddering waves. An erotic ebbing tide. Astonished, she closed her eyes and lay very still.

Fletcher felt her spasmodic quiver, knew it for what it was; delicious heat burst inside him, little fires of mounting ferocity. The thing that was man in him responded, pressing the air out of his lungs, disgorging itself, erupting out his loins, and he knew himself to be a man possessed. He leaned forward and took her lips hungrily until, at last, the eruption subsided.

CHAPTER ELEVEN

IT WAS SILENT on the pier except for their ragged breathing. Cleo thought, *So now I know.* She was Woman to her very core. The self-knowledge was exciting, magical. Lying next to Fletcher, her flesh cooling, she would not have exchanged places with any woman alive.

The sun had gone westward, behind a leafy poplar that now cast a dappled shade over the pier. A blue heron swooped down, alighting on a piling. It balanced on one stalk of a leg and glared at the naked humans. "Voyeur," Cleo called to it softly.

"I don't even have my eyes open," countered Fletcher.

"Not you, the heron. Oh, it's flying away now." She became aware of the hard bite of the boards against her shoulder blades, her buttocks. She sat up, hugging her knees and thinking she'd be showing bruises from fanny to backbone by nightfall. "You didn't pick a very good place for this, Fletcher."

"It's too soon for you to start feeling guilty."

"I don't feel any guilt. I feel..." She looked at him, but turned away, suddenly awkward, unsure about boundaries, the order of things.

He drew a fingertip down her spine, tenderly tracing the imprint of the boards that lingered on her skin. The contrast of his hand, large and tanned against creamy flesh low on her back made him acutely aware of her body; he found it impossible not to touch her. Hourly he was more in love with the sound of her voice, the look of her. She had become the single most important fact of his life. "Tell me how you feel."

"You'll think I'm silly."

"Try me."

"Sort of in awe," she said with a small catch of breath. "I've dreamed of what it might be like, but it's not something you can imagine at all, is it? You have to feel it first..."

It registered on him then, what she was saying. That it had been unmistakably the most complete time for her. He felt an exaltation of spirit, though exaltation did not stop at spirit, but became glandular, hunger building anew.

Cleo's gaze was caught by a hovering dragonfly searching for a place to land. It flew over the juncture of Fletcher's thighs, and lost its audience to the activity going on there.

"Fletcher?" she whispered with a small amazed laugh.

"I can't help it."

She lay down beside him, her head on his shoulder, lips at his throat, tracing with a fingertip a lazy circle from earlobe to his jaw, and back again. "Your knees are red raw."

"I'm not at all concerned with my knees."

"Well, I am." Her hand ventured slowly some distance down his abdomen, and lower. "Poor bony raw knees."

When her hand closed over him he had the feeling he'd just received a small electric shock.

"Does this make them feel better?"

"Makes them feel wonderful." His chest was tight, his breathing constricted, the words lost.

"If you would give up those towels?"

"What did you have in mind?" All this incessant talk . . . while her fingers were on him, feather-light, creating a mammoth fire.

She cleared her throat, still feeling her way. "You might think it's wicked."

He buried his face in her hair. "It so happens I love wicked." She slid a leg over his thighs, brushing his swelling appendage—deliberately—it seemed to Fletcher. Sinuous and sylphlike she mounted him. "Yep," he choked, feeling himself expanding inside her. "I like wicked."

"Don't look at me," she ordered, concerned about the indignity of her position, yet captive to the extraordinary sensations engulfing her.

"Right," he said, squinting at the white clouds sailing calm and stately overhead while she arranged the towels beneath her knees. Satisfied, she arched her back, thrusting her hips forward an inch, then two.

"It might take me a few minutes to get the hang of it. . . . Keep your eyes closed!"

"Take all the time you need." He felt her muscles contract, quick little butterfly touches. Just enough to drive him wild, make his voice crack. "I'm here for the duration."

She leaned forward, plucked open an eyelid. He got an askance view of her neck, damp hair on it in the frailest of curls. "You're making fun of me."

"Wrong."

"I'll just stop."

His hands shot out, locking her hips to his. "No stopping, darling. Not . . . just let me help you get started."

He drew her hips forward, gently, guided them back, and felt the fire spread through him as Cleo fell into the wondrous rhythm.

Through slitted lashes he watched the aroused pink tips of her breasts shiver, conveying a firm and welcoming invitation. Her mouth opened a little. Her face was radiant. In a flash of insight he realized it was more than sex to Cleo. It was a rending of her past, a ritual into full womanhood. Until now, with him, she had existed on the periphery of her sensual self. Now she was whole. Now she was his.

Her pace quickened in erotic abandon. Gasping, he succumbed to her wild rocking motion, glorying in it, senses alive to the sibilant whisperings of flesh on flesh. His. Hers. He stretched out his hands and gathered her to him. After a while he was hardly conscious of hearing anything at all.

"COME INTO THE WATER, Fletcher. It's lovely, especially in the shade."

"You want me to drown. I don't have the energy to wiggle a toe." He munched a sandwich, sipping beer to wash it down. A lizard darted onto the pier, inspected the cooler, a bread crumb, before dashing off.

"I'll have to make at least one trip back to Chicago," Cleo said, attempting to get him on the subject of marriage, the planning of it, wanting to hear him talk about their future. Her own brain was crowded with thoughts—ceremony, dress, house . . . babies. Did he want any? How many? When?

"I don't think so. I've developed a kind of proprietary feeling for you. Don't want you out of my sight."

"But, I have books, clothes—things."

"We'll hire a mover and send the key."

"I have a job."

"Right—me."

"Like you, the work ethic's ingrained in me, too. Besides, I've worked hard to get the credentials I have, such as they are."

"I'll concede work, after we're married and settled. I might even introduce you to my publisher."

"Pompous ass. I can find my own job." She paddled away from the pier, came back. "Probably I ought to read your book, find out what I'm up against."

He sighed. "If there ever was a thing I wish I hadn't done."

"That's not what you said earlier."

"Changed my mind."

Cleo laughed. "Fickle man. Shouldn't we be heading back? Magda's invited us to dinner, remember?"

He moved to the edge of the pier, dangling his feet and lower legs in the river. "That's hours away." His voice had sunk to a low purr, and it affected Cleo so that she swam over and rested her elbows on his knees.

"Had you thought how we might occupy those hours?" she whispered, holding his gaze.

He pulled her from the water. "I thought you might sit in my lap and we could talk nasty." He saw blood come up under the soft skin on her neck and face.

"You have no social panache, Fletcher, or maybe that should be, no sexual panache?"

His breath was warm, his lips and tongue catching droplets of water beading on her throat. "But, you'll concede to...other things?"

"Yes, wonderful...other things." She put her hands on his shoulders and quite naturally positioned herself. "Oh, Fletcher. Anything. Whatever you want. I love you so."

CLEO DIDN'T CARE if the world ended in the next five minutes. She was happier than she'd ever been in her life.

For too many years she had stood apart, fearful, specu-
lating, evaluating, raking over cold ashes. She didn't ar-
gue with herself anymore. Being loved was going to take
some getting used to. She basked joyfully in the thought.

Watching her because he couldn't keep from it, Fletcher
saw her lips, caught suddenly in a half smile. Another part
of him kept the boat in the deeper channel, guided them
safely around floating debris and sandbars. "A mysterious smile," he ventured. "Do I get to know what provoked it?"

It took Cleo a moment to focus on him, on his lean jaw
covered with beard stubble, his eyes alight with curiosity
and more. "No, just drive the boat."

"Keeping secrets from me already? This relationship's
going downhill early."

There would come a time, Cleo thought, when she could
tell him that until he came into her life she had lived in
limbo, barely alive, existing with demons and numbness.
But not today. Today was for unshadowed happiness.
"What's your house like, Fletcher?"

"You're already rearranging furniture!"

"I haven't even seen it. I've never lived in a house. Tell
me."

"It's a little ragged around the edges. Needs a woman's
touch."

"Oh? A woman's touch? You mean Comet cleanser and
elbow grease?"

"Do you know what it means when a defendant pleads
no contest? It means you plead neither innocent or guilty,
but leave it for the court to decide."

"I've decided," said Cleo, laughing. "Elbow grease."

"Bend your elbow right now and guide me up to the
dock," he commanded, cutting the motor.

"Look at your cabin, Fletcher. At all the cars. They're back early. You think something has happened?" Her heart lurched. "Katie...? Or maybe that awful man who's loose?"

"More like Horace got drunk and tipped the canoe." He secured the skiff opposite the dock where the old couple were still at their fishing.

"Have any luck?" the old man called.

"Real good luck," replied Fletcher, casting a salacious grin at Cleo.

"Pervert," she said beneath her breath, gathering up her camera and tote with the wish to be away before the old fisherman asked to inspect the nonexistent catch. "I have to go clean up, get some clothes ready for tonight . . ."

Even the way Fletcher cocked an eyebrow now was seductive. "Any old rag will do for dinner, 'cause afterward—"

"Afterward I'm getting a good night's sleep, which I haven't had since I met you."

"I don't have anything against sleep—properly done," said Fletcher.

Out of the corner of her eye Cleo saw the old man looking expectantly at the cooler. He put aside his fishing pole, lumbered to his feet, heading in their direction. "See you at dinner," she said, and fled.

AN HOUR LATER Cleo stood naked in her cramped camper, applying lotion to her skin. She was sunburned on the most tender places, body parts that had never before been exposed to sun—or other things. She winced at one thought, smiled at the other.

Suddenly the door was yanked open. Cleo whirled around thinking, Fletcher!

"Oops," said Katie, slithering inside and launching herself upon the bunk. Cleo retrieved her freshly ironed skirt and blouse only in time.

"Most people knock before barreling into somebody's house," she lamented, nonplussed as she held the outfit against herself for modesty.

"She's here!" howled Katie, punching up the pillow and shoving her satchel beneath it.

"Who?"

"My cousin, Lindsey. All she does is walk around sucking in and poking out. I can't stand it!"

Cleo attempted a soothing remark as she turned her back and stepped into fresh underwear, wincing as she hooked the brassiere.

"It's even worse than I imagined, Cleo," continued the child, too agitated for soothing. "Now she's got hair under her arms, too. She didn't shave it yet so she could show me. And all mine's falling out! Oh, I'll never have anything other girls do."

"You have beautiful gray eyes, and personality."

"But, I want breasts!" Katie wailed. She yanked up her knit shirt, displaying a pitifully thin torso, ribs countable. "Just look," she cried. "Just look! Both my nipples together wouldn't make a good-sized mole. God doesn't like me. I know it. He's probably never even heard a single prayer I've said. Probably won't even know who I am when I get to heaven."

"You'll be impossible to miss."

Katie sniffed, a sound full of scorn. "It'll be too late then." She dragged out the legal pad and pencil. "Can I stay here for a while? I've got to keep working on this. I need to leave it here, too. Lindsey's such a snoop."

"Runs in the family, eh?"

"You sound like Uncle Fletcher."

"Do I?" said Cleo, warmed by the comparison.

"Wanna hear an idea I got? About the prayer Reverend Dopple can say at my funeral? I got it out of the Bible."

Cleo wanted more than anything not to speak of dying and funerals; she wanted no shadows or sadness on the happiest day of her life. But there was Katie glaring at her, expectant, expression intense. "Okay."

"This is my version. It's from the Psalm of David. The Lord is my shepherd. He doesn't mean a dog."

"Katie!"

"Let me finish! He makes me lie down in green pastures. No cow patties, please. Thy rod and thy staff comfort me. Not if they're used to give a little kid a spanking. Thou preparest a table before me...hot dogs with ketchup, that's what I like best. We're getting them for supper tonight, too. And the part about, in the presence of my enemies—that takes care of Lindsey. Now the end. And I shall dwell in the house of the Lord forever. Breastless!" She looked up at Cleo with her gray, soulful eyes. "What d'you think?"

"That you're the most irreverent eleven-year-old I've ever met." But then she thought, the child wasn't afraid of the devils that plagued her as she herself had been. Katie was making fun of them, taunting them, challenging. Still...goodness! "You know very well no preacher is going to say or read that."

Katie made a face. "I could take out the part about breasts and put in, let not my enemies exult over me. Because that's just what Lindsey's going to be doing while I'm laying up there in my casket flatter than a pancake."

Torn between laughing and crying, Cleo sat on the bunk to buckle her sandals. She could offer only kindness, hope, love, and oh! she was brimming with it today. "Why don't

I add my prayers to yours and we'll see what happens. Now I want to hear all about your canoe trip."

Fretful, Katie sniffed. "You just want to change the subject. We just paddled around on the water is all, saw some alligators. The most exciting thing was when the park rangers came and got us and made us leave because fires were breaking out in the swamp. And driving home we went past a forest fire. It jumped the road right behind the car." Full of woe, Katie sagged visibly. "Now Mom is begging Daddy to take us home. My dress isn't finished, my will isn't finished . . . nothing's going right."

An awful feeling drove through Cleo. "It might not be safe here. Fires aren't anything to fool around with."

"We're perfectly safe. It's miles and miles to the fires. Mom's just looking for an excuse."

There was a soft knock at the door.

"I'll see who it is," volunteered Katie, scooting off the bunk and throwing open the door.

"Oh, great," muttered Cleo, scrambling deeper onto the bed. "All I want is five minutes to myself to finish dressing."

"It's Lindsey. Roger went and finked on me, told her where I am. You want to meet her?"

"Briefly," agreed Cleo, curious about the paragon upon whom nature had so generously bestowed her charms.

Katie drew herself up, as if standing tall might display her annoyance to better advantage. "You can come in," she said to her cousin, quoting with haughty disdain, "briefly. Cleo's got to dress."

The teenager stepped over the threshold, sat where Katie directed, gave a shy tight-lipped smile and kept her eyes averted from Cleo's underwear-clad figure. "Hi," she said.

"Okay," said Katie, formalities done, "you have to leave now."

Cleo sputtered at the quick rudeness.

"I'm going down to the machine for a Coke," said the cousin. "You coming?"

"I'll meet you there in a minute," Katie promised, and once the door was closed soundly on Lindsey, she turned to Cleo. "Did you see how smug? Did you? Flaunting herself. It's disgusting."

"What I saw was a painfully shy, awkward teenager wearing a ponytail, braces on her teeth, wire frames on her glasses and I didn't see anything poking out."

The narrow little back arched, defiant. "Now you're on her side, like Mom and Aunt Mary Ellen. They think I'm all freaked out because I'm sick." She threw up her pipe-stem arms. "Grownups are so blind!"

"You're right, we are blind sometimes," she said very seriously. "And, I am on your side, even if you don't think so."

"Then did you see the way Lindsey let her top slide off her shoulder to show off her bra strap?"

Defeated, Cleo shook her head. "Next time I'll be more observant. Now scoot."

Katie put her hand on the doorknob; she was looking at Cleo intently. "You're sunburned all over. I guess you went skinny-dipping with Uncle Fletcher."

"I guess that's none of your business," said Cleo in a voice that was not steady. The little twit!

"He's not married you know, but Mom says he deserves to be."

Cleo met that with silence.

"He's sunburned all over, too. He came out of the shower looking like a cooked lobster."

"I wouldn't know about that."

"Well, you do now because I just told you," said Katie, departing on a sly giggle.

Cleo put the latch on the door. Deserves to be married, Marilyn had said of Fletcher, meaning it in friendly rancor no doubt. Cleo laughed. She was moving toward something so settled, so dignified, so happy.

The years ahead of her seemed to have found their pattern at last. But that was future and right now minutes were ticking away—she felt an enchanting urgent need to be near Fletcher. She peered into the cracked mirror to arrange her hair, applying light touches of cosmetics, necessary to hide the sprinkling of freckles across her nose and cheeks, ending with a dab of perfume behind her ears.

All in gauzy pink, skirt swaying at her calves, she stepped from the camper into the twilight and came face to face with an elderly stranger. "Oh!"

"I was just getting ready to knock," the man said apologetically. "I didn't mean to startle you. I'm in number twelve and I can't find the water connection...."

Cleo glanced over through the thick brush. A small motor home was in the clearing.

"We just checked in. The state park didn't honor our reservations, something about a fire...."

"There's a double faucet in the brush, between our campsites, but you'll have to get the hose from Big Momma...from the office."

"Drinkable?"

There was admiration for her in **the man**'s eyes. Flushed, eager to find that admiration **from another,** Cleo took a step toward the path, toward Fletcher. "Yes, it's good water."

"The fishing any good?"

"I've heard it has been. Farther down the river though."

A woman called to him, her tone one of irritability. He excused himself with a mirthless laugh. "It's one of those weekends where nothing goes right. Well, I won't keep you. And, thanks."

The fishing camp hummed with a kind of controlled chaos. Every site and cabin had an occupant, and even the long grassy slope that Fletcher had mowed near the shower and laundry room was pitched with tents. Refugees from the fires in the state park? Cleo wondered as she arrived at Magda's cabin.

"The men aren't here just now," said her hostess. "Big Momma cornered them to fix the well pump, something to do with the float. Have you met Marilyn's sister, Mary Ellen?" she asked, making the introduction as she ushered Cleo onto the porch. The expression on the older sister's attractive face was strained. Marilyn looked as if she'd been crying.

"Is something wrong?" Cleo asked after Magda had pressed a paper cup of champagne into her hand.

"Just my whole life," said Marilyn. "Watching you and Fletcher..." She smiled wanly. "Ward and I have been living with Katie's illness for two years now. The laughter is gone and I can't remember the last time we made love. I'm not talking about sex, the pure bodily function. I'm talking about . . . love. We're at each other's throats all the time. How I wish I could recapture that feeling. I guess I'm envious of what you and Fletcher have.

"I mean you get married, live on sardines, have babies, save up to buy a house, live the perfect American dream, then—wham! And, there's no protection. None. You think, no matter what...no matter..." She crouched back in her chair, seeming to diminish before their eyes.

"Throw in with us, Cleo," said Magda. "We've been trying to convince Marilyn to take a break from the kids.

We think she and Ward ought to go off by themselves for a few days."

"It might renew your strength," offered Cleo, seeing that Marilyn wanted to go, but that she needed to feel good about it. "I don't know how much you've talked about it, but a few days might make a difference for Katie too. She . . . probably I'm breaking a confidence, but she's under a strain, too. She worries about you worrying about her."

"Did she tell you that?"

"Not in those exact words, but it's what she meant."

"See?" advanced Mary Ellen. "I'd be happy to take Katie back to Atlanta with me and Lindsey."

"Horace and I would be delighted to have Roger."

"Katie wants to be here. She's adamant, and Ward won't consider going against her wishes...like it's her last wish." Her eyes teared up again. "Oh! I hate this! I hate it! And I feel so selfish to even be thinking of myself."

"Sometimes selfish is where it's at," said Magda. "You're not doing Katie any good moping around red-eyed and arguing with Ward."

"I could help you out with Katie," volunteered Cleo. "If you showed me what to do, her medicine . . . I did volunteer work at a hospital back home so I'm not entirely unfamiliar with . . . terminal illnesses."

"What plans do you and Fletcher have?"

Cleo smoothed her skirt. "We haven't made any definite plans."

"Oh, Fletcher's got plans," laughed Magda. "Believe me! He just hasn't told you."

"We can include Katie, whatever they are."

An impish gleam ignited Magda's eyes. "So, ladies, now we see what's attracted our infamous bachelor. Backbone and independent thinking!" She paused, smiling like an apologetic child. "Of course feminine charms might have had a tad to do with it. And, we haven't any of us offered congratulations."

"You do look radiant," Marilyn said.

"Is she blushing or is that sunburn?" came from Mary Ellen.

Cleo gave a bewildered little laugh. "Thank you. But everything is really still up in the air."

"We don't mind," said Magda. "Now tell us about yourself. Start with your flaws, torrid love affairs, your greatest sins. Regular stuff."

"You'll know my flaws soon enough," Cleo murmured with a silvery laugh, relishing the moment of welcome, of being accepted, feeling she no longer stood apart.

A bevy of children skirmished past the cabin down to the river and back, throwing balls, yelling. Roger was among them, but not Katie or Lindsey.

"I'd better check on the girls," said Mary Ellen. She rolled her eyes heavenward. "Lindsey's discovered two hairs under her arms. They're shaving. Probably they've sliced all sorts of veins by now."

Magda refilled glasses. "And, I'd better set the corn to boiling. Compliments of Big Momma, by the way."

"I'll help," offered Cleo.

"No, no. You visit with Marilyn until the men get back."

"I wish I was better company for you, Cleo. This is such a terrible time in our lives. Everything is on hold—waiting. I'm..."

"Please, you don't have to explain. I understand. And, do consider allowing me to have Katie for a few days. In these few short weeks she's wormed her way into my heart. I think she likes me, too."

"You're all she talks about," confessed Marilyn. "Ward might agree. I suppose you're almost one of the family now—so to speak."

"I like that, being family. And we are going to be good friends in the coming years, aren't we?" It came to Cleo that those future years would be lived without Katie. The tears sat heavily in her throat, for then she understood more deeply how Marilyn was suffering.

The men came in and presently they were all talking of the overflowing park, the forest fires that had large and small animals on the run so that state park officials had ordered backpackers and those camping in tents to move out of the refuge lest there be confrontations between the bears and humans.

"Are we safe here?" Cleo asked of anyone, though she had eyes only for Fletcher. He looked quite handsome in polo shirt and Gurkha shorts that showed to advantage his long muscular legs.

"The fires are twenty-five miles to the east and south of us," said Ward.

"Fletcher and I saw that bear and her cubs again today."

"This is probably her regular territory, though."

"I could use some help dishing up," called Magda.

"I'll go," said Cleo.

"She means me," put in Horace. "I can tell by that tone of voice."

Ward went to find Roger, Marilyn to get her sister and the girls.

"Alone at last," sighed Fletcher, drawing Cleo out of the porch light into a shadowy corner of the cabin. He buried his face in her cap of red curls. "You smell nice. It does things to me."

Her face against his strong chest, she wanted to tell him not to squeeze so tight, that her flesh was tender, but the whole length of him was pressing her; she knew what she was doing to him, for she could feel the life in his thighs. It was a potent knowing. Her lips found their way to the tightening cords of his neck. She kissed him there and nibbled on his ear. A soft gutteral sound erupted from his throat.

"You know what I was thinking," he said, clearing his throat, "when we were working on the pump? That I'm going to be a husband. I'll be husbanding. What I know about being a husband wouldn't fit on a pin head."

Her eyes that had been closed opened, suddenly glowing as she looked up to smile at him. "You want to change your mind?"

"No! I'm possessed with you."

"What is it, then, that's made you—"

"I'm remembering how my friends and colleagues dumped on me about their problems, situations on the home front. Surely they had to feel what we're feeling, once, anyway. How does it get lost?" He tightened his arms. "I don't want us to lose what we have. It feels so good."

"Maybe they did it to hide the depth of their feelings. Men are notorious for masking emotions with male virtue and masculine brawn, or so I've heard."

"You've heard that?"

There was a dramatic surge of energy at the juncture of his thighs. Cleo laughed, voice thickening. "I've heard that, yes. Although I get the idea that you might not be so good at masking..." She put her hands on his, separating their bodies. "But you'd better learn in a hurry because here comes—"

"What're you two doing in that dark corner?" asked Horace, emerging from the kitchen carrying a food-laden tray.

"Talking," replied Fletcher, all innocence.

Stepping out of the shadows, Cleo's smile was serene. "I'll just go help Magda," she said.

"Ah! The glow of love," said the other woman when Cleo joined her.

"Does it show so much?"

"A woman notices these things. For instance..." she continued, her tone lilting, "there's a difference in you between last night and this. So! Today you made love the first time. I can tell."

Cleo riveted her attention upon forks, spoons, counting them out. "How many of us? I can't think."

"Ten. And after we eat, I'll read the cards for you."

"Oh, but I don't—"

"You'll want to know how many children—"

Cleo froze.

"I'm only teasing," said Magda, laughing. "Grab that ketchup for the hot dogs. I hear the kids."

Much later, after the steaks, hot dogs and corn had been washed down with wine, beer and soft drinks, and adult conversation had become desultory, Katie, acting important, sidled up to Cleo. "Mom says I can stay with you."

"It's been decided, then?" Cleo asked, taking the child onto her lap.

"What's been decided?" Fletcher yawned and rearranged himself in the lawn chair.

"Ward and I are going off by ourselves for a few days," said Marilyn. "We need some time...Magda's taking Roger back with them in the morning. Cleo's going to watch Katie here."

Fletcher looked dumbfounded at Cleo. "You decided that without discussing it with me?"

"Yes . . . I—"

"Fight! Fight!" hummed Horace. Magda threw her husband a look.

"Shut up, you."

"Look, if it's going to cause trouble, we can call it off," said Marilyn, disappointment threading each of her words.

Katie was following every single word that was said, looking from Fletcher's face to Cleo's to her mother's. Now she'd caused yet another argument. She hated herself. She ought to just run away, that's what she ought to do. "I can stay by myself or with Big Momma."

"You'll stay with me. I want you to." Cleo refused to look at Fletcher.

"Looks like you're outmaneuvered, counselor," Horace egged. "Hey, now, don't give me that dark look. I'm bigger than you are."

"Cleo," Magda said quickly. "Take Fletcher for a walk. Katie, you and Lindsey get busy on the dishes."

"Huh?"

"You heard me."

"But, I'm sick," wailed Katie.

"My nails!" cried the teenager.

"I'm deaf to excuses," said Magda, pulling one child out of Cleo's lap and pushing the other along in front of her.

"A walk sounds good to me," Cleo advanced, brushing wrinkles out of her skirt while surreptitiously watching to see if Fletcher was making motions to follow. He wasn't. Her heart sank, but, committed, she went.

Once down by the dock, she lingered, watching the moon ply its yellow path on the smooth water. Still

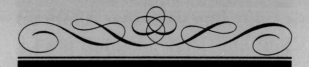

YOUR PASSPORT TO ROMANCE

HERE'S YOUR TICKET TO ROMANCE AND A GEM OF AN OFFER!

1. Four FREE Harlequin Romances

Book a free getaway to love with your Harlequin VISA. You'll receive four exciting new romances hot off the presses. All yours, compliments of Harlequin Reader Service. You'll get all the passion, the tender moments and the intrigue of love in far-away places...FREE!

2. A Beautiful Harlequin Tote Bag...Free!

Carry away your favorite romances in your elegant canvas Tote Bag. At a spacious 13 square inches, there'll be lots of room for shopping, sewing and exercise gear, too! With a snap-top and double handles, your Tote Bag is valued at $6.99 – but it's yours free with this offer!

3. Free Magazine Subscription

You'll receive our members-only magazine, Harlequin Romance Digest, three times per year. In addition, you'll be up on all the news about your favourite writers, upcoming books and much more with Harlequin's Free monthly newsletter.

4. Free Delivery and 25¢ Off Store Prices

Join Harlequin Reader Service today and discover the convenience of Free home delivery. You'll preview four exciting new books each month – and pay only $2.50 per book. That's 25¢ less than the store price. It all adds up to one gem of an offer!

YOU'LL GET A FREE MYSTERY GIFT, TOO!

USE YOUR HARLEQUIN VISA TO VALIDATE YOUR PASSPORT TO ROMANCE – APPLY YOUR VISA TO THE POST-PAID CARD ATTACHED AND MAIL IT TODAY!

"NO RISK" GUARANTEE

- There's no obligation to buy—and the free books and gifts remain yours to keep.
- You pay the lowest price possible and receive books before they appear in stores.
- You may end your subscription anytime—just write and let us know.
- If card below is missing, write Harlequin Reader Service, 901 Fuhrmann Blvd., P.O. Box 1394, Buffalo, N.Y. 14240-9963.

Place Your
VISA Here
to Validate
Passport Offer

- **4 Free Books**
- **A Free Tote Bag**
- **Free Home Delivery**
- **Free Mystery Gift**

YES! Please send my four new Harlequin Superromance Books Free, along with my free tote bag and my mystery gift. Then send me four new Harlequin Superromance Books every month as they come off the presses, and bill me just $2.50 per book (25¢ less than retail), with no extra charges for shipping and handling. If I am not completely satisfied, I may return a shipment and cancel at any time. But my free gifts remain mine to keep!   134 CIS KAZB

Name _____

Address _____

City_____ Province/State _____

Postal Code/Zip _____

NB: Offer limited to one per household and not valid for present subscribers. Prices subject to change.

PRINTED IN U.S.A.

RETURN THIS CARD TODAY WITH YOUR HARLEQUIN VISA FOR FREE BOOKS, FREE GIFTS AND FREE HOME DELIVERY!

How could she have been so naive to have believed Fletcher loved her? He had what he wanted of her and left. He was probably gloating over it this very minute.

"I've cleaned out the fridge," said Marilyn. "All the food's in that box, and there's still a case of soft drinks. Ward, you'll take that over to Cleo's camper?"

"I'm ready to go," announced Katie.

Cleo could see the parents were as anxious to be off as their daughter. "Is there anything I can help you do?" she offered, thinking that perhaps Fletcher had left a business card lying about, or company stationery. Not that she would call or write him. She had too much pride for that.

"Not a thing," replied Marilyn, giving Katie a hug, admonishing her to be good, take her medicines, stay out of trouble.

"I'm the sweetest little girl alive, Mom."

"Convince me," said her mother.

There was nothing for it, except to mouth platitudes, say goodbye, don't worry, take hold of Katie's small case and march out the door and down the path with Katie skipping lopsidedly alongside her.

"We're going to have all kinds of adventures," said the child excitedly.

"Were you up when Fletcher left?"

"He packed and left last night so Aunt Mary Ellen and Lindsey could have his bed. Everybody else left this morning."

Last night! Defeat crept into Cleo's bloodstream. She ached, she hurt and she had to hide it. One great and glorious day in life. Was that all anyone was allowed?

There were morning sounds in the park. Birds chirped, squirrels scampered, the river flowed, moss swayed, a great blue heron fished in the shallows. Maybe it was the same bird that had watched them making love. Fletcher, she

Fletcher did not come. She felt a blackness swirling about her feet, threatening to rise up, engulf her.

She'd done it again. The fights with Paul had always begun over some small matter, growing until the subject of the argument no longer mattered; only winning did. She'd never won. She'd emasculated him. That's what she'd done, and now with Fletcher... But he was wrong, too... he'd been too quick with his accusatory tone.

The boats and smaller skiffs bobbed, pulling at their ties, the ropes gone taut. She felt like those ropes, ready to snap, exhausted, unhappy. Then she remembered today! Today had been so grand, like a fairy tale.

But fairy tales weren't real. Oh, she wondered, heartbrokenly, how could she have made such an epic mistake, believing that falling in love was an end-all?

Later inside the camper, in the dark, she undressed slowly. Voices drifted. Her neighbors in number twelve were arguing. A boat motor coughed, probably someone going downriver to fish the night away. She waited for Fletcher to come to her, prepared to reason with him, to make things right between them.

Finally sleeping, she dreamed the old faceless dream, she thought she was back in the cramped apartment with Ellie and Gram. The demons were loose again.

CHAPTER TWELVE

THE SHOWER BUILDING WAS CROWDED and for the first time since she'd arrived, Cleo had to wait her turn. Of all mornings to have to make small talk with fellow campers—when she had to find Fletcher, talk to him, make everything right between them, somehow. Even humble herself, if that's what it took.

She paid attention as best she could to the task of showering, shampooing; but thoughts of Fletcher so sensitized her body, that her legs were weak.

Apprehensive, yet determined, she presented herself at his cabin, hesitating only a moment before she knocked.

"Cleo!" Marilyn ushered her into the cabin. She was smiling, her face flushed. "I was just about to send Katie to see if you were up. Ward was able to get us reservations at the Moonspinner in Panama City Beach. I can't wait! Oh, those lovely beaches, late-night dinners." She tore off a page from a note pad. "Now here's the number of where we'll be. The number of Katie's doctor, Ward's office and Mary Ellen's phone number, too...just in case. And on the back I've listed all of Katie's medicines and the times she needs to take them. I'll call every night at six. That won't be inconvenient will it? For you to be down at the office?"

"And, I'm all packed," said Katie.

"Packed?" Cleo looked at Marilyn. "Aren't I going to watch...I thought we'd stay here...."

"Ward gave up the cabin. What with Fletcher gone back to Atlanta for the week and—"

"Gone?" Cleo's voice shrunk, vanishing. Her blood seemed to have ceased circulating and her heart hurt with every beat. "Did he say when he'd be back?"

"Well, not to us." Marilyn gave her an odd look. "But he must've told you."

"He probably did," she replied airily, covering dismay. Now there was a liquid sensation in her stomach, almost a tingling. "I just wasn't listening."

"We just assumed that Katie would stay with you. What with the fires and all, Big Momma has a waiting list. Is the camper too small?"

"No, no. The table folds down into another full-sized bed. It's fine, Marilyn, really." Oh, everything was awful!

Ward came out of the bedroom, carrying suitcases. "You're sure you want to do this, Cleo? I feel like we're taking advantage. It's not too late—"

"Oh, yes it is," put in his wife.

"Right!" said Katie.

Cleo forced a smile. "Katie and I will be just fine." She glanced at the note. Nothing on it about Fletcher. She didn't have his phone number, his address; she didn't dare ask and make herself out a fool.

She knew every inch of his body, but not where he lived. She knew the sound of his voice, but not where he worked. She knew his every look, every nuance, every line on his face. She didn't know which side of the bed he preferred or if he slept in pajamas or how he liked his eggs in the morning.

When you loved somebody, when he loved you back, if he loved you back, you knew these things.

cried silently. She saw him with his mouth on her breasts, saw his fine hands moving up her thighs, saw him eagerly putting himself inside her, his dark, dark eyes heavy-lidded with love. Or had that been only lust? He *had* liked her. She knew it.

"Are you coming down with a cold or something?" asked Katie.

"No, why?"

"You were sniffing."

Cleo pulled herself together. "A touch of hay fever, I think. It's too dry. Come on, let's get your bed made up. We'll have to do some rearranging with the typewriter and my work."

"Yes, and now I can learn to type and if we go off anywhere in your car, I can learn to drive and I don't have to take naps."

Cleo went outside herself and laughed. "Try one out of three."

Katie took keen interest where things went in the camper, the manner in which Cleo did things—from brushing her hair, to glancing into the cracked mirror—so keen, that at times, Cleo felt herself under a microscope.

She wasn't in the mood for writing, or taking pictures, or working at all, but she forced herself to stay busy. Work, added to caring for Katie, who was company, kept her mind occupied and off the larger problem of Fletcher. Sometimes for as long as an hour at a stretch.

THE FIRST DAY of caring for Katie went by swiftly. The child had a thousand questions, which Cleo answered, and the newness of sleeping in the camper enthralled her—like playing house. The second day went much like the first; the third was disaster.

Early in the morning after they'd had breakfast and were at the picnic table, working, Katie folded her arms over the typewriter and rested her pointed little chin on them, eyeing Cleo. "Typing's not all it's hacked up to be. When you do it, it looks like fun."

Cleo set aside the letters she'd been going through looking for article ideas. "You're just too antsy to sit still. Do you feel okay?"

"I feel like a walk. Maybe I can meet some of the new kids."

"Okay, but stay in the camp, and check in with me within the hour."

Twenty minutes later an irate mother with two youngsters in tow stalked into Cleo's campsite. Katie trailed behind. "Your daughter has scared the daylights out of my kids," she yelled.

"But—"

"We paid good money for this vacation and now its ruined!"

"I didn't do anything!" protested Katie.

"You did! You told them the swimming hole under the diving tree was an alligator cave and that the river is full of giant turtles."

"But it is!"

"You see?" said the woman. "You see? Now my babies won't go near the water."

"I'm . . . I'm sorry," said Cleo. "The river is perfectly safe along here. The alligators mostly keep to the refuge. There's a dam—"

"Just keep your kid away from mine."

"I was just telling them what Big Momma told me," said Katie and slunk off before Cleo could stop her.

While Cleo was preparing sandwiches for lunch the man in number twelve banged on the camper door. He had in his grasp a squirming, twisting Katie.

"Is this your kid, lady?"

"I—yes."

"Well, you keep her away from me, you hear? I found her lying on her belly in them weeds, spying on me and my wife. Sneakin' little pest."

"It won't happen again," Cleo promised, taking Katie's hand and pulling her into the camper.

"I wasn't spying," said Katie a moment later, talking around a mouthful of bread and ham. "I was just looking. I don't like him anyway. He's mean to his wife. I was just watching him holler at her."

"People don't like to be eavesdropped on when they're having a quarrel."

At quarter to six they went down to the office to await Marilyn's call. Katie picked a fight with Big Momma.

"I don't see why you can't be sewing on my dress while you're just sitting in that rocker."

"I'm fair too tired to thread a needle, that's why."

"I'll just go to heaven naked then, and tell God it's your fault."

"Hah! You'll be tellin' it ter the devil if'n you don't watch that mouth of your'n."

"I'll bet Francine ran away because you said mean things to her."

Big Momma jerked herself out of the rocker and stormed into the house, letting the door slam behind her.

Katie plopped down on the step beside Cleo. "My legs hurt."

"I'll make you an ice pack before we go to bed."

"I guess you're going to tell Mom to come get me?"

"Do you want me to?"

"Sometimes I don't feel like being the sweetest little girl alive." Her voice quavered. "Sometimes I feel like just giving up."

Cleo put her arm around the child and pulled her close. "Maybe tomorrow will be a better day." One could always hope, she thought.

Katie snuggled deeper into the circle of Cleo's arm. "You smell good, Cleo. I guess that's why Uncle Fletcher likes you."

Cleo felt a sudden ache of loneliness. When Marilyn and Ward collected Katie she'd head on back to Chicago. After she gave up Katie, there'd be no one for her to care about, no one to care for her.

When the telephone shrilled she untangled herself and answered it on the second ring.

"Cleo?" The voice lilted with surprise. "Is that you?"

Her own voice lowered to a strangled whisper. "Fletcher?" There was a long silence. Cleo understood. He hadn't meant to speak to her. "You want Big Momma? I'll—"

"No! You. Wait! Cleo. I was afraid I'd call and find you gone. I realized I didn't know your address, or where you work or..."

The world was tumbling in on her. A happy world. "How do you like your eggs, Fletcher?"

"I beg your pardon?"

"Eggs!" Her heart was dancing. "Eggs. How do you like them for breakfast?"

"Fried, scrambled, any old way. But what do eggs have to do with anything?"

"Everything. Just everything," she cried as a swell of anger bubbled up and overlapped relief. "Why did you leave like that? Without saying a word?"

"I can explain."

"Well?"

"I meant later."

"Now!"

She heard his intake of breath. "You didn't discuss keeping Katie with me. It was so like the way my mother used to do with my dad... She'd buy things, big purchases, like a sofa or a dining room suite without talking it over with my dad first. He was always playing catch up."

"I'm not your mother."

"No."

"But, maybe it was wrong of me not to think of you, include you."

"And, I acted like an ass."

She sniffed. "Yes, you did." She searched her pocket for a Kleenex, blew her nose. "Are you... when are you coming back?"

"I got involved in a case. It'll take a day or two to hand it over to one of my associates."

A day. A lifetime. "That client of yours who escaped the police?" She couldn't bear it now if anything happened to him.

"No, no. He's gone to ground. Are you managing all right with Katie?"

"Yes, fine. She's a joy."

"I'm forgiven?" He could see her standing at the phone—tall, lovely, curls in wild disarray with that odd look of frailty on her face. He found himself very aroused, stunned that just the sound of her voice could do that.

"Yes..."

"I wish you were with me right now. Just hearing your voice does things to me."

Cleo met that with a thudding heart and silence because Katie had slipped up and was standing next to her, leaning against the wall.

"Fletcher, Marilyn calls every day at six. She might be trying to get through."

"All right," he said, hating to relinquish the connection. He was tempted to say something more, but he found his grip on the receiver was so tight his knuckles had gone white. "Think of me?"

"I can't keep from it."

The phone was no sooner in its bracket than it rang again. Cleo snatched it up.

"Cleo! You were right there. Is something wrong?"

"Marilyn. No. Everything's fine."

"And Katie?"

"She's wonderful."

"Katie? Wonderful?" Marilyn laughed. "Let me speak to the imp." Cleo handed over the phone.

"I'm being real good, Mom." After she hung up she looked at Cleo with hurtful eyes. "We both told lies."

"Let's just figure out a way to make them the truth."

"Maybe I ought to apologize to Big Momma."

They went through the office and down the hall, emerging into the kitchen where Big Momma was frying batter-dipped chicken.

"That smells good," said Katie.

"Beggar," groused Big Momma. She put a lid on the pan then sat at the table and began to peel potatoes.

Katie shifted her glance from the old woman to Cleo. "I wasn't hinting at supper," she said archly. "I was apologizing."

"Do tell. You be worse'n Francine tryin' to get around me."

"Try again," urged Cleo, seeing that the old woman was softening.

Katie edged over to the table and draped an arm around the old woman's shoulder. "I'm gonna do you the biggest favor ever, Big Momma," she said generously. "I'm gonna save you a place in heaven."

"On the off chance you get there?" She waved a potato at Cleo. "Turn that chicken for me. I'm give out."

"I can set the table," offered Katie.

The old woman sighed. "If we get lucky, a hant'll take her off'n our hands."

Cleo laughed. "I take it we're invited to supper after all?"

"I reckon, if'n you like chicken and doin' dishes," came the pointed reply.

"While Cleo's doing dishes, I can thread the needle," piped Katie.

"Law! I gives up."

Attentive to the frying chicken, Cleo took an apron off a nail and put it on. She was rife with a mixture of happiness and loneliness. Imagine Fletcher accusing her of being like his mother! An on-going obstacle to a successful marriage? she wondered, disturbed each time it came to the front of her mind.

Later that night she sat on the stoop of her camper, door latched open, listening to Katie turn in sleep. She suffered a pinprick of worry for the child, pausing in her thoughts to glance back over her shoulder. The pillows that she had put under Katie's legs to elevate them were still in place.

Closing her eyes, she turned her thoughts back to Fletcher. She'd better read his book, she mused. It might give her some insight into the man he was.

Angry voices drifted on the summer breeze. Cleo opened her eyes. The voices became more strident. Not demons, just her neighbors in number twelve.

Katie was right. The man was mean. Cleo could hear him berating his wife. She went inside and very quietly rummaged among her things to find *101 Ways*.

"CLEO?"

She woke up slowly, unwilling to give up the dream, liking the smell of it, the taste, the way it made her feel. She pushed the distant voice away, then brought it back to inspect more closely.

Katie!

She reached up and turned on the bedlamp. "What's wrong?"

Katie was hunched up in the corner of her bed. "I don't feel so good." Her voice was wispy with dread.

She went over to the child, touching her, stroking her, finding her skin hot and taut. "Are you feeling worse than you ever have before?"

"It's hard to tell. I try not to remember."

Cleo slid off the bed. "There's something for pain among your medicines."

"I don't want to take it. I can't! I might not wake up."

Oh, God! "Yes, you will."

"I might not. I feel all empty inside—airy."

Hands trembling, Cleo kept taking bottles from the shoe box in which the medicines were stored, looking at them, reading labels, instructions, unable to focus clearly because fear sat squarely in the center of her chest. "Here. Here's one for pain." She drew a glass of water, watching over Katie as she swallowed.

"I dreamed I was in my casket with the lid down and I couldn't breathe."

The camper was so small, cramped, crowded with two. Like a coffin. Closed. Cleo opened the door, allowing in the soft night wind with a swoosh. "We'll sleep with the door open. I think it's safe enough."

"Maybe I could get in bed with you for a few minutes."

"Of course." She moved the child, the pillows.

"I like to be on the outside."

They exchanged places. Cleo lay only half-reclined, head and shoulders propped against the camper wall. Katie squirmed and snuggled until her head was on Cleo's chest, an arm snaking up to curl around her neck. "I can hear your heart beating."

No wonder, thought Cleo; it was hammering on her ribs. "Go to sleep now."

"When I was in the hospital, Susie Stahl died in her sleep. If I stop breathing, you wake me up."

Cleo was torn apart by the monstrous incongruity, and forced to contemplate its meaning. She stared out the open door. The moon was high, stalking a path across the placid river, the angle of it enabling a golden finger to creep beneath the awning right up to the stoop. Not tonight, God. Not now. Not like this.

"I DON'T WANT oatmeal for breakfast. I hate oatmeal!"

"Put that thermometer back under your tongue."

"It is under my tongue, I'm talking around it. I'm expert."

"You're ornery, is what you are," said Cleo. "What about bacon and eggs?"

"No."

"Cereal?"

Katie shook her head. Cleo sighed and held hard onto her patience. Though, after the scare last night, she was only too thankful to have the opportunity to expend it. Katie's skin looked splotchy beneath her tan, her face pinched, thinner than ever.

She retrieved the thermometer, studied it and shook it down. "One degree above normal. We'd better keep an eye on you today."

"I might eat some grits," said Katie.

Grits. Cleo didn't know anything about grits, exclusively a Southern food. She found the half box that Marilyn had sent over, followed the directions and served up a lumpy congealed mess.

"You're supposed to stir it."

"I did."

"Well, it's gross. You better learn to cook before you have any kids or they'll starve to death."

Cleo slapped together a peanut butter and jelly sandwich. "Eat or starve," she said.

"Peanut butter constipates me."

Cleo snatched the sandwich and tossed it out the door. A pair of squirrels came at once to investigate the sudden manna. "Okay. Starvation it is."

Katie rearranged the bed clothes about her legs, folding them back neatly at her waist. "This is great. We're fighting just like I was normal again. I'll take some grape juice, please."

Cleo melted, but it still didn't solve the problem of getting proper nourishment into Katie. She opened the can of juice.

"I want a straw."

"Sorry, but I'm fresh out of straws." Cleo was convinced she was going to hate the rest of the day, and the whole of it remained before her. She understood where Katie was coming from with her scathing pronouncements. But arguing with a sick child made her nerves raw, made her feel guilty. She wanted to stay out from under guilt. She had lived with its debilitating force for too many years.

"After we get dressed I think we'll go into Fargo for lunch. At the café. I have to mail my articles. We can stop at the grocery."

"I'm too bald to go anywhere in public," said Katie.

Just grind your teeth, Cleo told herself, feeling resolve and patience and good intentions frittering away. "You can wear a scarf, like a babushka. I'll loan you one. Besides, Fargo is hardly public." The hamlet had a gas station, a cafe, a small motel, a grocery store boasting more bare shelves than full, a church and the post office.

"I couldn't possibly go anywhere looking like this. Can I borrow some of your makeup? Mom always lets me use hers."

"Next, I'll be hearing you smoke Horace's cigars," said Cleo, knowing she was being fibbed to and manipulated.

At lunch Katie ordered a hamburger. "Lots of mustard," she told the waitress. "Hey! There's Wesley," she said as the young man entered the café. She waved both arms wildly over her head.

So much for keeping a low profile in public, thought Cleo as Wesley pulled up a chair and sat down. His eyebrows were singed, his face blistered and beginning to peel. "Hi, Katie. You're Cleo, right? Fletcher's girl?"

"They're gonna get married," said Katie. She looked like a pint-sized Gypsy. The red and white kerchief tied about her head framed cheeks packed with blush, lashes so thickly mascaraed they drooped, and left splatters on upper and lower lids painted with blue shadow. The lip gloss had been licked off except where she had gone outside the lipline. It clung to the outer edges of her mouth, a sentinel to her unsteady hand.

Cleo let Katie's comment slide. "When did you get back from Florida?"

"Just now. I was going to get some lunch before I stopped at Big Momma's, see if she needs me. I passed a couple of burned out stands of timber coming in. Looks like ya'll have had some excitement here, too."

Around mouthfuls of food, Katie filled him in about the
fires in the refuge, the overflowing camp, the terrible man
in number twelve, the new kids. "Wimps and scaredy
cats," she announced scornfully. Batting her lashes, behaving the coquette, she added, "Wesley was gonna wait
for me to grow up so we could get married."

The boy sputtered.

"But he's off the hook now."

"She's making that up," he said to Cleo. "It's too bad,
too. I was going to ask her if she wanted to ride back to
camp with me in the truck."

"You were?" Katie said weakly, all sweetness and sy-
rupy. "You were gonna let me sit in your lap and steer?"

"I don't think—" Cleo began, seeing that Wesley had
every intention of doing just that.

"Oh, please, Cleo," begged Katie as if the invitation was
a given.

Cleo could see the truck wrecked, bodies lying all over
the road, everyone blaming her for letting Katie out of her
sight. "We were going shopping, remember?"

"It'll be all right," coaxed Wesley. "I used to babysit
Katie and Roger while Ward and Marilyn went night fishing."

"You never!"

"That's two lies in the space of five minutes, young lady.
You're on the road to perdition, certain."

"Is perdition good or bad?"

"Go wash that gunk off your face, first. I don't want to
ruin my reputation by being seen with a tarted-up
woman."

"I'm not a tart. I'm beautiful."

"Every time you flutter your lashes, they stick together. How're you gonna see to steer?"

Katie made a dash for the washroom. Reluctantly Cleo surrendered her into Wesley's care, regretting the decision the moment the truck was out of sight. She went across the street to the grocer's pushing down a frantic feeling in her chest.

She made her purchases haphazardly and broke speed limits driving the seventeen miles back to the fishing camp. Katie was sitting on the office porch safe and in one piece. The feeling in Cleo's chest eased. When she braked to a halt, the child limped to the car and got in. "Hurry—"

Big Momma came running around the office, out of breath and swatting at a chicken with a broom. "You keep that chit chained up the rest of this day, Cleo, you hear me? I fair got enough trouble 'thouten—" and she was gone around the other side.

"What'd you do this time?"

"Nothing. Just went to see if the chickens had laid any eggs."

"And?"

"The gate didn't close when I came out."

"Nap time for you, kiddo."

"Okay."

Katie's calm acceptance set Cleo to worrying again.

"Is anything going on that I ought to know about? What happened to Wesley?"

"I feel sort of draggy, is all. Wesley went on over to the state park to let them know he was back. He works there part-time y'know."

At the camper Katie accepted her medication, climbed upon the bed, fluffed a pillow beneath her knees, asked for an iced towel, and lay there staring up at her image in the cracked mirror.

She didn't feel good. And she was having bad thoughts. She imagined she could see the cancer inside her, imagined it gobbling up all the marrow leaving her bones hollow. She was getting weaker and she loathed being helpless. Worse, she knew what it meant. Out of some strange sixth sense she was aware that she stood on the brink of events.

Then she was going to disappear forever.

She just had to keep that awareness from Cleo and Big Momma. She had to make it until her dress was finished. She had to be more practical and conserve her strength. She focused on her image in the mirror; it began to wobble. Oh, no!

"Did you say something?" Cleo asked, turning to the child.

"I have to throw up."

Alarmed, Cleo yanked open the paper sack from which she'd taken the groceries. "Here, use this." She sat on the side of the bed, praying, pleading with God, holding Katie until she finished the terrible wretching.

"I ate the hamburger too fast," said Katie as she leaned weakly back on the pillows. "I want to brush my teeth. I hate throwing up!"

Cleo took a bowl to fill with water, but the spigot was dry. "The water's off, or maybe there's a kink in the hose." She opened a soft drink. "Here, sip on this while I go check."

She followed the hose to the faucet she shared with number twelve and found the woman from that camp twisting and turning the handle. "Did your water go off, too?" she asked, in her high whiny voice.

"I thought it might be a leak or a kink in the hose."

"Maybe we'll leave now," said the other woman. "I'm not much for nature. I like my air-conditioning, and small comforts, like indoor plumbing. Never take up with a man who likes to fish."

Cleo gave her a vague smile. "I think I'll check at the office."

A half dozen people were there with Big Momma fielding their complaints. "The pump quit on me. There ain't nothin' can be done till the part gets here on the bus from Valdosta."

There came a chorus of groans, requests for refunds and soon the camp was empty except for Cleo and the couple in number twelve. Cleo suspected when the man came in from fishing, they'd be gone, too. Big Momma gave her a piggin. "Ain't nothin' wrong with river water if'n you don't mind hauling it."

For the rest of the afternoon, in a whirl of conflicting thoughts and emotions, Cleo made the best of it. She hauled water in the rope-handled wooden bucket, kept Katie wiped down with cooling cloths, watched as the child napped restlessly and took her temperature each time she woke.

Perhaps it had been the hamburger that had made Katie ill, Cleo thought, pinning her hopes on that. As the hour drew close to six, Cleo was loath to wake Katie, yet she didn't dare leave her alone.

"Katie..." She shook the thin shoulder.

"What?"

Her speech was thickened with sleep, but desperate pride brought her head up, almost with alertness. Cleo was shocked at her look of exhaustion.

"Your mother will be calling in a few minutes," and perhaps Fletcher, too, Cleo hoped. "Let's drive over to the office."

"I can walk." Katie shook her head, trying to disperse the heavy drowsiness. "Did I sleep all afternoon? What did you do?"

"My nails. Are you sure you're up to walking?"

"Will you let me drive? I'm pretty good at it now, y'know."

"What I know is, we'll probably end up in the river," said Cleo, acquiescing. Her gaze went out the camper to look into the heat haze shimmering above the Suwannee. She'd ask Big Momma to observe Katie. If she, too, noted the child's failing health, then Marilyn would have to be told.

They found Big Momma sitting in her rocker on the porch. "Quiet as all get out, ain't it?" she said by way of greeting. "I ought to be hauling linens outen the cabins, but I'm too tuckered."

Katie stumbled going up the steps. She looked blindly down at her legs, then sat on the floor, clasping her knees hard. "Did you see me drive?"

"Seen you roll right over my lilacs," said the old woman, exchanging a stark questioning glance with Cleo.

A sense of helplessness descended on Cleo. Big Momma saw it; Katie was deteriorating.

"Come in the house, Katie," the old woman was saying. "I kin measure the hem for your dress. Reckon I ain't too tuckered to sew."

"I don't want it too short."

"Naturally not, got to hide them knobby knees."

"I don't have knobby knees. I have nice knees." But they were betraying her now; she had to grasp hold of the rocker to pull herself up.

After Katie had disappeared into the house behind Big Momma, Cleo leaned against the wall by the telephone. How could she be so calm on the outside when inside was pandemonium? Her heart raced, her throat was closing, her stomach undulated with dread. When the phone rang she snatched it off the hook, then couldn't speak.

"Hello? Hello? Is that some kid..."

"Marilyn, it's me, Cleo."

"Oh, I thought—"

"You've got to come back, Marilyn. . . ."

"Oh, God . . ." There was a long pause. Ward came on. "What is it, Cleo?"

"Katie's not . . . not well. She's feverish, throwing up. She's mobile, but just barely. She woke with a temperature this morning. It's been fluctuating all day. Up . . . down—"

"All right. Don't panic. We'll leave now. We've been through this before. Just keep her comfortable and . . . and happy."

"I am a little frightened."

"Can you stay by the phone? I'll have her doctor call you."

"That would be good, Ward. Yes, do that."

"Is Fletcher there?"

"No, not yet. He . . . tomorrow I think." She could see their perfect reunion, feel his hot breath on her ear, her throat, her lips; imagine the restraint he'd have to manage until they were alone. She choked back a sigh.

"The doctor's name is Caldwell. It may take an hour or so to locate him."

"I'll be here."

Cleo broke the connection and forced herself to breathe evenly before she went inside to find pen and paper for the doctor's instructions.

Chatter came from the kitchen. She went there. Katie stood atop the table in the dress of white chambray. A simple style, it had a Peter Pan collar, puffed sleeves and full skirt with which Big Momma was preoccupied. The child caught Cleo's eye and performed an unsteady pirouette to make the skirt lift, float and flutter.

"Isn't this the most gorgeous dress that ever was?"

"It's a-goin' to be a rag if'n you jerk it out of my hands like that again," said Big Momma, her tone querulous.

"It's a beauty," agreed Cleo, noting Katie's cheeks had begun to burn with a dry flush. She had the image now of Katie being caught in a current that was relentless, moving, speeding up, and there was no way of arresting the continuous flood, the inevitable. She felt a sharp piercing sadness, and shame that she had even given a single thought to Fletcher, to her own happiness.

"Look at the lace on the collar," insisted Katie, bending over and losing her balance. Cleo steadied her. "See that. Big Momma crocheted tiny angels right into the pattern."

"You're clever with your hands," said Cleo, complimenting the old woman. "I never could learn to knit or crochet. What're those slits on the back for? Ribbons."

Big Momma rolled her eyes. "You can ask her. I ain't about to say what them's for, exceptin' it's some foolishness she got in her mind. Get down, you, before you fall down," she said in an aside to Katie.

"It's not foolish. It's smart," said Katie archly, giving Big Momma a doleful look. "That's where my wings are gonna go."

"Wings...what wings?"

"My angel wings. No doubt as soon as I get to heaven they'll start growin'. I don't want 'em to tear a hole in my new dress trying to sprout."

"Oh," said Cleo, feeling a great and urgent need to sit down. She pulled out a chair and plopped down.

"Struck me sideways, too," commiserated Big Momma.

Katie glanced to the old wrinkled face then to the younger, smooth one, outraged at their comments, as if making angel was beyond her. It was going to happen. It just had to happen. What was the use of going to heaven if you didn't get to be an angel? "You don't think I've been good enough to make angel, do you?" she said hotly, glaring fiercely. Her jaw clenched in annoyance. The pupils of her eyes dilated with obstinacy; feverish, they looked intensely black. "Reverend Dopple said I only had to follow the Ten Commandments to make angel and I have.

"I don't have any gods before the real God, and I never took His name in vain, and I remember every Sunday, and I honor Mom and Dad—I only watched them doin' it once, an' that was only because I was too little to know better. I never killed anybody, especially Roger, and he deserves it. I'm not big enough to commit adultery, and I've never stolen anything. Just borrowed it. I never did a false witness against a neighbor—only Lindsey. She's not a neighbor, she's a cousin. I've never coveted a neighbor's ox or ass, because none of them have any." She ran out of breath and flung herself into one of the cane-bottomed chairs. "I know I'm goin' to be an angel."

Cleo's heart beat suffocatingly. She could no more move than could a rabbit frozen in a light beam.

The only sounds in the house were the distant ticking of an old wind-up clock and Katie's ragged breathing. Big Momma moved to the sink, her slippers swishing on the floor.

"Do tell," she said, her voice sounding odd, as if she'd suddenly lost track of what was going on. Something of what she was feeling conveyed itself in a look she gave Cleo.

Oh, Katie, darling, she thought, *have you no regard for the impact of the things you say? Such single-mindedness makes the rest of us feel so inadequate, lost, forcing upon us all this charade called life.* Cleo's gaze shifted outward, and there was Katie, staring fixedly, waiting for a reply. Her bulldogish expression indicating she wanted no neat little lectures about bodies to dust, souls to heaven. Only acceptance that she had planned her immortality. Cleo wet her lips. "You're going to be the best-dressed angel in heaven, sweetheart."

Appeased only a little, Katie's chin lifted perceptibly, her level dark brows drew down. "That's the idea."

The telephone pealed. Cleo started, then leapt up. "Oh, that's . . ." she swallowed doctor, burrowing into deception. Later she could mention to Katie that she had spoken to her doctor. If it was necessary. If—

"That's for me. Quick, Big Momma, pen and paper."

"On the counter in the front room," she said, and Cleo grabbed them up as she ran through.

CHAPTER THIRTEEN

THE CAMP WAS THE DARKEST Cleo had ever seen it. No friendly lights spilled from empty cabins or campsites. From her perch on the office porch she had a dim view of the lights in the motor home in number twelve, but only when the wind blew, moving moss-draped limbs. Stars were beginning to carpet a velvet sky, but as yet, the moon had not risen. As the shadows grew darker the silhouettes of trees and shrubs all merged into an indistinguishable haze.

There seemed to be a lack of harmony in nature tonight, too, for there was a deathly stillness upon the swamp. No frogs croaked for mates, no crickets chirped, birds were oddly silent. Now and then a fish leaped in the river. The splash as it plopped back into the water sounded uncommonly loud. The quiet seemed menacing. But that was absurd, thought Cleo, resisting an urge to shudder. It was just a tranquil summer evening, much like her first night in camp those many weeks ago. The person she'd been then was connected to the person she was now only by threads of memories, none of which held personal terror for her today. It was just the conversation she'd had with the doctor about Katie that had her at sixes and sevens.

Dr. Caldwell's words still rang in her ears, signaling doom. "Katie is beyond any medication or lasting procedure I can prescribe. She has been for two months. She's surviving on indomitable will, or perhaps, God's. Most of the medication she's on now will alleviate pain, some of the symptoms—''

''But, there has to be something...!''

The doctor had been silent for long seconds, and Cleo could tell that he was vacillating between anger and sympathy. ''We've tried, done everything. But, anyway, I'll be at the hospital when Ward brings her in tomorrow. We'll exchange her blood. That may rally her somewhat.''

''You don't think I should take her to a hospital near here. There's one in—''

''Miss Anderson, if that will make you feel better, do it, and they can call me. But you did say Katie's kidneys were functioning, her respiration is good and that her temperature hasn't climbed above 101. What you're seeing is the natural deterioration and the progression of the disease. There's no stopping it. I think it would be more harmful to frighten Katie unduly by putting her among strangers.

''And, there's another thing. Katie has my phone number in that tattered notebook she carries with her everywhere. She promised if she ever got to feeling too badly, she'd call me. She hasn't. She does know how...''

''She might not—''

''She would. Even if it was just to say...goodbye. We've been good friends, through a lot together. Katie has her own ideas about dignity and death. I trust her. I think you should, too.''

''But how can you tell which way it will go? How can she?''

A heavy sigh came over the wire. ''I can tell you she's dying. I can't tell you when. I don't *think* she's going to die tonight, but if she does, it'll be a better death than what I'll have to put her through tomorrow and the days after. Look, do you want me to speak with her?''

"No, she doesn't know I've called her parents home or that I'm so worried."

"Ah. She's manipulating you, too." He sounded amused, proud of his patient, in cahoots with her.

The conversation had ended on that. Now, on the darkened porch Cleo searched for her interior self, looking for support, for direction; she concentrated hard, trying to find that personal vision, but no vision came, no second voice. No help. She was on her own. With a dying child on her hands.

Be happy! How could she when she was so frightened? She should never have accepted the responsibility. Hindsight! She looked at the slender form that was Katie, lying there in the shadows, the matchstick legs only a little darker than the white shorts.

Cleo grieved, then abruptly she stopped, appalled at her own audacity. Others were in charge. Ward, Marilyn, Dr. Caldwell. Katie and God. Well, she'd put her money on those two. It was a safer bet.

She and the child had the porch to themselves, Big Momma having decided to sew in the kitchen where light was easy on her eyes. Supper had been a joint effort. The older woman provided leftover chicken, and Cleo had contributed apples, grapes, cheese and crackers she'd bought that day.

Now Katie lay on her side, elbow propped on a cushion borrowed from a rocking chair. She was quite still, seeming to be gazing out across the river. Cleo wanted to speak to her, but she didn't yet trust her voice.

She should gather up Katie and drive back around to the camper, get Katie's things ready for her parent's return. But she couldn't make herself move. Fletcher might yet call, and she didn't want to miss talking with him. His loving reassurance was what she needed now to make the evening right, to rid herself of this peculiar anxiety that lay low in her belly. She glanced at Katie again. The stillness was so out of character. Cleo took a breath.

"You've been quiet for so long, Katie. What're you thinking about? Anything important? Want to share it with me?"

The girl stirred, turning over, putting her hands behind her head. "You know something. You're the first grownup to ask me what I think. Grownups just don't. I guess they think kids don't have brains."

Cleo smiled. How well she recalled making that same observation when she herself was a child. "I can hear yours ticking away. What's it saying?"

"You'll think it's silly."

"I might, might not."

"I was thinking about the two sides of fate."

Cleo felt a shock in the pit of her stomach. This was serious, and she wasn't sure she could cope. "I didn't know fate had two sides."

"But, you believe in fate?"

"I guess."

"You're superstitious, too. That cracked mirror you won't throw out."

"Guilty again."

"What I was thinking is this: Suppose I had been born February fifteenth instead of Valentine's? Wouldn't that put me on the other side of fate, a day later in life. Would I have still gotten sick? Suppose Roger had been born first? Would he be sick instead of me? If I knew just where I was standing when the germ found me, could I have moved over an inch and let it fly right on by?"

They were up-against-the-wall questions, ones with no redemption, all *ifs*. "I don't know," said Cleo. "There're some things to which we never find answers—at least not the answers we want.''

Turning back to gaze at the river, Katie expelled one of her trademark sighs. ''Well, that's what I was thinking—''

It was also on Katie's mind that she was in deep cosmic trouble. She could tell. She was hot on the outside, cold inside. It took all of her willpower just to keep from shivering. She could almost feel her blood slowing down. No matter which side of fate she was on, it was going against her.

She sighed again. ''I tell you, Cleo, it's awfully hard to make your life count for something when you only get to be eleven. I wish nothing would ever change, like the river...I wish everything would just go on and on and never end....'' Until she grew some breasts, anyway, and maybe a little bit of hair. Going to heaven breastless and bald was the pits. *Oh!* she thought, *I'm going to miss so much.*

Now, thought Cleo. *Now is the time to mention that Ward and Marilyn are coming back tonight, that she's going into the hospital tomorrow.* But those words just stayed suspended at the back of her throat. ''When I have children,'' she said instead, ''As soon as I get them home from the hospital I'm going to start asking them what they think.''

A soft giggle floated on the night air. ''They'll say wah...wah...wah...then you'll have to figure out what it means.''

Cleo smiled. Babies came after marriage...to Fletcher. What joy if she could find herself magically alone with him somewhere, their bodies entwined.... She expelled a sigh that could have matched one of Katie's.

Katie propped the side of her head in the palm of her hand. She felt the fever flush rising along her cheek and forehead. Bending and drawing her knees up only confirmed what she knew, emphasizing the aching pain along her spine. She had to hang on for a while longer, and she could. It was just a matter of mind over body. Concentrating, willing her body to do her bidding, she stared sightlessly at the far riverbank. A flicker of light caught her attention, then another. She raised her head.

"Look at those fireflies, Cleo. There must be a whole swarm of them."

"I don't see them."

Biting her lip against a dreadful stab of pain, Katie pushed herself up and pointed. "Not in the yard, across the river, near the ground. They keep flickering on and off."

"Oh, yes, now—" But even as Cleo watched, the tiny flickers hopped along the dry mulch and grew into flames that suddenly went racing up a tall tree. A huge ball of light flared when moss caught. "My God!" she breathed, and hard little knives of fear moved in her lungs.

"The swamp's on fire," said Katie, awed. "I saw it happen. It just . . . did."

Then Cleo was speaking, moving the way one does when very frightened after the first panic dies. "Katie. You stay right there, don't move!" She whirled and dashed into the house, startling the older woman with her abrupt appearance.

"There's a fire just started across the river. You'd better come have a look."

"Law! I knowed it was bound to happen. Sure as my bones ache and my hair's gray. Knowed it certain when the pump quit."

In the moment it took them to return to the porch the fire had leaped across treetops, engulfing them; smoke furled into the sky, disappearing from view once it got beyond the light cast by flames. But the smell hung chokingly in the air. Small pieces of flaming debris dropped to the forest floor. The fire in them was extinguished as oxygen was sucked up by higher flames. Only when a great pine exploded and fell, did ground mulch begin to burn in earnest.

Mesmerized by the flames, Big Momma's mouth worked, deciding on words. "I ain't...I ain't seen nothin' like that in better'n fifty years."

"Suppose it jumps the river?" Cleo whispered.

"Law! An' me 'thout'n a drop of water to wet things down. I better call the park rangers. That there side of the river is refuge land."

A huge poplar on the riverbank swelled with flame, then tottered and fell into the river. Sparks flew, and there came a great hissing like a caldron steaming. Several limbs jutting skyward continued to burn fiercely, their flames reflected upon the coppery surface.

"I bet all your hants are running for cover," said Katie, teasing Big Momma. Then, worriedly, she said, "Say, Cleo, maybe you'd better get our stuff out of the camper. I don't want my satchel to burn up. I need it."

"They're a-comin'," said Big Momma, hanging up the phone. Then she called the county fire department. "They ain't comin'," she said with disgust.

"Why not?"

"Because they're at a fire down on 441 what's jumped the highway and life's in danger. I shoulda told them..." She glared at the leaping flames, judging. "Well, I 'spec we're safe enough for the time being."

"With a fire not more than fifty yards away?" said Cleo, rocked with disbelief. "I'd better go hitch up my camper, be ready to pull out...." And, go where? she wondered, to wait for Marilyn and Ward.

"Law! I wish Wesley was here. It wouldn't hurt to sink all the boats."

"Maybe the man in number twelve will help," said Cleo. "I'll ask." She knelt down beside Katie, passing a hand over the child's forehead, finding it hot. "How're you feeling?"

"I don't have a fever. It's just the excitement...."

"I think you'd better go in the house, perhaps lie down on the sofa?"

"I want to stay out here and watch the fire. But I wouldn't mind a blanket, in case some sparks fly this way," she added quickly.

While Big Momma went to the sheds to find a mallet with which to knock the bungs out of the boat bottoms, Cleo got a blanket and draped it around Katie. "I know you don't feel well, sweetheart. I want you to promise that you'll tell me if you..." *If you feel as if you're dying? Dear God!* "If you feel something happening that you don't understand or if you get scared. Okay?"

"I'm perfectly fine," she said, giving Cleo a fierce gray glare.

Saucy twit. Darling girl. Sad, and oh, so courageous. "Perfectly stubborn, you mean," returned Cleo. "I'll be right back."

Once at her campsite she positioned her car so that she could hook the camper tongue to the hitch. That part was never easy, and she'd never done it in the dark.

However, there were many other preparations called for first; the awning had to come down, drawers had to be taped shut, glassware packed into boxes. Clothes... Best to speak to the couple in number twelve first. It was peculiar, Cleo thought, that they had not come up to the office at the first sign of the fire. Disasters always seemed to bring people together, if for no other reason than curiosity.

As she cut through the shrub she had her answer. She could distinctly hear the man shouting at his wife.

Her steps slowed. Off to her right, across the river another great tree exploded into flame, the sound drowning out the voices from within the motor home. Something warm and furry brushed against Cleo's leg. She yelped.

The motor home door was thrown open. "Who's out there?"

"It's me," said Cleo, spying the silver tabby slinking off. But it just as easily could have been a wild animal running from the fire. A mink, a panther, bear or possum. She gave in to the shudder, letting it take hold of her.

"Who?"

The man was peering out the door. In the week he'd been in camp he hadn't shaved, and without his hat to keep springy gray hair in place he looked untidy, slightly menacing. Cleo stepped into the spilling light. "I'm your neighbor in number eleven. I just wanted to—"

"We're not leaving," said the man. "I paid my money to fish and I'm going to fish!"

His wife pushed him aside. "If you're leaving, will you give me a lift to the nearest town? I got to get away from here," she said, sounding desperate. "I can't abide—"

"Get back, you," her husband said, giving her a rough shove.

The moon was up now in full regalia, and above Cleo's head bats flitted in black silhouettes, wheeling and dipping in their flight, racing away from smoke that was beginning to drift into the camp.

"I didn't come to ask you to leave," explained Cleo, embarrassed at having witnessed the altercation. "But park rangers are on their way, and we may be ordered to evacuate. Mrs. Freeman needs some help. She wondered if you'd knock the bungs out of all the boats and sink them in case the fire jumps the river."

"If the fire jumps the river!" the woman wailed. "We're gonna be burned up...."

"It's just a precaution," Cleo said, attempting to remain calm in face of the woman's fright.

"Sure, I'll help. You got a hammer or a mallet?" He turned back to speak to his wife, then stepped out, closing the door on what she was saying. "Don't pay any attention to Evelyn," he said to Cleo. "She's just high strung." He walked to the riverbank and stared at the fire. "It looks to be burning away from us, going deeper into the swamp."

"But if the wind changes..."

"Then we might have a problem."

Cleo handed him the mallet. "Do be careful. The river's narrow where the pier is. If that diving tree caught and fell..."

"Cypress doesn't burn all that easily."

He started off down the path.

"Would you like for me to look in on your wife, talk to her?" Cleo called.

"No!" he said sharply. "I mean, no. Evelyn's fine. Mostly she's aggravated because we forgot the television and she's missing her soaps. She figures if she can make me miserable enough we'll go home."

He capped that with a small laugh. Cleo thought he sounded disdainful. On the other hand, she didn't really know the couple and who was she to interfere? More urgent matters were at hand. Shrugging, she returned to the task of scuttling camp.

Within ten minutes she was frustrated. She needed three hands, two to wrestle the camper tongue onto the hitch and one to hold the flashlight so that she could see what she was doing. She could hear the woosh as the fire gobbled up more trees, and the thump-thump of the mallet. Maybe the man's wife would lend her a hand....

"Say, are you in need of a white knight?"

That voice! Cleo whirled around, then just stood there immobile, filling space. "Fletcher!" she choked dazedly. "If there was anyone in the world I needed to see, to..."

"I leave you alone for a few days, and what do I find? Hell and havoc. Is that an indication of what our life is going to be?"

She couldn't answer. Words and phrases tumbled over themselves in her mind, but she couldn't form a sentence. What should she speak of first? Katie? The fire? How much she loved him, had missed him?

He reached for her, gathered her close, inhaling the fragrance of her hair. Her arms went around his neck, clinging tightly; she pressed her face against his shoulder, content for the moment to be in his arms, safe and close.

He tilted her face up and kissed her eyelids, her cheeks, the tip of her nose...finally, touching his lips against hers, but only lightly. "If we got into any heavy necking now, I'm afraid this place would burn down around us before I'd be willing to stop," he said, disengaging himself with reluctance.

"I didn't expect you until tomorrow," said Cleo, in shaky control of herself.

"I told you, I'd be here as soon as I could. C'mon, let's get you hitched up." He looked back over his shoulder at the fire. Burning embers were floating and swirling on drafts of heated air. The wind was shifting, bringing with it not only hot ashes, but the roar and crackle of destruction. It was only a matter of time before the fire jumped the river. "We don't have time to dally."

"We can't leave! Marilyn and Ward are on their way. Katie's got to go into the hopsital."

"They can catch up to us in Atlanta. We're not staying here."

Cleo considered that, agreeing. "The sooner we get Katie to the hospital, the better, as far as I'm concerned. What about Big Momma? We can't just abandon her."

"Mostly likely we'll have to tie her up and haul her into Fargo. Now where's that flashlight?"

Amid all the smoke and smut and confusion, Cleo was thinking, Atlanta. Home. Fletcher. Loved and loving. Life could be good if you let it. She was willing. She stood off to the side while Fletcher got behind the wheel of her car, driving forward a yard or two to test the hitch. He pulled the camper over a stump. It wobbled and she heard a crash; glass breaking.

"What was that?" he asked.

"Just an old mirror. I forgot to take it off the shelf."

He shook his head. "Oh, hell! Seven years bad luck."

"Not for us," said Cleo. "It was somebody else's mirror." Somebody else's luck, she thought, determined never again to borrow trouble that rightfully belonged to another.

"DID YOU GET my satchel?"

"It's on the front seat of the car," Cleo said, skirting Big Momma's ancient pickup. The boarded up truck bed was piled haphazardly with linens, pots and pans, clothes, the rocking chairs off the porch. Cleo thought it looked like something out of *The Grapes of Wrath*. She waved as

Fletcher drove her rig past to line it up behind his own car close to the entrance gate. "Where's Big Momma?"

"Turning the chickens out to fend for themselves. I want my satchel." The child huddled deeper into the blanket, facing away from the yellow porch light.

Cleo clasped the porch railing, clasped it tightly. "Katie . . . we're all of us going to be leaving here in a few minutes. We're . . . we're taking you to Atlanta, to the hospital. I've already spoken with Dr. Caldwell."

"No! You can't! Please, Cleo. I'm not ready!" she cried, and burst into tears.

Cleo gathered the frail bundle into her arms and carried her into the house. She sat on the old sofa, cradling Katie, rocking back and forth. "I know you aren't," she said feeling a lump forming in her throat. "But, you need—"

"I'll die this time," Katie said, wailing, gulping air in and hissing out words around hard gasps. "I know I will. I've been in hospitals till I can't stand it. They do things to you, and you get so tired . . ."

Cleo didn't know what words of comfort to offer. She didn't think there were any. She pressed her lips against the pink scalp. "Try to get some sleep, Katie. Try. It'll make you stronger." *And, close your eyes,* Cleo thought. *Close your eyes, because I can't bear looking into them.* She arranged the child on the sofa, stroking the gaunt young face, the thin arms. "I need to see what I can do to help Big Momma. I'll check on you every few minutes, okay?"

She grasped Cleo's arm. "Please, can't we stay? Just another day or two?"

"It's not possible," Cleo said gently. "First because you're too ill, and the fire's gaining. It's not safe."

Katie sniffed and let her arm fall back to her side, her mouth quivered. "I guess that's it, then," she whispered, talking more to herself than Cleo. "Don't forget my dress. I guess Mom can finish hemming it."

"I won't forget." She stood by the sofa for a long moment, then turned away. Out on the porch, the phone rang, and she ran to answer it, turning so that she could watch the encroaching blaze.

"Cleo? Is that you?" Ward asked.

"Yes—"

"How's Katie?"

"Worse, I think. But I might be overreacting. She's resting now. We've got a problem—"

"We do, too. Highway 441 is closed. We're going to have to backtrack—"

"Fletcher's here now. He says we'll meet you in Atlanta. We'll just go straight to Emory hospital. The swamp is on fire here."

"Oh my God!"

"It's across the river. We're not in any danger yet." She spied Fletcher coming around the side of the house with Big Momma in tow. Cleo gestured for him to take the phone. "It's Ward," she said and moved away to allow him a measure of privacy.

Big Momma was wringing her hands. Cleo hurried to her. Close up, the wrinkled old face seemed to have sagged away, the bones no longer supporting the skin.

"I thought the park rangers were coming."

"They're there," said Big Momma, waving her hand to indicate the blazing swamp. "They went in from the back side to cut a break. Can't you hear them tractors?"

Cleo couldn't, not above the roar of the fire. But now she could see the machinery, small in the distance, barely illuminated by the blaze. "I thought they were coming here!"

The old woman shrugged. "Guess they ain't. The fire's yonder." But even as she spoke a shower of burning embers swept ashore. The dry grass on the riverbank smoldered, then burst into full flame. "Law!" she cried. "I been a-savin' this place for Francine. Been a-workin' to keep it up, paying like. Now there won't be nothin'! Likely she'll take one look and fly off again." A brief dry sound punctuated the words.

Fletcher came over and put his arm around Big Momma. "We'll all help you rebuild. Now, we've got to get out of here." He turned to Cleo. "Everything's set with Ward and Marilyn—"

In the middle of this the woman from number twelve came running up, panting. "The bushes in front of our campsite are burning. Have you seen my husband? He hasn't come back." She threw an accusing look at Cleo. "You sent him off—"

"Oh...! Fletcher? I forgot. He's sinking the boats."

"I'll go look for him. You get Katie, and move on out. Wait for me in Fargo. Big Momma, you follow Cleo."

"I can't. I can't just leave what it took me and four misters to build."

"Okay," said Fletcher. "But tell me quick. What do you want on your headstone? Something like...Here lies Big Momma Freeman. She up and died. Francine got the last word."

Big Momma's chin shot up, eyes flaring with anger. "I ain't giving her that satisfaction. She's the one what run off. Outta my way," she said, giving Fletcher an elbow. "I got to get my moneybox and my Bible."

The smoke was getting thick now. It stung Cleo's eyes, making them tear. Nearby a moss-covered tree fanned into flame, shooting sparks high into the night sky.

"Oh, law!" gasped Big Momma, glancing back. The woman, Evelyn, squealed.

"You can come with us," Cleo told her and went to get Katie. The child's breathing was shallow and short, little gusts of breath through her lips as though she were blowing dandelion fluff. Katie didn't awaken as Cleo fashioned the blanket into a warm cocoon. She felt an urge to pray. Not the frenzy of raised voice of which Gram had been so fond, or the cry of anguish she had issued when Ellie had died. Cleo thought, *If you don't ask for too much...if you don't ask for the impossible...* Her prayer now was a plea to God to give this crumpled broken little person another day, another week.

She went into the kitchen for Katie's dress, rolled it up and tucked it inside the blanket. She couldn't think of anything else needing to be done. Her purse and Katie's satchel were on the front seat of her car. She scooped the child into her arms.

In the front yard, Cleo found Evelyn, dazed and wavering on her feet. She looked back at the building that served as office and home to Big Momma. The porch roof was afire. The smell of hot tarred shingles was thick in the air. "Did you want to get your purse or anything?" she asked.

"I don't want to leave without my husband. This is supposed to be our honeymoon."

Cleo had no time to sort that out or offer a pleasantry. "Fletcher will bring him along. Please, we have to go." She shifted Katie's head onto her shoulder. And where was Big Momma, now? Damn! She called the old woman several times and from somewhere beyond the house came the reply. Big Momma was hunting up her silver tabby.

All along the camp lane palmetto fronds were bursting into flame, dying as quickly, but adding puffs of furling smoke into the air which was getting thick and acrid.

Cleo's throat stung, and holding onto Katie, her arms began to ache.

Panic was beginning to seize Cleo; she forced it down. She'd make Katie comfortable on the back seat of the car, then round up Big Momma. She turned to go to the car, but was stopped by Fletcher's shout.

"I didn't see anybody down by the pier."

"But, that's where he went."

"He's burned up!" screamed Evelyn.

Fletcher grabbed the woman by her arm, dragging her toward the vehicles.

"Big Momma's off looking for her cat," Cleo told him, hurrying at his side, not sure he could hear her above the screaming Evelyn, the crackle of the fire and the squawking chickens running crazily about the camp.

He muttered a curse, shoved Evelyn into the back seat, then took Katie from her arms and laid her on the front seat. "How is she?"

"Sleeping." Or unconscious, thought Cleo.

"You can't just make me leave," whimpered Evelyn.

"Shut up!" Fletcher ordered as Cleo moved behind the wheel and started the car.

"Now...now, counselor, that ain't no way to speak to a lady."

Fletcher whirled, searching in the dark for the source of the voice. A figure stepped through the light beams. "Knowed if I stayed here long enough you'd show."

"B. B. Bostwick," uttered Fletcher.

Cleo's heart was in her mouth. The few seconds when the man had revealed himself in the lights had shown he had something other than the mallet in his hand. A gun. Now Fletcher was calling him by name. B.B. Bostwick. The client who had escaped jail.

"Billy! You're safe!" squeaked Evelyn, scrambling out of the car. "Oh, Billy, I was so afraid—"

B. B. Bostwick knocked her aside. "Shut your cater-wauling," he said. "And, stay out of my way. I got a score to settle here with the counselor."

"You won't get away with this," Fletcher said, sounding grim.

"Haw! Famous last words."

"Cleo, pull on out," Fletcher ordered.

"No, little lady, don't do that." Bostwick's pale eyes protruded, cold and staring, neck stretched forward menacingly. He pointed the gun at Cleo, then swung it back to Fletcher. "You owe me. You took my money and set me up. They said you was the best. You'd get me off."

"I promised you'd get a fair trail. You did."

"You call a life sentence, fair?"

"I call it cheap considering how many old women you fleeced out of their savings." Fletcher moved a cautious step toward Evelyn, reaching out a hand to help her to her feet. "This is your most recent victim, isn't she?"

B. B. Bostwick laughed, a sour sound. "Had her all lined up—ripe for picking. Now get back against the car."

"What do you propose to do?" Cleo asked.

"That ain't a polite question, miss. Get out of the car."

"We have a sick child in here, we've got to get her to the hospital."

"Too bad. I said, Get out!"

"Why're you doing this?" Evelyn whimpered. "I love you."

"Shut your sniveling!" He waved the gun toward Cleo. "I said, out!"

"Do as he says," urged Fletcher.

Cleo picked up Katie, holding the limp form tight as she slid out of the car. She looked at Fletcher. His face was bloodless. "It'll be all right," he said softly.

"Sure will," sneered Bostwick. "Got me a lucky fire, counselor. Of course, they'll write you up as a hero, trying to save women and children and all."

Cleo stumbled. Things like this didn't happen to ordinary people, she thought. They just didn't....

Fletcher took her arm as Bostwick, gun pressed against Fletcher's spine, shepherded them back toward the inferno. "Can you manage Katie?" he asked quietly. "I have to keep my hands free."

Cleo nodded.

"No talking!" growled their captor.

The office porch was engulfed in flames. Cleo could feel the heat of it, could feel sweat trickling down between her breasts, the cold sweat of fear.

Bostwick stared at the fire. "Okay. Go around back."

"Wait a minute," Fletcher said. "Your grievance is with me. Let the women go."

"Leave them to testify, you mean. I ain't that stupid."

Cleo was too sacred to cry. The smoke was choking, the heat from the blaze reaching out, unbearable. She pulled the blanket over Katie's head, and buried her own face in it. Breathing was easier that way.

The roof of the porch collapsed, blasting out a sudden shower of sparks and burning embers. "My hair!" cried Cleo, feeling the stabbing heat, getting a whiff of the acrid odor of burning hair and flesh. At once Fletcher was at her side, brushing away the burning ash. Evelyn danced around, yelling.

Something dark was flung through the air. "God's provenance!" shouted Big Momma as her precious family bible smacked B. B. Bostwick in the face. Surprised and distracted, he flailed his arms and in the next instant Fletcher was barreling into him, the gun went off, then Fletcher dragged him to the ground and sat on him. Still trying to do her part in the fray, Big Momma was swinging the mallet. It connected with Fletcher's head.

Groggily astonished, he looked up at her. "Why'd you do that?"

"Meant to flack that moldwarp you're a-sittin' on, my aim was off. Ain't got the eye like I usta. Fair good thing, ain't it, that I stayed behind to bury my money box? Law! Hope I ain't set myself up for goin' in the wrong direction," she said, picking up the Bible and dusting it off with the wet towel she had draped over her shoulders. "Tossing the Good Book ain't rightly what the Lord calls for us to do with it." She looked at Cleo. "You and the girl be all right?"

"My legs feel like rubber. That bullet whizzed right by my ear," she backed away from the snaking gray smoke and sat on the ground in the lane, laying Katie out to check on her. Her breathing was still coming in little puffs. Asleep or unconscious? Cleo wondered, shaking Katie gently, then not so gently, calling her name, until finally Katie roused, eyelids fluttering. "Quit moving me around, Cleo," she moaned weakly. "It hurts."

Fletcher didn't think his heart would ever stop pounding, though in a very male and primitive way, his pulse throbbed exultantly in his throat. He kept his knee firmly on Bostwick's stomach. The scum! Trying to sully, to kill those he loved most in the world. His hands balled into fists, then slowly he let them relax. "Get me something to tie him with," he told Big Momma. When Bostwick's hands and feet were secure, he tossed the man in the back of Big Momma's pickup. "When you get into Fargo, call the state patrol. They'll take care of him."

"What...what about me?" asked Evelyn, timidly. "He...he was going to kill me...us, wasn't he?"

"He was trying his damnedest. Can you drive your camper?" Evelyn shook her head. "Well, maybe Big Momma can send somebody back for it." He looked down the lane. None of the cabins had caught yet, but campsites fronting the river were burning out of control. There wasn't much chance of saving the motor home now. He hurried to where Cleo was sitting in the middle of the road, cradling Katie's head in her lap. He knelt down beside her, touching her face, brushing soot-streaked tears and sweat from her cheeks. "Are you okay?"

"I am now. I'm trying to be. Can we leave?" She attempted to lift Katie by herself and couldn't. A small surprised laugh escaped her. "My legs are like Jell-O."

"Do you think you can drive at least as far as Fargo? We'll leave your rig there, I'll send someone for it tomorrow."

"We can drive to Atlanta together?"

"That's the idea," he said, helping her to her feet. He scooped Katie into his arms, jutting out his elbow, offering it to Cleo. She tucked her arm through his, and moved in unsteady step beside him.

"I had thought about going to the Grand Canyon this summer," she said, "but I changed my mind. I thought it would be too dangerous for a woman alone." She spoke in a faraway voice, like someone talking in her sleep.

She was trying to pull herself together, Fletcher saw, but she was close to tears. He could see her lower lip trembling. He suffered an icy stab of fear—aftershock—that she could have been lost to him. He felt his legs were suddenly functioning in slow motion. "Just hang on for a few more minutes," he said, as much for his own benefit as hers. "The worst is over."

"What about Katie?"

Fletcher winced, recalling the past two terrible years, the lost hope and pain and indignities Katie had suffered. He clutched his godchild closer to his chest. The worst was probably over for Katie, too. But he didn't think Cleo was ready to accept that. "She'll be fine," he said. "This hour of night with no traffic, we'll make good time to Atlanta."

THEY MADE a sad and blistered caravan as they drove away from the burning fishing camp, thought Cleo, guiding her car into line behind Fletcher's.

Driving her old truck, Big Momma was first in line so that Fletcher's beams could keep her truck bed in view against B. B. Bostwick's rousing and trying to throw himself off, thus escaping. Evelyn had insisted on riding in the back of the truck with him. She sat high in the rocking chair, face grim and somewhat dazed.

As they made their way away from the fire and smoke, Cleo rolled down her window breathing very welcome fresh air. Her lungs felt scorched; blisters raised on her bare arms where hot ash had fallen.

Katie had escaped such injury, although the blanket had scattered ember-burned holes. The child lay inert on the front seat, head to door, feet in Cleo's lap. Cleo wanted them there, for now and then she could touch the toes, the instep and finding warmth, knew Katie was still... Cleo felt an obstruction in her throat. She couldn't think anymore, couldn't plan anymore... Mechanically she focused her eyes on the back of Fletcher's car and drove.

SHE HEARD the sirens long before the flashing red lights came into view. Brake lights flashed ahead. The caravan moved off to the side, and halted as two pumper engines went racing past. Cleo hoped they wouldn't be too late to save something of the camp. Before they could pull back onto the narrow road, Wesley drove up and screeched to a halt.

"I got the parts for the pump," he yelled. "But that isn't all that came in on the bus from Valdosta. I got a surprise for you Big Momma."

"I'm past surprisin'," she said wearily.

Cleo hung her head out the window. "Fletcher, we need to keep moving."

He got out of his car and walked back to hers, bending down to gaze in. "Just give me a minute, something's going on here that I don't understand."

Wesley was helping someone out of his truck. "Run up on her at the bus station," he said. "She was asking about for directions to the fish camp. So I offered her a ride, seeing as I was coming this way. You coulda bowled me over with a feather when she told me..."

The girl walked in front of the truck lights. Big Momma started screaming. "Francine! Francine! I knowed you'd come back, I knowed it!"

Not Francine, Cleo saw. It couldn't be. Francine had been gone forty years. The girl being guided by Wesley was young. Big Momma was hysterical. Seeing things. Cleo went to help.

"I'm not Francine," said the girl. "I'm Fanny."

"You looks the spittin' image of Francine," choked Big Momma, leaning heavily against the truck. "You give me a start."

"Francine was my grandmother. Are you Big Momma Freeman?"

"That be me," Big Momma said, dazed, trying to sort what she was hearing. "You looks just like Francine," she said again.

"Grandmother told me if I ever needed help, I should come to you. She told me all about you. I—I'm all alone now. You're the only family—"

"Where's Francine?"

"She died. She and my mother both, in a car crash."

"Francine...dead?" Big Momma's hand fluttered to her throat. "That don't seem possible. I had a presentiment, but it didn't feel like it was my own flesh and blood, an' when little Katie come off bein' sick... All this time I been a-waitin'..."

Hesitantly, the young girl reached out to touch the old woman's hand. She seemed to sense the agony that was mingling with pride, the tragedy of lost years. "Grandmother...Francine always meant to come back," said Fanny. "But Momma got sick."

"Law!" said Big Momma softly. "I had me a granddaughter and never knowed it. I can't hardly countenance Francine gettin' bewitched. She was allus uptight, like, when I took up with my misters."

"A great-granddaughter ought to do you," injected Wesley. "You want her or not?" He looked at the girl shyly. "If you don't, I might. But right now, I got to go help put out a fire." He had a brief word with Fletcher, asked about Katie, then moved off.

"Do I want...?" Big Momma was saying. "Law! You're welcome, child. And, this here's some of my reg'lars, Fletcher and Cleo, and in the back of the truck is a couple of moldwarps, shiftless as they come. We be gettin' rid of them..." She suddenly stopped talking and blew her nose heartily. "Get in the truck, you can catch me up on Francine while I'm drivin'."

"We always baked bread on rainy days," said Fanny.

"Shame! Coopin' you up in a hot kitchen like that."

"It was the best bread I ever ate."

"Do tell. My recipe, no doubt. Pure puzzles me how-somever that Francine would go to bakin' after leavin' me. I allus had to take a stick to her, balkin' like she did."

"Grandmother told me that baking days were the happiest of her memories of home, the good cooking smell in the kitchen, you and her talking."

Big Momma looked startled. "My kitchen done burned up, but we'll build another. An' get us a good cook stove, too. Electric." She jerked the truck into gear, clutch growling and lurched off with no mind for her passengers in the truckbed.

"That solves the issue of Francine," said Fletcher, shaking his head. "Let's check on Katie, then get on the road ourselves." He put his arms around Cleo's shoulder. She derived a measure of strength from his touch, and pressed her lips to his swollen knuckles. She was happy for Big Momma, but problems of her own were pressing.

"If Katie doesn't make it," she said. "I'll never be able to face Marilyn and Ward again—or myself."

Katie was sitting up on the front seat. "What's going on?" she asked groggily.

Reprieve! thought Cleo. For once, God was on her side. "I'll tell you all about it tomorrow," she said, then pressed her lips together to keep from crying or shouting her relief.

"Where's my satchel?"

"On the floor. Go back to sleep." She smiled up at Fletcher, her eyes communing with him. Something had lifted inside; she felt lighter. "No more delays, okay? We join up in Fargo, then no stops to Atlanta."

"No stops." He kissed her briefly on the lips. "You're something rare, Cleo. I'm a lucky man."

Cleo's head was still ringing with those words when, twenty minutes later in Fargo, she and Katie transferred to his car.

CHAPTER FOURTEEN

THEY DID MAKE one stop after all, an hour outside of Atlanta, to phone ahead to the hospital to alert them that Katie was coming in.

"Ward and Marilyn are already there," Fletcher said when he returned to the car. "Ward's calling Dr. Caldwell."

"Do hurry," urged Cleo, hanging on to any thought to blot out Katie's face and the frantic clutter under her ribcage.

Katie lay with her head in Cleo's lap, her feet in Fletcher's. The young features seemed old and feeble, a wax works belonging to some stranger. Some fluke of perseverance on Katie's part had roused her to speak earlier. In the past four hours she had not so much as fluttered an eyelid.

At the hospital Katie was snatched from Fletcher's arms, swiftly placed on a wheeled stretcher and taken away. Cleo could not look the distraught Marilyn in the eye. "This is my fault. I should've called you sooner, I should've..."

Marilyn said nothing, only gestured toward Cleo with one hand as if disparaging of the merciless waves of fear and hope and dread and loss that were washing over her. Cleo was taken aback by the other woman's seeming disregard of her feelings, of Katie's condition, until she noticed Marilyn's other hand so tightly clutching Ward's, he had to peel the fingers from his own.

An all-efficient nurse began leading them down the corridor. "Dr. Caldwell said he'll see you in the ICU waiting room in a few minutes. If you'll just go there now."

Another couple was in the room, their faces strained, clothes rumpled. They looked up, then away so quickly that Cleo knew her own and Fletcher's and Marilyn's and Ward's expressions must be reflecting the same look of dread.

"You both look as though you could use a bed here yourselves," said Ward quietly as he ushered Marilyn to one of the plastic-covered sofas. "You smell like smoke and is that a bruise on your forehead?" he asked Fletcher.

While Fletcher filled Ward in on events, Cleo tried to engage Marilyn in conversation, but Marilyn answered in monosyllables, lost somewhere inside herself.

The few minutes before Dr. Caldwell's arrival stretched into an hour. By the time he appeared in the doorway, his aristocratic features solemn and weary, conversation had long ceased among them all.

Ward and Fletcher shot up, but the physician urged them to be seated again. He pulled up a chair, sinking into it. "The long and short of it is that Katie has just about worn herself out in the struggle to live."

Marilyn dug her fist into her mouth, stifling a sob.

"There must be something you can do," Cleo blurted.

The doctor averted his eyes and thrust long and elegant fingers through his hair. A tragic gesture. Defeat.

"We should've...last November..." sobbed Marilyn. Ward put his arm around his wife.

"No. We crossed that bridge. It was the right thing—"

"What happened last November?" asked Cleo.

"We should have let them amputate..." cried Marilyn.

Katie? Without legs? Cleo started to choke and shudder, seeing a Katie who couldn't hop, skip, sneak around in bushes, climb into laps or pirouette to show off the best dress that ever was.

"It would only have added a few months. We knew the cancer had already traveled to Katie's spine."

Dr. Caldwell stood up, shook hands with Ward. Cleo could see the question they all wanted to ask in Ward's hesitant demeanor. He looked at his wife with pain-filled eyes, then his shoulders seemed to sag. "How long?" he finally asked, the words trailing out of his mouth in a sibilant whisper.

"She's losing ground very quickly. I have to tell you, I think...a few days...a week." His mouth curved in a small sorrow-filled smile. "But with Katie, who knows? She's proven us wrong before."

"We can't take her home?" asked Marilyn through twisted heavy bursts of sound.

Dr. Caldwell stood there for a long moment, a sorrowful look on his long unshaven face. "Not this time, Marilyn."

"Can we see her?"

"Not now." Doctor Caldwell exchanged a glance with Ward. "We've stabilized Katie, but we've still some work to do. Go home now, get some rest..."

"I hate those words!" cried Marilyn. "I hate them! I can't go home! I can't abandon my daughter. We haven't talked...we haven't...there's so much...I haven't told her...said—"

Cleo put her arms around Marilyn, holding her, but she was unable to speak for there weren't any words to ease Marilyn's kind of suffering. After a moment, Fletcher put his hand on her shoulder, drawing her away and out of the room, leaving Ward and Marilyn clinging to each other. "Home sounds good to me," he said. "I'm beat."

"I'm like Marilyn. I hate to leave Katie." But she allowed him to guide her out of the hospital into the early light. The sky was streaked with deep purples and pinks, prelude to a bright dawn.

SUNLIGHT BORE DOWN on Cleo's eyelids, quite destroying her uneasy sleep. She began to rummage around on the bed, tossing this way and that until she realized where she was—Fletcher Fremont Maitland's bed. She bolted up, wide awake.

Last night, or rather, this morning, Fletcher had driven into his garage, shepherded her through the kitchen, down an unlighted hallway and into his bedroom. Their systems, overloaded with stimuli had finally short-circuited. Together they had collapsed upon the bed, fully clothed, too utterly weary for love or sex or conversation. But now...

Except that Fletcher was not in bed, nor to be found anywhere in the house. She went to the kitchen, peering out the door into the garage. The car was gone. So much for retrieving her suitcase, she thought, wondering where he'd gone and why. A sudden savage grip of panic assailed her. She grabbed the phone off the cluttered kitchen counter, fingers trembling as she dialed information, then the hospital.

"There's no Katie Miller listed as being in ICU," said the woman in information.

Cleo felt faint. "Oh, yes, there has to be—"

"There's a Kathleen Miller—"

"That's it!"

"—Moved to the children's ward."

"Her condition?"

"You'll have to check with the charge nurse," said information and hung up.

"I'll do that," Cleo said to the dead phone, redialing and learning Katie was listed as guarded.

"What does guarded mean? Good? Fair?" she asked the nurse.

"Guarded," the woman answered with some exasperation.

"Is she awake? Can we see her?"

"Katie's awake and her usual charming self," came the dry reply. "Visiting hours are four to six."

Cleo cradled the phone and dropped her head into her hands. Prayers answered! God was good, not all-punishing as Gram had preached. She gave a thought to Ellie, realizing now how strong her mother had been to survive those last bed-ridden years; to Gram, whose overpowering strength had been flawed, a facade behind which she had hidden all womanly wants and needs. It was a good feeling to be free of them both.

She'd tell Fletcher about that other self. She could do it now. She opened her eyes and caught a glimpse of her reflection in the sunny window, aghast at what she saw. No wonder Fletcher took off! She looked like some wild creature just risen from the bowels of the earth. She smelled like one, too!

She was fresh from the shower, naked, reaching for Fletcher's robe on the closet door when he burst into the bedroom.

"Oh, my..." he said softly.

"Don't you know how to knock?" she squeaked, shrugging quickly into the robe.

"In my own house?"

"You do have a point," she said, giving him a doleful smile. "Katie's better. They've moved her out of ICU."

"I know."

"Where've you been?"

"To the deli for our breakfast. Chinese. That okay?"

"Chinese? For breakfast?"

"Late lunch?" he said, just standing there on the threshold, devouring her with his eyes.

Tying the sash on the robe, Cleo looked at him in quick scrutiny. "You have a funny look on your face."

He glanced in the dresser mirror. "That's a look you'll have to get used to. It's called lust."

Cleo felt suddenly like her old self, inept, an alien being in strange territory. "But, there are so many things we need to talk about, get straight, about my car and camper, moving my things—"

"We'll talk about them." He advanced a step in her direction, at the same time unbuttoning his shirt, unbuckling his belt.

"I haven't had a chance to look at the house. Really look. Except I can tell you're messy."

"I'll take you on a tour, lots of mess to see."

"Now?"

"Not now," he said in that voice that he could make do anything. He dropped his shirt, kicked off his loafers, tossed his slacks toward the wooden valet in the corner and missed. "Do you realize we have yet to make love on a bed?" He discarded his underwear.

"I—I hadn't actually thought about it." He was naked, muscular, magnificent, wanting her. He brushed against her thigh, tantalizing her with his erection. His fingers tugged at the sash, loosening it so that the robe fell open.

"Give it some thought now," he said throatily, sweeping the robe off her shoulders, using it as it dropped down her back to lock her body against his own. He sighed heavily. "Have I ever mentioned how good you feel?"

"Maybe once or twice," she whispered as he bent to nibble on the pink shell of her ear. The nibbling had the effect of diverting her attention away from the activity at the juncture of her thighs, though the diversion lasted only a moment, because his sex was as erect as a sentry and seeking satisfaction with persistence. There was the matter, too, of her nipples touching the hair on his chest, which sent shivers down her spine to lodge with the urgency in her moist womanly core.

His lips brushed hers. "Have I said how much I love you, how I've missed you, how—"

"All of those things," Cleo managed somehow, lifting her arms from the robe to trail them over his shoulder and down his arms, reveling in the feel of his ropy muscles, the texture of his skin. Her legs were going rubbery. "Fletcher... you did mention the bed."

"Don't want to stop doing this to get over there," he murmured against her neck, shifting his hands between their bodies so that he could cup her breasts.

"I'm melting, Fletcher. And I'm going to fall down." Her voice had an edge to it. Fletcher stepped back.

"We'll have to work on building up your resistance."

She reached the bed, burying her face in the pillows. They smelled faintly of smoke so she turned her head and watched Fletcher align himself next to her. He locked his hands beneath his head, lying there staring up at the ceiling. His behavior confused Cleo. Upon her was an urgent primeval need. Just lying next to Fletcher on the bed was not what she had in mind. "You really want me to build up resistance to you?" she asked, wondering if she was being put to a test of some sort.

"You'd better not even think of it."

She straightened the bed clothes beneath her body, managing to inch closer to him as she did so.

"Comfortable, now?" he asked.

"Yes, very." She gave him a smile that did not quite come off.

"You know what's incredible to me? That I'm lying here in my own bed, naked, in the middle of the day, with the woman who's going to be my wife. My wife. I'm going to be a husband, doing things that husbands do. Coming home to supper every night . . . a clean house. Now that'll be a nice change." He looked over at her and smiled. "I'll probably have to balance your checkbook, too."

"You will not! But you can depend on having to clean up your own messes." A quick glance in the direction of his thighs told her his need was still evident. She put a hand on his chest, running her fingers through the wiry hair. Just for a little something to do, she told herself.

"You noticed the house has three bedrooms?"

"I noticed they were uninhabitable."

"Just trial papers, old clothes, things from my parents' house that I didn't want to get rid of. You could move them out of the way."

"For what?"

"For kids. We're going to have some, aren't we?"

Cleo sighed. "I don't see how."

He looked at her through slitted lashes that hid the effort with which he was controlling himself. "You do have a one-track mind, Cleo, my heart."

She sniffed. "I am known for seeing a task through to the end, no matter how unpleasant."

"Unpleasant?" His voice was going husky, shaking a little.

"You shouldn't have started something you had no intention of finishing."

"Oh, but, I have every intention . . ." He shifted on the bed, turning toward her, maintaining only a small space between them, yet enough so that he could look down the length of her, committing all to memory. With one finger he traced the fair line of her level brows. Cleo closed her eyes and strained against him.

"I thought you might like to know that B. B. Bostwick is safely behind bars again."

Cleo pressed her lips to his neck, discovering the telltale throbbing pulse in his throat. "That's good news," she said, and moved a bit so that she could press her ear against his chest, listening to his heart beating.

"I've made arrangements for us to take our blood tests this afternoon. We can—"

She licked his nipple. "We can what?"

"I can't think while you're doing that."

"Just tell me when to stop," she said, having no intention whatsoever of doing any such thing. She allowed her hand to trail down his abdomen and lower, fingering lightly what she encountered there. A murmured sound of pleasure erupted from him. Cleo withdrew her hand, forcing herself to breathe evenly while gazing at him with wide innocent eyes. "Oh, I'm sorry. What were you saying? About blood tests?"

"I thought . . . I was thinking . . . you can put your hand back—"

"That's okay. I don't want to distract you."

"I'm finding I sort of like being distracted."

"You mean . . . like this?"

His Adam's apple bobbed, but no words came forth.

Cleo said, "I suppose with all that's happened since we left the camp, you weren't able to get in touch with Big Momma?" She was trembling all over, close to having to give up all pretense at game playing.

"Cleo," he choked, guiding her onto her back. "You talk too much."

"Sorry," she whispered and opened herself to him.

SIGHING WITH CONTENTMENT, Cleo snuggled deeper into Fletcher's arm. She very delicately placed the tip of her tongue in his ear. "We're very good together, aren't we?"

"What?" he said groggily, then added more forcefully, his voice in a croak, "Get your tongue out of my ear."

She nibbled on the lobe. "Can't help it. I'm hungry."

"Have you no consideration for an older man? Don't you ever get headaches?"

Cleo laughed. "Well, just this once, I'll settle for Chinese." She wrapped herself in the bedsheet and headed for the bathroom. "You can serve today, since you know where everything is in the kitchen. After we get our blood tests, I want to go see Katie."

"So that's how they do it," he muttered.

"How who does what?"

"How wives train their husbands. The guy gets three choices—hers, hers and hers."

"Second thoughts, already?" she asked, feeling a flutter of alarm.

"No. I'm just going into it like a tail-wagging lamb." But he couldn't keep from wondering if this was how it had been for his own father. First, thralldom, then…it was like waiting for the other shoe to fall.

"I'm not so certain about the lamb part, Fletcher," Cleo said, her eyes sparkling with mischief. "But, your dingus has the ferocity of a tiger."

"Pervert," he said, moving away from doom-and-gloom thoughts.

"Name calling so soon into our relationship?" she said with a laugh, closing the bathroom door on him. A moment later she opened it. "Go fetch this pervert's suitcase out of the car. And, don't forget my knapsack. It has my makeup kit and iron in it.''

"Do I hear a 'please'?"

"Oh, by all means, please."

Prodded thus, Fletcher rolled off the bed and shrugged into the robe Cleo had left lying on the floor. Look on the upside, he told himself. Cleo was learning to joke in ways she had not dared to before, learning to let her feelings show more; her spirit had blossomed into a riper thing. He was just suffering normal bridegroom jitters.

He looked at the bathroom door, open just a sliver, and listened to the shower running. His heart beat so fast he didn't think he could breathe. Better not, he thought, or he'd be so weak by the time they got to the blood lab, they'd have to give him a transfusion instead of taking a sample.

ON THE WAY to the lab Cleo said, "You know what, Fletcher? I've never made love in a car."

He almost missed the red light and rear-ended an auto. "It's no fun—"

"You mean, you have?"

"Maybe just wrestled—"

"Either you have or you haven't. The light's green."

"I had it in mind," he said carefully, "that we'd start off arguing about which brand toothpaste we'd use and reach Armageddon because I always leave used towels on the bathroom floor."

"Oh," she said flatly. "So you have done it in a car."

He looked over at her with a wondering clarity. "Ah! I understand it all now."

She sniffed. "Understand what?"

"Why my colleagues dumped on me. They were trying to figure out why it was they never got in the last word, never won an argument. It's the convoluted way women get to conclusions. Amazing,'' he said, as if he'd just discovered the eighth wonder of the world. ''If I admit, which I don't, that I've done it in a car, you'll get mad. If I say no, you won't believe me. Either way, I'm done for.''

''Really? Perhaps you ought to write another edition of your book. Add that pearl of wisdom.''

''See what I mean?''

''I suppose your legs or elbows or other body parts would get all caught up in the steering wheel.''

Fletcher opened his mouth, but nothing came out. Cleo put her hand on his thigh. Last word, indeed, she thought, giving him a wide-eyed golden smile.

At the hospital they ran into Magda in the lobby. Roger was sitting on the floor tossing a ball up, catching it in a tattered glove. Greetings and questions overlapped until Magda asked ''What's with Fletcher? He's white as a sheet.''

''We just had our blood tests. He didn't like the needle. Have you been in to see Katie yet?''

''You kidding? I don't dare leave Roger on his own or every plate glass window in the hospital would be shattered. Ward will be down in a minute to relieve me.''

Fletcher ruffled Roger's hair. ''Why don't I sit with Roger, and you two go on up. After Ward collects him, I'll come along.''

There were two beds in Katie's room, separated by curtains. Cleo clutched the footboard of Katie's, gazing horrified at the small emaciated figure with wires and tubes sticking out of her flesh. The volunteer work she had done back home had prepared her for what to expect in hospitals. But those children she had read to, joked with, or merely sat with, holding hands, had been strangers. Katie was no stranger. Katie was . . . ''They lied to me,'' she said in a strangled voice. "They said Katie was improved, awake."

"She is improved, she was awake. She's just sleeping, now," said Marilyn.

"Here, Cleo, you'd better take this chair," urged Magda.

"No, I'm all right." She hovered at the bedside, fidgeting and fussing, crooning soft words. She couldn't get it out of her mind that while Katie was lying there, trussed to machines, she'd been making love to Fletcher. She'd been happy!

"Cleo," said Marilyn. "I didn't thank you last night...for watching Katie, for everything you've done... I feel ashamed for going, but Ward and I needed it. We were on the verge—we did have a good time," she added, almost defiantly, looking at Ward.

"We've been here most of the day," he put in. "What say we collect Roger and take him to McDonald's. He's probably feeling a bit left out."

"Bring me a double cheeseburger," came weakly from the bed.

Cleo whirled. Katie's lids were fluttering, so much so they could all tell the fluttering was gamey pretense. "You've just been pretending to be asleep," accused Magda.

"I was only waiting to see if anybody was gonna say anything nice about me."

"If we didn't you'd make it up," returned Magda. "You little twit. You gave us all heart failure. Shame on you." She turned to Ward. "I think I'll join you. I always have to feed a fright. We'll send Fletcher up," she added in an aside to Cleo. "You want us to bring you something?"

"No, we had a late lunch. We'll stay until you get back, though."

"French fries, too, Mom," said Katie in a small voice as Marilyn bent to kiss her.

"You probably won't be allowed to eat hamburgers and fries," Cleo said, after the other adults had gone.

"I know," Katie replied, sighing one of her great sighs, which sent icy terror into Cleo because Katie was already so breathless. "Roll the curtain back. See if Cissy's awake. She can eat 'em."

"I'm awake," the girl answered, smiling at Cleo. "This is my first broken leg," she said proudly, as if the prospect of many more was a good omen.

Cleo could only nod. All of her attention was centered on Katie. "How do you feel?"

"For real?"

"For real."

"Weird, like I'm floating away. I can't seem to keep from floating. So far, I've floated back every time." She tried to lift her hand, hampered by the IV tube. "Nothing hurts, though. And, I'm shrinking. At least, I feel like I'm shrinking." Her voice was getting faint, her lids beginning to droop.

"See . . . ? Floating . . . Must . . . be . . . somethin' . . . the IV . . . ."

A nurse came in, shoes squeaking on the polished floor. "Who opened these drapes?" she asked, frowning.

"I did," said Cleo softly. "The girls—"

The rings rattled on the metal rod as the nurse jerked the drapes room length again.

"What's the harm of opening the curtain?" Cleo asked, following the woman into the corridor, piqued by her attitude.

"It could traumatize a less-ill child."

"What could traumatize?"

The nurse suddenly looked as if she'd said too much. "Excuse me."

Cleo felt sick. *It* was death, dying. She slumped against the wall, eyes closed until Fletcher touched her.

"What is it? Why are you out here? Are they working on Katie?"

Cleo forced a smile. "No, I just had word with the nurse. Katie's resting." She clutched his arm. "Fletcher...I don't think she has much time left."

"No." His fine features suddenly looked careworn and ravaged, like a living sculpture that had been terribly vandalized. Cleo reached up and touched his face with her fingertips as if to smooth out the lines of despair.

"I've been selfish. You've known her since birth. I've only wondered how I'm going to handle it." There it was again, *It*. "But, I ache so."

"We all do." He gathered her into his arms, holding her tightly, until a group of visitors came down the hall and stared.

When they entered the room, the little girl with the broken leg hissed at Cleo. "Give this to Katie for me, will you?" She thrust out a bit of note paper. "And, don't worry about that old nurse. When Katie's awake we talk through the curtain."

Cleo slipped the paper into the pocket of her slacks. "What's your name?"

"Cissy McWilliams."

"I'm glad Katie has you for a roommate."

"Oh, me, too. Do you think her mom will really bring that cheeseburger?"

Cleo laughed. "You can count on it."

Thirty minutes went by before Katie was again alert. "How'd you get that bruise?" she asked Fletcher.

"Big Momma hit me with a hammer," he said, then entertained her with the tale of the fire, B. B. Bostwick and the arrival of Fanny.

"I told you he was a mean man," she said to Cleo, with a tone of justification, both of them remembering the day Bostwick had found her spying on him.

"Next time, I'll listen." There wouldn't be a next time, Cleo knew. But, how did one stop referring to the future?

"Did you give me blood?" Katie asked, eyeing the Band-Aid in the crook of Fletcher's elbow.

"Nope, gave it to the health department. Cleo and I are going to get married. Checking out blood is a rule before we can get our marriage license."

Katie became animated, her gray eyes alight with excitement. "Oh! I'll be your flower girl. That'd be okay with you, wouldn't it, Cleo? I could wear my new dress. Promise me you won't get married until I get out of here."

"But…" began Fletcher, stricken, then looked at Cleo.

Katie followed his glance, reading the sad and sorrowful look they exchanged. Her own eyes veered away, fingers plucking weakly at the sheet. "Well, never mind…"

"Hospitals have chapels, don't they," Cleo said. "I don't see why we couldn't get married there as easily as City Hall. Or, if Katie isn't up to a wheel chair, what's wrong with right here?"

Fletcher had a dazed look on his face. Cleo laughed, feeling stiff muscles relax. "Miss Kathleen Miller, I officially invite you to be my maid of honor. That's more important than flower girl."

"Uncle Fletcher?"

"Why ask me? I'm only the groom."

"Uh-oh. I'm fixing to float off again," complained Katie, visibly trying to fight the drowsiness. "Cleo…! Bring my dress…to…mor…"

"I will," she replied, bending down close to Katie's ear. She placed her hand on the thin chest, feeling the heartbeat. Steady on, she prayed.

Hours later, after she and Fletcher returned home and she'd made the bed with fresh linen, Cleo was getting undressed when she found Cissy's note. Oh, damn! she thought, glancing at the childish scrawl.

The note said:

My sister's name was Judy McWilliams. She was hit by a car on February 11, 1983. Ask her if she remembers me. Tell her I'm ten years old now and I don't wet the bed anymore.

Signed,
Cissy McWilliams.

Cleo clutched the note to her chest. "Oh, Katie," she wailed forlornly.

Fletcher came out of the bathroom wearing the bottom half of his pajamas, carrying the top in his hand. "Here—darling, what's wrong?"

She passed him the note. "That little girl with the broken leg asked me to pass this to Katie. I forgot," she said between gulps of air. "She's still collecting people to say hello to in heaven."

He read the note and laid it aside, then coaxed Cleo into bed. In the dark she lay in the crook of his arm, head resting on his shoulder. "I wish there were miracles, Fletcher," she said fiercely. "I wish it so hard."

"There are," he whispered with deep conviction, pressing his face into her sweet-smelling hair. After a long while when he thought she was sound asleep she poked him in the chest.

"After we pick up our license tomorrow, I want to go shopping."

"All right," he murmured, and lay for an hour wondering at her mood swing. He'd never understand her. With that knowledge came a new awareness. Once the chemical element—alpha waves, odylic force, whatever—had you by the throat . . . or wherever it got you, the connection was made. It was done, mating was inevitable, fates dovetailed. It followed there had to be miracles. How else could he explain what had guided Cleo to the fishing camp at precisely the moment he was there? There was to be no miracle for Katie though. He couldn't explain that either.

For a few minutes he contemplated God, fate, life, death, souls. Cleo murmured something in her sleep, then turned out of his arm, reaching for a pillow. Once she was still again, he pressed himself against her back, moving his hand along her side and down her hip. He'd tell her all about his thoughts in the morning . . . but for now . . . the odylic force or whatever, was making his dingus swell.

CHAPTER FIFTEEN

CLEO SAT at the kitchen table, sipping a second cup of coffee and making a "to do" list. While Fletcher was in the shower she had counted and recounted her dwindling supply of traveler's checks. She'd just have to buy something practical to get married in, otherwise she'd have nothing left over to get Fletcher a wedding present. Too, there was a little something she wanted to get Katie. She became aware of Fletcher's presence and glanced up to find him smiling. "What's so funny?"

"I like coming into the kitchen and finding you here. Did you know when you're concentrating you have this little V between your brows, and you nibble the end of your pencil?" His smile widened. "I'm just a tiny bit jealous of that eraser."

"Have you noticed the bags under my eyes, too?" she asked, unable to resist a little friendly sarcasm. "Some man kept me awake half the night."

"Oh? Doing what?"

"An activity too vulgar to mention at the breakfast table, so if you don't mind I'd like to go on to a more suitable topic."

"Such as?"

"When do you think my car and camper will get here? I'd like to sell the camper. That will give me enough cash to move my things here. I think I can get one of my neighbors, nosey old Mrs. Petrosky, to oversee the movers. It'll give her a chance to snoop."

"I'll pay for all that."

"No you won't. There're some things I have to take care of myself. And, I will have to work, I'm still paying off the student loans I borrowed to see myself through college." She perused her list once more. Needle and thread to finish hemming Katie's dress. She could do that at the hospital. Put film in to be developed. Write a note to her boss, resigning, but asking for a position as contributing editor.

"I already agreed you could work until we started having children. Speaking of which, I'd like to go back to bed.... A bit of practice at getting you pregnant can't go amiss."

"No way! We're going shopping!"

"Afterward."

"Before."

"Okay, you be the judge." He opened his robe. "In your considered opinion, do you think I can walk around malls like this without attracting attention?"

Cleo looked out the window, but only for a moment before her gaze was drawn back. "Is that how you win trials, Fletcher? Presenting irrefutable evidence?"

"Only when the jury is sitting across from me at my own kitchen table, wearing my pajama tops unbuttoned down to the naval so that I can see she doesn't have on a stitch of underclothing."

"There aren't any buttons on this thing! Anyway, suppose I'm not in the mood?"

He came around the table and slipped his hand inside the pajama top, fingertips feather-light on her breasts. Then he bent his head and very delicately put his tongue in her ear. "Remember this little trick?" he asked, his voice husky, scarcely a thread of sound.

"I—I might," she said, her speech thickened slightly. His hand began to travel lower, tracing every rib before trailing down the ever-tightening muscles of her abdomen. Cleo felt a rising sting of intolerable pleasure erupt in the center of her body. "All right," she said faintly. "Afterward."

An hour later, once more taking up her "to do" list, Cleo wrote, Buttons—Fletcher's p.j.s.

"YOU SHOULD SPEND the night before your wedding at my house," said Magda, while they stood outside Katie's room during Doctor Caldwell's examination of her. "The groom isn't supposed—"

"Like hell!" howled Fletcher, and that was that.

"Just think, counselor," crooned Horace, grinning, "you're joining the world of the down-trodden, the suffering, the begging for a night out with the boys."

"Cleo isn't like that," said Fletcher.

"Yes, I am," she put in, laughing at his surprised expression. Only moments earlier Dr. Caldwell had been consulted, and through him, permission secured for the wedding ceremony at Katie's bedside on Sunday afternoon. The prospect of a happy event lifted everyone's spirits. Everybody wanted to get in on the act, due in no small part to Katie, who informed all her nurses that she was to be maid of honor in her godfather's wedding.

When Doctor Caldwell emerged from Katie's room, his face was grim. He motioned Marilyn and Ward aside. Cleo clutched Fletcher's arm as she watched dismay cloud Marilyn's features. After a moment of conversation Ward continued down the corridor with the doctor.

"They've decided to take Katie off all medication," Marilyn said, disconsolate. "It's only making her weaker, trying to fight off the side effects. She's complaining about floating. Floating!'' She looked as if she'd been struck in the face. "Why didn't she tell me? Me! I'm her mother!"

Cleo braced herself against Marilyn's misery and anguish to no avail. A mother had a right to know what her daughter was up to, Cleo told herself. And, the knowing might ease some of the suffering. "I know why," she said softly. "Fletcher, why don't all of you go on in? Marilyn and I will be along in a minute." She took the mother's arm, guiding her gently down the hall. "Let's go find a cup of coffee."

They had to settle for instant, machine brewed, but Cleo found a quiet corner in the waiting room. The coffee's just a prop, anyway, she told herself, taking a deep breath in the face of Marilyn's growing confusion and resentment.

"Katie's told you something, shared secrets with you, hasn't she?" A lilt of terrible envy edged every word.

"Everything Katie has said or done," Cleo began, "has been to protect you from hurt and pain. That's all. She worries about you worrying about her. I want to show you something." Reaching into the shopping bag she held, Cleo pulled out and displayed the dress. "Katie engaged Big Momma to make this. It's her burial dress, her shroud."

"Oh, God!"

"If you could see your face, Marilyn..." said Cleo, feeling necessarily brutal. "That's what Katie is trying to prevent. So, ask yourself, could Katie have approached you about a shroud?"

"I couldn't bear to talk...." Her voice trailed away, her face fiercely distorted as clarity dawned. "Oh...Katie needed to talk...?"

"For her own reasons. She's got very specific views about dying and God and heaven. And, she had a view as to how this dress was to be constructed. It has a very special feature." Displaying the garment on her knees, Cleo poked her fingers through the buttonholelike slits. "These are so when her angel wings grow, it won't ruin the dress. She's thought of everything. Planned everything. She got Fletcher to help her with her will, me to help her with spelling. How could we refuse? But, all she's done is so that you won't have to deal with it. I think it would hurt her very badly if she thought she'd failed. She feels guilty about being sick. If there's anything I know about, it's guilt."

"But, it isn't her fault. It—it just happened."

"I know, but when bad things happen, our first thought is that we're being punished. Katie has gotten past that to the point that she just wonders if she could've moved out of the way of the germ."

"I'm the one that's being punished—"

"No! Katie's illness isn't your fault. That's what she's trying to make you see by doing all of this. That it isn't your fault." Cleo sighed. "I'm doing this all wrong, not saying—"

"No, you're not. I'm getting the message," countered Marilyn. "I know what I've been doing. I've been grieving for Katie and she isn't even gone. No wonder..."

"There's more." Cleo paused. "Katie's taking names of people to say hello to when she gets to heaven." Marilyn's tear-filled eyes widened, an abyss of disbelief. "It's true," Cleo said, half laughing to swallow back a lump in her throat. "Before she...well...I think you ought to be prepared. She's probably going to ask you what you want her to say to your mother. If she were my little girl, I don't know how I could...I know all this is painful." She searched the other woman's face. "Do you have any reserves left?"

"I don't know. I thought . . ." Her eyes brimmed with tears. "I guess I can muster as much grit as my own daughter." The archness came through, so patently like Katie that for a suspended moment Cleo saw what the child might have grown up to be. Marilyn took the dress, spreading it out upon her lap, stroking the chambray as if it were a delicate, live thing. "Angel wings?"

"Positively. I'd hate to have to be the one to talk her out of that dress. She's adamant that she's earned those wings."

"It needs hemming."

"I bought some needles and thread."

"I'll do it," Marilyn said with difficult dignity. "If . . . if you don't mind, Cleo, I'd like to sit here by myself for a few minutes."

"I hope when all of this is over—"

Marilyn clasped Cleo's hand. "We'll be good friends. I've just been so scared, hating, because of all the things Katie is going to miss."

"She expects to rule the roost when she gets to heaven, though."

"She probably will." Marilyn smiled through her tears. "Can you imagine the celestial havoc she'll cause? I'd hate to be God, wouldn't you?"

"I've done you an injustice, Marilyn. All this time I've been thinking Katie got her wit from Ward."

"Ward wouldn't know wit if he ate it for breakfast."

Gently Cleo disengaged her hand. "You'll be all right, now?"

"Fine. I'll be fine."

"I WAS just getting ready to go looking for you," said Fletcher, when Cleo entered Katie's room.

"He's probably going to lock you in the house all day when he's at work," Horace said out the side of his mouth. Fletcher gave him a dirty look.

Magda hurriedly kissed Katie goodbye and began marshaling her hulk of a husband out of the room. "I know you won't believe it, Cleo, but this is the man who was screaming bloody murder to get Fletcher some police protection against B. B. Bostwick," she said on her way out. "We'll see you at the wedding. Count on us for the champagne."

"Where's my mom?" Katie asked worriedly, sounding pitifully feeble.

"Having a cup of coffee." Cleo made her self look at Katie, assessing, smiling away the anguish that clutched at her. "Fletcher, will you give us a few minutes alone? Without balking?"

"Why?" asked Katie, which took the words right out of Fletcher's mouth.

"Because I have a little something for you and I thought—"

"A present?" The little peaked face, so white, took on the flush of excitement.

"I guess I could round up Ward, have a word with him about being best man."

On his way out he said something to Cissy that made her giggle.

"Roll me up a little bit, Cleo," Katie ordered. "Is it a wrapped present?"

"Not with ribbons and stuff, no. Close your eyes." She took the tissue wrapped gift out of the shopping bag and crinkled the paper at Katie's ear. "You get one guess."

"Something soft?"

Cleo let it dangle from her fingers in front of Katie's face. "Good guess. Open your eyes." She watched the astonished expression, the gray eyes lighting up, the faint flush coloring the pale cheeks and knew she'd bought just the right thing.

"Oh!" the child gasped. "Oh!"

"Well, what is it?" cried Cissy from the other side of the curtain.

"A bra," came Katie's whispered reply.

"What size?"

Katie looked at Cleo. "Thirty double A. Want to try it on?"

It was elasticized, but still it hung limply on the small frame. Katie was not at all disappointed. "Pass me the Kleenex," she said, sniffing. Her hands trembled with the effort, but she managed to wad up a couple tissues and stuff them down her front. Then she pushed the call buzzer that was pinned to her bed. When the nurse came rushing in, Katie said, "We need a pair of scissors."

The nurse cocked an eyebrow, but drew a pair from her pocket. "For what?"

"Cleo needs them to take a tag off something. She'll bring them right back, okay?"

The nurse left.

"I already took the tags off."

"Just cut a little bit along the shoulder seams of my night gown...please."

"Cut...? Why?"

"So the straps'll show. Aunt Mary Ellen and Lindsey will be here any minute. Hurry up before I float off," she pleaded desperately. "Oh, Cleo, make sure I get buried wearing my bra. And don't forget the Kleenex. Oh, I love it," she rasped as Cleo helped her back into the gown. "Yank the shoulder down. Do they show?"

"Yes," said Cleo, regretting the impulse to buy the bra in the face of the promise Katie was extracting from her. She left the room to return the scissors in confusion, her feelings a jumble of gratification, irritation and a vague, disembodied helplessness.

When she returned to the room, Katie was off on one of her "floats" but Marilyn was there, smiling. "I noticed," she said, waving her hand to indicate the twin mounds that were so patently false. "She's ecstatic. It was exactly the right thing to buy her." There was no tone of resentment now.

Cleo's hand fluttered. "Except she...she wants to wear it under her dress."

There was a heartbeat of silence while Marilyn fumbled with the sense of Cleo's statement. "I'll see to it," she said resolutely, and began tidying the bed clothes.

"Including the Kleenex," Cleo said lamely.

"Oh."

"Please...Mom..." Katie's voice was weak, but full of intensity.

"Kleenex, too," agreed Marilyn, moving to rearrange flower vases lining the windowsill until she'd worked her way around next to Cleo. "What in the world will Reverend Dopple think?" she croaked in a whisper.

Just then that august man, rotund and red faced swept into the room on Fletcher's heels. "I found the man to marry us," said Fletcher.

Cleo and Marilyn wheezed soft laughter, then spent an embarrassed five minutes trying to explain without ever touching on the unexplainable topic.

In the bed, Katie sucked in a lungful of air and twitched her shoulders as much as lethargy would permit. "Hello,

Reverend Dopple," she flung with an immense courtesy that belied her failing strength. "Have you told God I'm coming, yet?

Cleo and Fletcher left while the kindly cleric was still sputtering.

"I DON'T KNOW what's wrong with me," complained Fletcher. "I've put a tie around my neck five days a week for the past sixteen years. Now I just want to take my neck in the bathroom and cut it."

"You're hogging the mirror, Fletcher," Cleo said, trying to maneuver him out of the way so that she could position the chair she'd brought from the kitchen. "I have to put my makeup on."

"Can you tie a tie?" he asked, staring at his hands, betrayers over which he seemed to have no control.

"I know about jabots, and your socks don't match."

He uttered an epithet and went to look under the bed. "Somehow I always thought cleanliness was supposed to be admirable, matched or not."

"Nobody is going to be interested in your feet," said Cleo brushing her red curls back, securing one swath with a gold-colored comb and admiring the sophisticated effect.

"If that's so, why do my socks have to match?"

"Well, they might be interested," she replied, leaving Fletcher to worry with the illogic. "Just put your tie in your pocket. There's bound to be somebody at the hospital who can tie—"

"A cute little nurse, maybe."

"Or hang you with it," Cleo shot back as she was stepping into the beige silk dress so as not to muss her hair or face. The bodice was fitted, the skirt hugging her hips before flaring becomingly.

"Do you think everyone will be on time?"

She eyed his reflection in the mirror. "Everybody except the bride and groom, if you don't hurry up."

"My zipper's stuck."

"You've got an entire closet full of pants. Find another pair."

"No, these are my lucky pants. Every time I wear them the last day of a trial during summing up, I win."

Cleo crossed the room to him. "Fletcher, do you . . . do you think our marriage is going to be based only on luck?"

"Love and luck. Phew! You look exquisite."

"You're being too breezy and you're trying to change the subject."

"How do you want me to be? I'm going to be married in an hour and I'm a nervous wreck! Oh, damn!" He enclosed her in his arms, kissed the tip of her nose, nibbled on her exposed ear. "I don't know what's come over me. The jitters; it's a big step."

"One you'd rather not take?"

"If there's any single thing certain in my mind, it's that I want to marry you. It's just that I want to be married wearing clean socks with my tie proper and my pants zipped."

"Now I know why you're such a good lawyer," laughed Cleo. "You've completely mastered the art of talking in circles. I think I can help you with the zipper," she said, and sat on the bed to manipulate it.

"Don't get me riled up down there," he warned.

"I wouldn't dream of doing such a thing on our wedding day," she told him as the zipper came loose from the nap, adding, as she kissed him lightly on his whiskered cheek, "I'll just get your boutonniere." He had forgotten to shave. She wouldn't dream of mentioning that, either.

CHAPTER SIXTEEN

THE WEDDING CEREMONY WAS kept blessedly short, for which Cleo was everlastingly grateful. In a high state of anxiety Fletcher kept slipping one hand into his breast pocket, reassuring himself that the marriage license was there; with the other he kept patting his hip pocket for the ring box, which was not—for Katie had preempted the best man's duty of ring bearer. Every time he glanced at the beaming child, she waved the box reassuringly, which had the effect of distracting Reverend Dopple. "Where was I?" he muttered.

"Just get to the ring part," hissed Katie.

"In sickness and health," prompted Cleo. Fletcher lost his voice on "I do," which provoked a snicker from Horace. When they were finally pronounced man and wife, Fletcher was in a daze.

"I'll never do this again," he groaned.

"Me, either," said Cleo, but the play on words was lost on him as everyone sang out congratulations.

Alcoholic beverages were forbidden, a hospital rule blatantly ignored by Magda, though she served champagne in paper cups to preserve a semblance of decorum.

The wedding cake, produced by the hospital kitchen and set up on a makeshift cart was wheeled into the already crowded room. During the ceremony the cake had been left in the corridor where it had gathered a bevy of ambulatory, pajama-clad, pint-sized admirers. The bottom line of icing trim and roses had disappeared.

The separating curtain had been dispatched by a stern-faced Nurse Tomball and wedding gifts were displayed on the foot of both Cissy and Katie's beds. Much to their joy, Cleo allowed the girls to open them.

A pound of beluga caviar with all the trimmings, a gift from Fletcher's office staff, was delivered by his secretary, a beautiful willowy blonde. Cleo suffered an instant spasm of jealousy. "Can she really type?"

"I'll transfer her to research first thing Monday morning," said Fletcher.

"How can I make a toast without champagne," wailed Katie, pleading with her mother.

Cleo looked past Mary Ellen and Lindsey, exchanging a sympathetic smile with Marilyn. Katie was behaving the prima donna. She had on her special dress beneath which she wore her well-stuffed bra to the consternation of Lindsey. "New medical advances," Katie had said blithely. Her head had been swathed in gauze and the gauze decorated with freesias and forget-me-nots garnered from flower arrangements.

The age rule had been bent to allow Roger to attend the wedding and visit with Katie, but he sat on the floor in the corridor entertaining the icing culprits with his baseball cards. In the midst of a toast offering and picture taking, Cissy's mother arrived to visit and was introduced to the bride and groom.

"Fletcher Fremont Maitland?" she said, offering best wishes. "The author of *101 Ways*? You're Katie's Uncle Fletcher?"

Fletcher made a strangled noise in his throat.

"I'm a reporter for the *Atlanta Constitution*. I just can't pass up an opportunity for an exclusive." From her shoulder bag she whipped out a pad and pen.

"No!" said Fletcher.

"Just a quote from your wife," she said, turning to Cleo. "How'd you snag the most eligible bach—"

"With kindness," Cleo said swiftly and sweetly, watching Fletcher out of the corner of her eye. In the background Ward and Horace laughed.

"Will my name be in the paper?" piped Katie.

"And your picture," promised Cissy's mother. "If your uncle and aunt will pose with you." From the depths of her bag she drew out a camera."

"He's my godfather," Katie corrected. "Cleo's my godmother-in-law now...I think."

"No pictures," said Fletcher.

Katie looked at him with pleading eyes. "Just one," she wheedled, trying to sit straighter against a bank of pillows while the reporter kept prudently silent.

He gave in and the photo was taken, Cleo and Katie smiling at the camera, Fletcher looking mulish.

Katie sighed happily and burrowed back into the pillows. Cleo bent to kiss her cheek and found it cool. "Are you feeling okay?"

"I'm wonderful," she said, but her eyes traveled the room, collecting the sight of it, of her parents and Roger, Mary Ellen and Lindsey, Horace and Magda who were chatting with Reverend Dopple and a nurse in the doorway.

"I'll send you copies of the picture," said Cissy's mother who seemed only then to take in Katie's fragile existence.

After an hour or so, Nurse Tomball bustled in and pulled the curtain, which had the effect of breaking up the reception. "Everybody out for ten minutes," she said over Katie's weak and worn protests.

In the hall, Reverend Dopple checked again to make sure the marriage certificate had been signed, shook hands all around and after a private word with Ward, he left, as did Mary Ellen with Lindsey in tow. Horace pounded Fletcher on the back in parting. "I've got an extra ring in my nose anytime you want to borrow it," he wisecracked.

"Thanks," Fletcher said dryly.

"My, my. How marriage mellows a guy," laughed Magda, giving Cleo one last hug and a promise to telephone.

As visitors and wedding guests left, the corridor gradually resumed a hospital quiet. Fletcher slipped his arm about Cleo. "Hello wife," he said. "How's it feel to be Mrs. Maitland?"

"Lovely, tiring..." She drank in the shape and hue of him, admiring, absorbing the strength of his arm that was about her.

"What do you say we get out of here, have dinner someplace romantic, then go home and get that way?"

"That's the second nicest offer I've had all day. Let's just spend a few more minutes with Katie."

"What was the first?"

"When Reverend Dopple asked, 'Do you take this man...'"

"I don't remember that part," said Fletcher.

"That's all right. You said your part. That's what counts."

"I kept smelling your perfume. It was distracting me."

"Really? I kept thinking I wish I'd reminded you to shave."

He fingered his chin in disbelief. "Damn!"

There came a low pain-filled wail from the hospital room. Cleo froze. Marilyn sagged against Ward. Roger edged up to Fletcher. "What're they doin' to Katie? Cuttin' her open?"

He put his hand on the boy's shoulder. "No, but maybe the nurse is doing something Katie doesn't like."

"Sounds to me like she doesn't like it a lot."

"It's the catheter," whispered Marilyn.

Knowing the indignity of the procedure, Cleo shuddered.

Nurse Tomball emerged from the room, cheeks splotchy, her eyes red. "Five minutes," she said indicating the trio that was Fletcher and Cleo and Roger. She stopped in front of Ward. "Dr. Caldwell's ordered a cot if you both intend to stay the night. The other patient will be moved after dinner."

Cleo's mind raced. Ward and Marilyn were staying at Katie's side overnight? Dr. Caldwell had said he would allow that only when... only when... Cleo kept her voice neutral, the better to fight the sensation of being disconnected to the world and the people around her. She shooed Roger into the room. "Go keep Katie company."

She meant to take a step toward Marilyn, but Fletcher held her fast. She looked at him; he was shaking his head, his expression stark. "I tried to get you out of here. In any case we won't be allowed to stay."

Cleo was crushed. "Why didn't any of you tell me?"

"This was your day. We didn't want to spoil it for you. It's been touch and go for two days. But, you were happy, Katie was hanging on..."

"But she seemed so much more... more vibrant today."

"Anticipation, adrenaline..."

"Come on," Ward said, looking even more forlorn and lost than Marilyn. "Mary Ellen is waiting for Roger in the lobby. Maybe you two could see him down when you leave?"

With hollow feelings and pasted-on smiles they reentered the hospital room. Cleo felt as if her legs were functioning in slow motion.

Roger and Katie were engaged in a heated argument. How could Katie sound so boisterous if...? Cleo wondered, succumbing to a seductive, treacherous hope.

"For sure you're going to see Babe Ruth and Roger Maris," the boy was insisting, fingering his baseball cards. "You could get me their autographs if you wanted to!"

"I am not going up to a perfect stranger in heaven, Roger, and ask for an autograph. Besides, how would I get it back to you?"

"You're never coming back at all?"

"Once you're there, God keeps you. Isn't that right, Mom?"

"That's right, sweetheart," Marilyn answered with a thin, ghostly smile, summoning a reserve that joined forces with her maternal instinct.

They could all see Roger pondering the reality of it. "Is heaven dark?"

"I don't know..."

"Are you scared?"

Katie turned pensive eyes on her mother. "A little."

"When are you going?" Roger pressed.

Katie shrugged. "Pretty soon."

"Maybe you could stop by pet heaven and pick up Champ. He could keep you company."

"Roger, you're the stupidest brother a girl could have! God isn't going to let a dog in heaven, and even if He did, Grandma Baily wouldn't."

"He might. Champ's house-trained."

"Scoot over," Fletcher said, climbing up on the bed to lie down beside Katie.

"If Tomball catches you!" she giggled.

Watching him, Cleo saw beyond his smile, the ashen face, the melancholy he was suffering, that they all were suffering. Except Roger, who was only bewildered.

"Are you going to forget me, Uncle Fletcher?"

"Nope."

"Are you going to tell Cleo about taking me to the zoo?"

He wrinkled his nose. "That old story?"

She tilted her face up to his, painfully, slowly. "That's a good story. I was such a darling little thing."

Ward lifted Roger down from the foot of the bed. "Time to go, sport."

"Another minute, please," pleaded Cleo.

Fletcher kissed Katie. "Goodbye sweetheart."

"I was a pretty good maid of honor, wasn't I?"

"You were a pretty good everything."

"See, Mom. I told you you did a good job of raising me."

"If we're goin', let's go," said Roger. "I'm hungry."

"Wanna kiss me goodbye, Roger?"

He backed away. "I'm not doin' that again!"

"Hand me my satchel, Daddy. I want to scratch Roger's name off my will."

Roger shoved his hands in his pockets. "You really have a will?"

"Typed and everything."

Greed won out. "What do I have to kiss?"

"Just my cheek," she said, turning so he could reach.

Feeling battered, Cleo took Katie's bruised hand, warming it between her own, gently stroking the black and blue marks left by the IV needles.

"If you bend down," said Katie, "I could give you a hug." The spindly arms went around her neck. Then, "Don't cry on my dress, Cleo. I've got to wear it again, y'know."

"Right. Sorry." Goodbye, goodbye, was like a refrain in Cleo's head, making it ache, but the word just clotted in her throat.

"I hope you learn to cook grits."

"Me, too."

"Don't forget to tell Big Momma goodbye for me."

"No, I won't forget anything." Cleo looked up to find Nurse Tomball standing at the foot of the bed.

"It's long past visiting hours."

"Marilyn . . ." Cleo's voice trembled, trailing off at the thought of the approaching night-long vigil.

Katie sensed what lay ahead, understanding that the darkness was already planted inside her—and growing.

"Tomball, will it be all right if my mom lays down by me?"

"After we get you into a nightgown."

Cleo's palms were sweating; she grabbed up a Kleenex to wipe them, foraging for time, but Fletcher was at her elbow, taking it, ushering her toward the door. "Wait! Nurse Tomball? You won't forget about the leftover wedding cake?"

"No, the children are already anticipating it for dessert. They'll all get a slice."

Cleo chanced one last look over her shoulder at Marilyn. The soft pretty mouth was set with tragic determination. The pencil-thin body that was Katie was hidden from

view by Ward and Nurse Tomball, who was busily un-
wrapping a sterile package.

"Maybe I ought to stay with Mom and Dad," Roger
said, sounding lost, as they emerged into the corridor.

"Not this time, sport," Fletcher said, feeling lost himself.

"But Katie sounded funny. Do you think she'll be all
right, going off to heaven by herself? If it was me, I'd take
Champ." His small hand trembled in Fletcher's grip.

"Katie will be fine," Fletcher managed, exchanging a
glance with Cleo. Her eyes looked like golden motes, far
too bright for the strain and intensity in her face. In a way,
Fletcher thought, the long, long siege was over—at least
for them. Walking away was the most painful part. Seeing
a child out of this universe into another was the personal
province of the parents, a moment that was close to the
hurting heart; private, no intruders allowed. Letting go
hurt.

He gave Cleo a careful scrutiny. Again he had that odd
sense that she was struggling with more than Katie's dying.
She was his wife, and yet, some mysterious part of her remained aloof, impregnable. He was wondering how to
pierce that aloofness, strip it away to make her wholly his
when she caught him staring. "Home?" he asked.

She nodded, speaking hoarsely, "That's the best place
to be, isn't it?"

CHAPTER SEVENTEEN

CLEO WOKE with a pleasant warm feeling about her heart, an unusual thing for her these past trying days. Most mornings she woke on the thought, Katie isn't here anymore, and then a dull-bladed knife seemed to stab her heart with each waking breath. She inhaled, relishing the freedom from the ache that had begun to seem a pronounced part of her. She moved her arms and legs. The paralyzing numbness that had been with her since the funeral was gone. It's over, she realized.

Yet, one thing still caused her a deep burning anguish. She had finished reading Fletcher's book. The tongue-in-cheek suggestions he had made to husbands to retain their independence were funny. But hadn't someone once said that there was great truth to be found in humor? In those suggestions she had fathomed Fletcher's Achilles' heel—he thought others should live up to his own ideals. When they didn't, he suffered disillusionment.

How long did she have before he became disillusioned with her? she wondered. Plagued so, how could their marriage survive?

She smelled coffee, longing for a comforting cup. *I must get up,* she thought, and snuggled further down into the bedclothes to ponder the many unsaid things between herself and her husband.

As if he had read her mind, Fletcher came into the room, bearing two steaming mugs. "I was wondering when you were going to stir. I was thinking about hiring a brass band."

"You've been trying to wake me?" She scooted up on the pillows and took the cup, inhaling the steam before she took a sip. She smiled at Fletcher over the rim. "You make good coffee."

"I haven't seen you smile like that in weeks." He felt a glowing sense of relief. It had taken Cleo far longer to work through her grief than himself. But then, he and Ward had worked it out together. Cleo had hugged her grief to herself, kept herself aloof.

She eyed him as he sat on the bed. He was wearing shorts, an old shirt; beard stubble was thick on his jaw. "Aren't you going to work today?"

"It's Saturday."

"Saturday?" she repeated, as if the day had only come into existence. "Oh!" She threw back the covers and leapt out of bed, heading for the bathroom. "I have a luncheon engagement."

"With whom?" asked Fletcher, indignant. Cleo was the center of his world. It was only right that he be the center of hers, especially now that she was back with him.

"Elsie McWilliams. Cissy's mother, you remember—"

"I don't like her."

"Fletcher...she's really very nice. She was mortified that our wedding picture with Katie ran on the society page the same day of Katie's obituary notice. She came to the funeral, too."

"So, what's her attraction?"

Cleo turned back to face him. "I knew this discussion was going to happen. I just didn't expect it to happen today, now."

"Well, let me in on the secret." Sarcasm overrode his wanting to take possession of her right then. She still wore his pajama top for sleeping gear, primly buttoned now, which served only to enhance the long elegant length of her legs. She had magnificent legs. He wanted them wrapped around him. He had been too long without her, honorably so, he thought, because he had not pressed her while she grieved.

"I finished reading your book. I know you meant it as a joke. But what it said to me is that you think a husband should rule his house...his wife, his children, like your own dad did not."

"You're way out of line, Cleo," he said, getting angry. "You don't have the right to make judgments like that."

"I'm not judging. I'm trying to understand you. I may not say this right, but you worry that you'll be weak like you think your dad was. I don't know if he was or he wasn't. Besides, how do you know what promises he made to your mother, what their dreams were?"

She drew a deep breath and paused to gather her thoughts. "You're one of the strongest persons I've ever known. The way you perceive strength frightens me. I don't want to pretend to be less strong than I am because you see strength in women as a flaw. I've overcome so much, Fletcher. I don't want to give up... Imagine what your life would've been had your mother outlived your dad instead of vice versa. You may have been proud of your mother's strength then. Maybe your dad provided what he did because your mother prodded him. I'm not saying that's the right way."

Fletcher sat on the bed and dragged a hand through his hair. Every sinew in his neck was taut. "I admit there's some truth to what you're saying. I loved my dad, but—"

"You wanted him to be more?"

"I would've liked that, yes."

"Maybe he was all that he could be, maybe he was locked in. Like Gram. Like my mother. I don't want you to stop loving me because you see things in me that remind you of your mother."

"I'll never stop loving you," he said with feeling. "I'm mesmerized by you, though you philosophize before breakfast and before anything else—for that matter," he added pointedly.

Just as pointedly, Cleo responded. "You sound as if you're in court. I'm not canceling my lunch. Before Elsie was hired on at the newspaper, she freelanced. She knows editors all across the state and then some. She's a good contact for me. Besides..." Cleo's face flamed. "I've written a story about Katie...her faith in God, which was so different from Gram's. Katie believed in a good God, not a punishing God. It helped me to let go, helped me to stop wishing for a thing that couldn't be."

"I'm glad for you, Cleo. But why go out today of all days? You agreed that you'd discuss things with me beforehand."

"I know. And, I will, but you always go to the office on Saturdays. You said it's the only day the phones don't ring, you said—"

"I know what I said." He looked glum. "But I'm not going today."

"Then you should've mentioned it. Why aren't you?"

"This feeling has taken hold of me. I can't think around it."

"What kind of feeling?" she asked, concerned. "Are you sick?"

"Not sick. I just have this airy feeling."

"Where?"

He pointed.

Cleo laughed. "Go mow the lawn, Fletcher. That ought to occupy you until I get home. I won't be late, I promise. Then we can spend all afternoon in bed, like the decadent souls we are. And, next time, before I make an appointment on a Saturday, I'll check with you first."

Behind the closed door in the bathroom Cleo inspected her face in the mirror. It was a good mirror, no waves, no cracks, but there was her second self nevertheless.

We haven't talked in a long while, Cleo.

No.

And, you've never mentioned me to Fletcher.

I—it was a hard thing to explain. He knows everything else.

It's just as well because I'm leaving. I'm taking the faceless dream with me.

Oh, but I haven't seen—

You couldn't put a face on it because the face was yours. I thought you knew that.

Not mine!

Your face, Cleo. Before, you couldn't love yourself, now you do. And others do, too. You're looking outward now. It was all so simple. You should've seen that long ago. You don't need me anymore. I'm going now.

Wait!

Be happy, Cleo.

Cleo closed her eyes tightly, so at the last, she never saw it go. For several chilling seconds she felt abandoned, exposed, like a child again, uncertain and unsure of herself.

Fletcher banged on the door. "Who're you talking to in there?"

Cleo froze. "No one, just myself. You drive me to it." She glanced at her reflection once again, trying to call up her other self. No one came, no voice dictated to her.

Suddenly she felt lightheaded, weightless—free. She stepped into the shower.

"You're the most unsympathetic woman I've ever known," Fletcher yelled over the sound of running water.

Cleo flung open the bathroom door, standing there naked and dripping wet from the shower. "I think you're the best husband a woman could have—the kindest, the most understanding, the most indulgent . . ."

He watched a rivulet of water drip from her hair, down her neck, onto her breast, and bead on a taunting pink nipple. Kind, was the last thing in the world he felt like being. He glared at her. "Fat lot of good that does me."

Cleo straightened her shoulders, the bead of water splashed on the floor. "Fletcher, I know what marriage means more than anything."

"Goody for you."

"It means compromise," she said undaunted. "When you want something, you get it. When I want something, I get it."

Fletcher regarded her levelly with clear brown eyes, which took some doing considering the manner in which she stood before him. "I promise to surround us with compromise, to think compromise, to—"

"I also wanted to mention—" she interrupted, lowering her lashes, offering a promise of her own, "—that I've never made love in the shower."

"Oh."

Suddenly, being the best and kindest and most indulgent husband was wonderfully appealing, thought Fletcher, managing to fling off his clothes as he covered the distance between himself and his wife.

A few moments later Cleo said, "You seem to know exactly how to go about this."

"No experience at it whatsoever," Fletcher replied, watching the dance of water on her flesh. Her mysterious frailty seemed to have disappeared; in its place an exciting cachet. She looked prettier, fuller of ripeness, more beautiful than when he'd first met her.

"No experience whatsoever?" She gave him a look of loving forbearance. "Your instincts are uncanny, darling. Show me more."

Harlequin Superromance

COMING NEXT MONTH

#230 ONCE A STRANGER • Megan Alexander
Holly Jones is happy working at her pottery in
Oaxaco, Mexico, until her former husband,
renowned filmmaker Christopher Brooke, arrives to
make a documentary. Suddenly Holly's
determination to protect her heart begins to
slip away....

#231 A DANGEROUS SENTIMENT • Lynn Erickson
When Daphne Farway joins forces with Wes Leroux
to prove her fiancé's death was not accidental, time
is not on their side. Only three weeks remain for the
cookbook writer and the secret service agent to
uncover motives, to snare a traitor . . . to fall in love.

#232 SEE ONLY ME • Shirley Larson
Investigating Jessica Moore turns out to be the
toughest assignment Rourke Caldwell has ever
had as a corporate crime specialist. Every time he
stumbles on evidence that could convict her,
Rourke remembers that day seven years ago when
the blind farm girl had lovingly traced his features
with trembling fingers as they kissed in the rain....

#233 FINAL PAYMENT • Evelyn A. Crowe
What price will JoBeth Huntley have to pay for
getting the man she has always wanted? In the fourth
and final book in this series, Brandon DeSalva agrees
to marry JoBeth, but wedded bliss may cost them
their lives.

HARLEQUIN HISTORICAL

Explore love with Harlequin in the Middle
Ages, the Renaissance, in the Regency, the
Victorian and other eras

Relive within these books the endless ages of
romance, set against authentic historical
backgrounds. Two new historical love stories
published each month.

HIST-A-IR

ATTRACTIVE, SPACE SAVING BOOK RACK

Display your most prized novels on this handsome and sturdy book rack. The hand-rubbed walnut finish will blend into your library decor with quiet elegance, providing a practical organizer for your favorite hard-or soft-covered books.

Only $9.95

Approximately 16" x 8" when assembled

Assembles in seconds!

To order, rush your name, address and zip code, along with a check or money order for $10.70 ($9.95 plus 75¢ postage and handling) (New York residents add appropriate sales tax), payable to *Harlequin Reader Service* to:

In the U.S.

Harlequin Reader Service
Book Rack Offer
901 Fuhrmann Blvd.
P.O. Box 1325
Buffalo, NY 14269-1325

Offer not available in Canada.

Take 4 books & a surprise gift FREE

Harlequin Intrigue

Because romance can be quite an adventure.

Available wherever paperbacks are sold or through

Harlequin Reader Service

In the U.S.	In Canada
901 Fuhrmann Blvd.	P.O. Box 2800, Station "A"
P.O. Box 1325	5170 Yonge Street
Buffalo, N.Y. 14269	Willowdale, Ontario M2N 6J3

INT-6R

She had the pride of Nantucket in her spirit and the passion for one man in her blood.

Until I Return
Laura Simon

Author Laura Simon weaves an emotional love story into the drama of life during the great whaling era of the 1800s. Danger, adventure, defeat and triumph—UNTIL I RETURN has it all!

Available at your favorite retail outlet in OCTOBER, or reserve your copy for September shipping by sending your name, address, zip or postal code along with a check or money order for $7.70 (includes 75¢ for postage and handling) payable to Worldwide Library to:

Please specify book title with your order.